DEATH AT
SWAYTHLING COURT

DEATH AT
SWAYTHLING COURT

J. J. Connington

COACHWHIP PUBLICATIONS

Greenville, Ohio

CONTENTS

ALFRED WALTER STEWART / J. J. CONNINGTON
(1880-1947)

CURTIS EVANS

DURING THE GOLDEN AGE of the detective novel, in the 1920s and 1930s, J. J. Connington stood, along with R. Austin Freeman, Freeman Wills Crofts and John Rhode (Cecil John Charles Street), as one of British mystery fiction's foremost exponents of the science of true detection. I use the word "science" advisedly, because the man behind "J. J. Connington," Alfred Walter Stewart, was an esteemed scientist who held the Chair of Chemistry at Queen's University, Belfast, for twenty-five years, from 1919 until his retirement in 1944, three years before his death. A "small, unassuming moustached polymath," Stewart was "a strikingly effective lecturer with an excellent sense of humor, fertile imagination, and fantastically retentive memory," qualities that served him well in his detective fiction. During his years at Queen's University, the talented Professor Stewart found time to author not only a remarkable piece of science fiction, the apocalyptic novel *Nordenholt's Million* (1923), but also a mainstream work of fiction, *Almighty Gold* (1924), and, between 1926 and 1947, a string of two dozen mysteries, all but one tales of true detection. Among these latter works are at least eight examples of the Golden Age detective novel at its considerable best. Critics at the time doubtlessly reflected the views of many mystery genre devotees when they avowed that "Mr. Connington is one of the clearest and cleverest of masters of detective fiction now writing" and that "for those who ask first of

7

all in a detective story for exact and mathematical accuracy in the construction of the plot, there is no author to equal the distinguished scientist who writes under the name of J. J. Connington." Nor are such assessments off the mark.

Born in Scotland, Alfred Walter Stewart was the son of a prominent professor of divinity at Glasgow University. Yet despite his parentage and his marriage into the wealthy and devout Coats family—probably the most socially prominent Baptists in Scotland—Stewart himself throughout his life remained markedly materialistic and skeptical in his own philosophical outlook. "I prefer the *Odyssey* to *Paradise Lost*," the author once remarked, while the pseudonym "J. J. Connington" he derived from a nineteenth century Oxford professor of Latin and translator of Horace. Stewart's most renowned series investigator, Chief Constable Sir Clinton Driffield, who appears in seventeen novels, is one of the most sardonic and acerbic detectives in the literature of mystery fiction, sometimes behaving, especially in the earlier tales, in a ruthlessly highhanded fashion. Yet whether one finds Driffield's behavior appealing or appalling, the Chief Constable is, I believe, one of the most impressive and interesting Great Detectives in British crime fiction.

We see Sir Clinton at nearly his most ruthless in his debut in *Murder in the Maze* (1927), the novel that established "J. J. Connington" as one of Britain's premier detective writers. No less a literary figure than T. S. Eliot praised *Murder in the Maze* in *The Criterion* for its plot construction ("we are provided early in the story with all the clues which guide the detective") and its narrative liveliness ("the very idea of murder in a box hedge labyrinth does the author great credit, and he makes full use of its possibilities"), deeming it "a really first-rate detective story." For his part, the prominent English critic H. C. Harwood declared in *The Outlook* that with the publication of *Murder in the Maze* its author "demands and deserves comparison with the masters." Harwood urged mystery fans, "buy, borrow, or—anyhow get hold of it." Two decades later, in his 1946 critical essay, "The Grandest Game in the World," the great locked room detective author John Dickson Carr echoed Eliot's assessment of the novel's virtuoso setting, writing:

"These 1920s . . . thronged with sheer brains. What would be one of the best possible settings for violent death? J. J. Connington found the answer, with *Murder in the Maze*."

In his first recorded case, Sir Clinton Driffield—who, we learn, served in "a big post" in the South African police—returns to England to claim ownership of a landed estate and the office of Chief Constable of the county. Driffield is given his fullest description in *Murder in the Maze*, where we find that deliberately concealed under a conventional façade is a masterful individual:

> Sir Clinton was a slight man who looked about thirty-five. His sun-tanned face, the firm mouth under the close-clipped moustache, the beautifully-kept teeth and hands, might have attracted a second glance in a crowd; but to counter this there was a deliberate ordinariness about his appearance. . . . Only his eyes failed to fit in with the rest of his conventional appearance; and even them he had disciplined as far as possible. Normally, they had a bored expression; but at times the mask slipped aside and betrayed the activity of the brain behind them. When fixed on a man they gave a curious impression as though they saw, not the physical exterior of the subject, but instead the real personality concealed below the facial lineaments.

Debuting with Sir Clinton Driffield in *Murder in the Maze* is Sir Clinton's best friend, Squire Wendover. The Squire appears in fourteen of the seventeen Driffield novels (he is entirely absent from three of the first five Driffields, but appears in every one from 1931's *The Boathouse Riddle* through 1947's *Commonsense Is All You Need*), serving as Driffield's Watson figure as the Chief Constable marches from one investigative triumph to another. As in *Murder in the Maze*, Driffield often is staying over at his fellow bachelor's ancestral country estate, Talgarth Grange, when he is called into a local murder investigation. Driffield seems to have a dry affection for his friend, but that does not prevent him from frequently twitting the Squire, whose enthusiasm for the art of amateur detection somewhat exceeds his skill at practicing it.

Although the resemblance of Driffield and Wendover to Holmes and Watson is specifically referenced by the pair themselves in *Murder in the Maze* ("I see," announces Wendover at one point. "I'm to be Watson, and then you'll prove what an ass I am. I'm not over keen."), in *Maze* Connington takes pains to make clear that Wendover is no mere "idiot friend," as the Watson figure in the detective novel was often labeled:

> [Wendover] was one of those red-faced, hearty country gentlemen who, on first acquaintance, give an entirely erroneous impression of themselves. Met casually, he might quite easily have appeared to be a slightly fussy person of very limited intellect and even more restricted interests; but behind that façade lived a fairly acute brain which took a sly delight in exaggerating the misleading mannerisms. Wendover was anything but a fool, though he liked to pose as one.

Squire Wendover indeed is a more interesting character than Agatha Christie's Captain Arthur Hastings and many of the other "fairly acute" to outright dim individuals who filled the stolid ranks of the Watson phalanx in Golden Age detective fiction, though he was never as fully limned by his creator as he might have been. We learn, for example, that Wendover has an instinctive and indulgent sympathy for "pretty girls," but Connington never really lets us glimpse any deeper emotional life that the Squire might have (even Watson had a wife, however briefly). Yet Wendover's warmer, more humane presence admittedly provides relief from the brilliant but formidable and sometimes forbidding Sir Clinton Driffield.

Like many 1920s Golden Age detective novels, *Murder in the Maze* is centered on criminous events at a country house. Attending a weekend house party at *Murder in the Maze*'s Whistlefield, the estate of Roger Shandon, are the following individuals: Roger

DEATH AT SWAYTHLING COURT   11

Shandon himself; Shandon's fraternal twin brother, Neville, and his other brother, Ernest; his niece and nephew, Sylvia and Arthur Hawkhurst; his private secretary, Ivor Stenness; and his charming young houseguests, Vera Forrest and Howard Torrance. Ne'er-do-well Ernest's continual presence at Whistlefield is a constant source of mild irritation to Roger Shandon, but of more concern to him of late is his nephew Arthur, who has exhibited a disturbing lack of mental balance after coming down with "sleepy sickness" (encephalitis lethargica). Further, both of the elder Shandon brothers are involved in contentious business matters: Neville, an attorney, is King's Counsel in the controversial Hackleton case; while Roger, who made his fortune from mysterious doings in South Africa and South America, has been vaguely threatened by a former colleague, who accuses Roger of having cheated him. Finally, the private secretary, Ivor Stenness, clearly is up to something untoward.

After both Roger and Neville Shandon are felled in Whistlefield's famous hedge maze by curare-tipped darts, Sir Clinton arrives to restore order at this fractious country estate. Sir Clinton's performance as a criminal investigator is dazzlingly acute and the novel boasts several bravura scenes, all centering on the sinister hedge maze of death. Surely *Murder in the Maze* is one of the very finest country house mysteries produced by a British detective novelist in the 1920s.

Connington followed *Murder in the Maze* with additional fine Clinton Driffield tales, including *Tragedy at Ravensthorpe* (1927), *The Case with Nine Solutions* (1928), *The Boathouse Riddle* (1931), *The Sweepstake Murders* (1931), *The Castleford Conundrum* (1932) and *The Ha-Ha Case* (1934). Like *Murder in the Maze*, four of these novels we may properly term country house mysteries. One of the very best of the Connington country house mysteries, in every way a worthy successor to *Maze*, is *The Castleford Conundrum*. In this tale the author does an extremely effective job of portraying an odious, stupid woman, Winifred Castleford, and her detestable, sponging in-laws. Even her seemingly sympathetic second husband, Philip Castleford, is offhandedly dismissed with contempt by Clinton Driffield as a cringing weakling. Only Philip's daughter (and Winifred's stepdaughter), Hillary, is portrayed by the author with real sympathy. If one desires to read a novel with a houseful of scheming, contemptible relations and a cleverly arranged murder of the one person with all the money—and what fan of classical English mystery does not—one could not do better than to choose *The Castleford Conundrum*.

The novel opens at Winifred Castleford's country house, Carron Hill, with the author detailing the multiple after-dinner animosities (all centering on the very wealthy Winifred) simmering among the various people there that night. In the one camp we find Philip Castleford and his daughter Hillary, in the other Winifred's designing relations: Constance Lindfield, Winifred's half-sister and companion; Laurence and Kenneth Glencaple, her brothers-in-law from her first marriage (a country doctor and a struggling businessman respectively); and Francis Glencaple, Kenneth's brutish, seemingly near semi-moronic fourteen-year-old son. Not part of the menagerie at Carron Hill, but of great concern to the three women who live there, is Dick Stevenage, an utter waster nevertheless found intensely interesting by the local female population.

In *The Castleford Conundrum*, Connington casts his scorn for humanity about in heaps. Winifred is an utterly worthless being—pushy, selfish and common—eminently deserving of murdering. Thirty-five and with "calves like a sturdy dairy-maid's," "Winnie," as she likes to be called (one of her irritating qualities is her insistence that everyone, even adults, be addressed by diminutives), despises her younger, prettier stepdaughter and makes her life miserable in every petty way that she and her half-sister can devise. Constance is resentful of the presence of Phillip and Hillary at Carron Hill and does all she can to undermine them. Thirty-three years of age and, like Winnie and Hillary, powerfully attracted to the handsome Dick Stevenage, she also is intensely jealous of Hillary Castleford. The main concern of the calculating Laurence and the piggish Kenneth is to secure as much as they can of the fortune Winnie inherited from their deceased brother, by getting Phillip and Hillary essentially written out of Winnie's will. Kenneth's son is possibly the worst of the worthless lot, a horrid young brute whose favorite pastimes are torturing animals and playing with the rook rifle his doting Aunt Winnie has given him. "I could shoot you, Aunt Winnie. Look!" he yells proudly on receiving the weapon, foreshadowing his aunt's imminent demise. Soon the egregious Winnie Castleford is discovered shot dead in a chair on the porch of her summer chalet.

Clinton Driffield and his friend Squire Wendover do not appear on the scene until the final third of the book, but they then find their hands full with a highly complex crime. Before the relentless Sir Clinton reveals all in a classic drawing-room lecture to the suspects gathered at Carron Hill, he sportingly provides Wendover a list of the nine key points in the case, for the Squire to work his way through, if he can. Cryptic clue tabulations like this one were eagerly devoured by the puzzle gluttons of the Golden Age, and Connington certainly does not stint his readership its meat and drink in *The Castleford Conundrum*, a novel full of good things.

The Castleford Conundrum presented crime fiction critics with no puzzle as to its quality. "In *The Castleford Conundrum* Mr. Connington goes to work like an accomplished chess-player. The moves in the games his detectives are called on to play are a delight to watch," raved the reviewer for the *Sunday Times*. He added that "the clues would have rejoiced Mr. Holmes' heart." For its part, the *Spectator* concurred in the *Sunday Times*' assessment of the novel's masterfully-constructed plot: "Few detective stories show such sound reasoning as that by which the Chief Constable brings the crime home to the culprit." Additionally, writer E. C. Bentley, much admired himself as the author of the classic detective novel *Trent's Last Case* (1913), took time to praise the purely literary virtues displayed by Connington in *Castleford*, noting: "Mr. Connington has never written better, or drawn characters more full of life."

The tenth Clinton Driffield detective novel, 1935's *The Tau Cross Mystery* (In England *In Whose Dim Shadow*) moves away from a country house milieu that by the mid-thirties was becoming clichéd to a well-conveyed setting in an English suburb beset with a multitude of sins. The mystery itself is meticulously clued and compelling and the kicker of a closing paragraph is a classic of its kind, showing a pithily sardonic Sir Clinton to great advantage. Additionally, the author paints some excellent character portraits, including an ambitious young police constable, a pushy freelance journalist, a callow Christian evangelist, a careworn Frenchwoman in a marriage of convenience and an introverted, elderly clerk who dreams of traveling to Japan. Connington in particular portrays the clerk, Mr. Mitford, with considerable poignancy. Mitford's one great goal in life is to visit the storybook Japan of his dreams before it is vanquished entirely by the forces of modernization, but, alas, he may not be destined to achieve his goal.

I fully agree with the *Sunday Times* reviewer's enthusiastic assessment of *The Tau Cross Mystery*: "Quiet domestic murder, full of the neatest detective points. . . . [T]hese are not the detective's stock figures, but fully realised human beings." The American humorist and crime fiction reviewer Will Cuppy was similarly discerning in his praise of *Tau Cross*. Having a keen appreciation for data and material fact, Cuppy was dazzled by the tale's "abundance of clews and many other aids to armchair sleuthing," including "an extra pair of shoes, a handkerchief soaked in gore . . . an overturned paint pot . . . the fact that the corpse wears rubber gloves . . . a small bludgeon, a crumpled piece of brown paper and a little gold ornament in the shape of a Tau cross." With such fascinating aids at Clinton Driffield's disposal, the delighted Cuppy concluded, "Sir Clinton can hardly fail, especially as he's letter perfect on 'The Golden Bough,' can quote Sir Thomas Browne's 'Garden of Cyrus,' and can speak any language—we mean, he's smart."

When nearing the end of his composition of *The Tau Cross Mystery* in the spring of 1935, Connington found his own eyesight was going dim. "I was really surprised on looking over the book," Connington later recalled to a friend, the great horologist Rupert Thomas Gould, "to find how I managed to keep up the lightheartedness of dialogue toward the end, for the latter part of the book was written when I was so blind I couldn't read a word I was typing." The author found that he was blinded by cataracts in both eyes. Later that year he underwent successful operations to restore his eyesight. Yet fate had not tired of hazarding with Connington's health. In May 1936 the author had his first heart attack, an event he detailed, with the mordant humor of his creation Sir Clinton Driffield, in another letter to Gould, "written in bed, recumbent, with a drawing board looming over me": "[On May 29] woke up at 3 am feeling Browning was mistaken when he said 'All's right with the world.' An hour later, felt quite sure he was wrong + clammored for morphia to dull the pain. If I'd had only myself to consider, I'd have given in + passed in my cheques, I imagine." Not until August 21, nearly three months later, would doctors allow Connington to "descend and ascend a stair once per diem, and resort to my study four hours a day."

Connington never fully recovered good health after 1936. Eventually he was able to complete a much-interrupted Clinton Driffield detective novel, *A Minor Operation* (1937), but this was the last of his major fictions. Though there are a few bright spots in his later work, most notably *For Murder Will Speak* (1938), *The Four Defences* (1940) and *No Past Is Dead* (1942), overall the last ten years of Connington's life saw a serious diminution of his writing powers. Ill health finally forced Connington's retirement from Queen's University in 1944. "I am afraid," Connington wrote a friend, the chemist and forensic scientist F. Gerald Tryhorn, in August, 1946, eleven months before his death, "that I shall never be much use again. Very stupidly, I tried for a session to combine a full course of lecturing with angina pectoris; and ended up by establishing that the two are immiscible." He added that since retiring in 1944, he had been physically "limited to my house, since even a fifty-yard crawl brings on the usual cramps."

After what he bleakly but forthrightly characterized as "my complete crack-up," Connington admitted that he "didn't feel inclined to write a tec yarn." Instead he relaxed for a time from the technical requirements of mystery plotting and composed a dozen essays on a diverse array of subjects, among them a fascinating French true crime case (which he earlier had used as the basis for his novel *No Past is Dead*), drug use, atomic power, and Scottish legends (including that of the Loch Ness Monster), indicating a wide range of imaginative scope on his part. In these elegant short works, Connington's daughter Irene Stewart avows, "there was something of [the man] himself." The author collected his essays into a volume, *Alias J. J. Connington*, which was published, along with his final detective novel, the pithily titled but over-hastily written *Commonsense Is All You Need*, in 1947, the year of the death, at the age of 66, of Alfred Walter Stewart, Emeritus Professor of Chemistry at Queen's University, Belfast. After Stewart's death his entire body of fictional work fell into decay, despite strong praise in 1972 for the author from Jacques Barzun and Wendell Hertig Taylor in their *Catalogue of Crime*.

In my view Barzun's and Taylor's highly laudatory assessment of J. J. Connington's books is amply justified. The author's work has lasting value, both for the ingenuity of the puzzles and the soundness of the detection as well as for the bracing, sometimes acerbic, narration, so at odds with the "cozy" stereotype of tales from the Golden Age of detective fiction. J. J. Connington has a distinct and memorable voice in mystery fiction, setting him apart from his contemporaries in the genre. The author put not merely his great scientific and technical facility into his J. J. Connington detective novels, but his own distinctive personality as well. The best of the Connington mystery tales—which certainly include *Murder in the Maze*, *The Castleford Condundrum* and *The Tau Cross Mystery*—should give considerable enjoyment to mystery readers of today, just as they did with mystery readers of the Golden Age.

BIBLIOGRAPHICAL NOTE: For much more on Alfred Walter Stewart and the J. J. Connington detective novels, see "Alfred Walter Stewart (1880-1947): Survival of the Fittest," the fourth chapter in my book *Masters of the "Humdrum" Mystery: Cecil John Charles Street, Freeman Wills Crofts, Alfred Walter Stewart and The British Detective Novel, 1920-1961* (McFarland, 2012). On Stewart's life and academic career see also his entry in the *Oxford Dictionary of National Biography* (Oxford and New York: Oxford University Press, 2004), vol. 52, pp. 627-628. The quotations from the Stewart-Gould correspondence are by permission of Jonathan Betts, Sarah Stacey and Irene Stewart.

DEATH AT
SWAYTHLING COURT

NOTE

A READER BEGINNING a detective story has two methods open to him in following the narrative. He may regard it simply as a tale and not trouble his head about the solution of the mystery until he reaches it in due course at the final chapter. Or he may treat the book as an exercise in reasoning and pit himself against the author in an attempt to work out the mystery for himself.

Unfortunately in many cases his labour is made futile because the author allows his detective to pick up some undescribed clue of supreme importance; and this generally happens in the middle of the book, after the reader has expended much mental energy in working his way through the tangle of incidents.

In the present book I have tried to play quite fair by my readers; and I believe that they will have a full knowledge of every essential fact before they reach the last chapter. They may therefore, if they so choose, embark light-heartedly on the task of detection with the assurance that they will at least know as much as the character who is attempting to solve the problem.

This statement may perhaps excuse my breach of literary etiquette in putting a prefatory note in front of a mere detective yarn.

J. J. C.

1
THE GREEN DEVIL OF FERNHURST

Colonel Sanderstead looked gloomily at his wrist-watch for the third time. Punctual to a second himself, he expected an equal clockwork precision from others; and even his long series of disappointments in the matter had failed to reconcile him to humanity's slipshod methods. He gave another glance down the empty avenue which fell away from the terrace of the Manor towards the gates on the Fernhurst Parva road; then he addressed the dog at his side:

"If that young man doesn't put in an appearance soon, old boy, we shan't get our two rounds before lunch. I can't think what this generation's coming to."

The dog, gathering from the tone of the remark that the Colonel was wounded but courageous in the face of adversity, wagged his tail mournfully through a small arc. Suddenly, however, he pricked up his ears and gave a short bark. From far down the avenue came the ascending roar of an engine; a motor-cycle, furiously driven, flashed from behind the trees at the turn, skimmed up the slope and stopped beside the terrace.

"Hullo! Hullo! Colonel," the rider remarked breezily, "I must apologize for being late and all that; but I forgot to ring up a man before I left home, and I had to swoop into the grocery emporium and ask old man Swaffham to let me breathe a few words through his wire. Hope I haven't kept you waiting for the golf-bag parade?"

"No harm done, Jimmy," his host reassured him.

With young Leigh's arrival, the Colonel had forgotten his previous fidgetings. He liked the younger generation, even if, as he regretfully admitted, he did not altogether understand them. Although only in his early fifties, the Colonel in some mysterious way left the impression upon strangers that he was a belated Edwardian who had survived into the Georgian era with all his mild prejudices intact. His social psychology seemed to have become truncated in the early years of the century. When motor-cars came in, he had been abreast of the times and had become a keen driver; but the high-powered motor-cycle appeared too late to secure his approval.

Golf had come into favour early enough to catch him in its net; and he had laid out in his park a private nine-hole course. He took golf, like everything else, very seriously. Once on the links, his conversation was confined to the putting-greens; and even there it was not abundant. It was, in fact, restricted to two words: 'My hole,' if he had been successful; 'Your hole,' if fortune went against him. At the eighteenth green he was accustomed to vary this by saying: 'Your game,' or 'My game,' as the case might be.

"Come along, Jimmy; we've just time for a couple of rounds," said the Colonel, moving towards the path which led down to the first tee. Then, noticing that his dog was following them, he invited it, in the most friendly tone but with unmistakable firmness, to remain behind.

"Towser has never learned to be anything but a nuisance on the putting-green," he explained, half-apologetically.

"Towser?" mused Jimmy Leigh aloud, "Towser? What sort of a name's that? I never heard of any dogs called Towser."

The Colonel rose to the bait.

"One of the dogs at Fernhurst Manor has always been called Towser," he explained with dignity.

"Oh, I see." Jimmy assumed the expression of one who suddenly fathoms a mystery. "Just as one of our family has always been called Leigh, eh? A positively coruscating idea. Saves confusion and wear and tear on the brain-cells. When you call for Towser in extremity, you get Towser. Perhaps not the same Towser as you had yesterday, but a sound, reliable article with the identical label on the bottle."

"You young scoundrels have no respect for tradition," said the Colonel, with a faint grin. "Your forefathers, Jimmy, were decent country gentlemen; and now you come along—a black-faced mechanic, spending your time in that grubby laboratory you've fitted up at the Bungalow, down there. If you dug up the churchyard you'd find most of your ancestors turned in their graves by the thought. . . . By the way, I've got one of your new sound-boxes fitted to my gramophone. My congratulations; it's a wonderful improvement. Voices sound less like Punch and Judy with your fitting."

"Overwhelming applause and sound of boots in the gallery. Don't all shake hands at once. As a matter of fact, it's not a patch on a new affair I've just finished."

"Is that the thing I heard about the other day, something like a ray that kills without leaving any marks?"

Jimmy Leigh assumed a disconcerted expression.

"Somebody's been talking. The Secret Out or the Inventor Betrayed, tragedy in one fit. Who can it have been? Concentrate your attention on the name; and without apparatus of any kind or even the assistance of a confederate, I shall now proceed to divulge the artist's cognomen. . . . It's coming. . . . I have it! . . . The Reverend Peter Flitterwick, Vicar of Fernhurst Parva. . . . How's that for mind-reading? The collection will not be taken."

"It was Flitterwick, of course," the Colonel admitted. "But I thought you were pulling his leg, to check his enthusiasm for gossip."

"Dear! Dear! Terrible wave of scepticism extending from Iceland to the west coast of Ireland. Indications of secondary doubts farther east. Local patches of disbelief in Lethal Rays will be found in Southern England. Direct by wireless from the Psychological Bureau. I tell you what, sir. I'm giving a practical demonstration to-morrow morning: come along yourself and see what science can do."

The Colonel examined his companion curiously.

"You'll never get anyone to take you seriously, Jimmy. They say you're sound on the scientific side; but you're not impressive."

"True bill, Colonel. The flesh-and-blood scientist is very human, most disappointingly unlike Sherlock Holmes. But with all my failings I manage to impress some people. Why, the other night at the 'Three Bees,' old Summerley was boasting that he could 'p'ison a man so that nobody, no, not even young Master Leigh at the Bungalow, could find it out.' That's a tribute of respect that even your favourite Sherlock never got. James Leigh, the great detective of Sleepy Hollow!"

The Colonel winced slightly. Fernhurst Parva was very dear to him; and he hated to have fun poked at it, even by one of a family that had been as long on the ground as his own forbears. Twenty years ago he had settled down on his small estate, determined, as he put it, "to do his duty by his tenantry"; and in the doing of that duty, as he saw it by his simple lights, he had considerably impoverished himself, and had captured the difficult affections of the slow-moving country-folk of Fernhurst Parva. To them, the Colonel's least word was more than law, not because he could put the screw on them, but because they trusted him to do his best for everybody. He had gradually become a minor Providence in the district. To him, Fernhurst Parva was very important; and he disliked to hear it described as 'Sleepy Hollow.'

"Fernhurst Parva is a very decent place," he rapped out. "They're not a lot of half-baked, semi-educated towns-folk, anyway. They stick to the old ways; and that's uncommon in these times."

"True," Jimmy conceded, thoughtfully. "By the way, one of your favourite old traditions has bobbed up again lately. There's talk in the village that the Green Devil's reappeared. Somebody's 'for it' this time, it seems."

The Colonel glanced uneasily at his companion, suspecting another attempt at leg-pulling. The Green Devil of Fernhurst was a local superstition of which he was archæologically proud, but which he was rather ashamed to find cropping up at the present day. The phantom's manifestations were supposed to be a portent of sudden and violent death in the neighbourhood; but its last recorded appearance had been far back in the nineteenth century; and the Colonel had believed that the legend was almost dead.

"Where did you get that?" he asked, suspiciously.

"Broadcasted by Local Information Bureau—Flitterwick."

"Who saw it?"

"Somebody who told a boy who told a girl who told a man who repeated it to Flitterwick who gave it to me. Sounds a bit like the House that Jack Built, doesn't it? But Flitterwick never had any notion of sifting evidence. All's grist that comes to his gossip-mill, you know."

The Colonel was inclined to pursue the subject; but by now they had reached the first tee, and he dismissed all minor matters from his mind.

"You can have the honour," he said, pulling out his driver.

For three holes, Jimmy Leigh respected his host's silence; but as they came to the next tee, his irrepressible loquacity broke out once more.

"There's young Mickleby—the locum that Crabtree put in when he went off on holiday—driving Crabtree's old Ford along the Bishop's Vernon road. I envy Mickleby. He can look dignified even driving a tin Lizzie. Some lad, that. Sainted liver-flukes! Here comes the Micheldean Abbas Express with the fat proprietor at the wheel. See 'em pass each other. Mickleby's dignity won't allow him to give anyone else much of the road. I wish I were near enough to hear old Don Simon's remarks; they must be fruity."

"Your honour," said the Colonel, testily.

He hated Simon: pestiferous fellow, setting up a motor-omnibus service to Micheldean Abbas, and bringing all sorts of new ideas into Fernhurst Parva. Always against constituted authority, was Simon; a man with no respect for territorial connections, next door to a Socialist. But what could one expect from a townsman? The fellow was forever trying to stir up trouble in the village; one couldn't have a quiet meeting on local affairs without him getting on his feet, making would-be acute comments and trying to rouse dissatisfaction in the country-folk. If Colonel Sanderstead had not been capable of immense self-restraint he might have foozled his drive, so much irritated was he by the mere name of the motor-bus proprietor. There was no further conversation between the players until the end of the round.

"Yours," said the Colonel; and with that he put away his taci- turnity until the first ball had been teed for the new round.

"I've just been wondering," he went on, dropping the flag back into the hole, "what relation you will be to me when that nephew of mine marries your sister. Her decree *nisi* will be made absolute in another three weeks or so, Cyril told me the other day; and then I suppose they won't put off much time."

A cloud seemed to pass momentarily across Jimmy Leigh's face; but it had gone before the Colonel could be sure that he had really seen it.

"Mind if I smoke a cigarette before we start the new round, Colonel?"

He pulled out his case and began to smoke as they stood at the teeing-ground. It was not until the cigarette was well alight that he answered the Colonel's implied question.

"They ought to have married eight years ago. Hilton was never her style. No girl ever seems to know a bad hat, somehow."

"The thing that passes my comprehension is why she did not get rid of him long ago."

"Because he was too smart for that. He's a queer card, is Mas- ter Hilton. He's not tired of Stella; he's as jealous of her as a couple of Othellos rolled into one: and yet he's been after dozens of women in the last few years."

"Then I don't see much difficulty," said the Colonel. "He's given enough away to establish a cruelty charge, all right. I've seen bruises on her wrists myself; and anyone could guess how they got there."

"Yes, Colonel, but you don't begin to understand Master Hilton even yet. He's a bright fellow, a nap hand when it comes to this sort of thing. He goes off—untraceable; we've had private 'tecs on his track often enough and he shakes them off every time, like water off a duck's back. Then he comes back, the loving husband, you know, and tells Stella all about it—full details—except for names and places. That's his way of being humorous. No evidence at all. It was the merest shave that we nabbed him once at his games, a pure fluke. And that's why everything's been staked on that single case. If it were to break down—any hitch of any sort—I doubt if we could get him again."

"Couldn't he be thrashed into some sort of decency?"

"Not by me. You forget there's been a war and that I didn't manage to pick all of myself off the stricken field when I had had enough of it."

"Why doesn't Cyril do it, then?" growled the Colonel. "I'm not particular, Lord knows, but women are my weak point. I can't stand seeing them hurt."

"Stella and I have kept Cyril in hand—difficult job at times, I can tell you. No sinecure. He was all for knocking friend Hilton into the next county. But Stella and I made up our minds there was to be none of that. We want no grounds for people sniggering and hinting that Cyril had staked out an illicit claim on Stella; things are bad enough without that complication."

"Well, perhaps you're right." Then Colonel Sanderstead's simple code came out. "All the same, a man who treats a woman badly shouldn't be allowed to go on existing. That's my view; and if I were twenty years younger I'd like to take on Hilton myself, just on general principles."

He pondered for a moment or two in silence, as if brooding over the case. Then he seemed to dismiss the subject.

"Your honour again, Jimmy."

They played the second round in silence; and, ended up all square. Whatever the Colonel's reflections may have been, he evidently decided to say no more on a sore subject; and when the last putt loosened his vocal cords, he opened a new line of conversation.

"Have you seen much of our next-door neighbour, Jimmy, the fellow who took Swaythling Court?"

"Hubbard, you mean? I've come across him. Ardent butterfly-snatcher, I judge. His talk about Purple Emperors, Red Admirals, and Painted Ladies gives me a fine spacious feeling—as if I were being received at Court, almost. But apart from that, I don't find much interest in his society. Greasy fellow, one of the kind that can't talk to you without crawling all over you—putting his hand on your shoulder and spraying saliva into your physog."

"The country-side's getting infested with undesirables. First of all we have that damned fellow Simon with his stinking motor-omnibus coming in and trying to stir up discontent in the village; and now, instead of poor old Swaythling, there comes this fellow Hubbard—not our sort—and plants himself right down in the middle of us. Never spends a penny in the village, of course, though he seems to have plenty of money. I wonder what brand of profiteer he was in the war?"

"Ask Flitterwick," Jimmy suggested. "But you're wrong about his distaste for spending money locally. He's most anxious to finance me—only we don't quite seem to be able to hit off the relative values of Bradburys and brains. Perhaps we'll get to it yet, though."

"Look here, Jimmy," interrupted the Colonel, anxiously. "Don't get mixed up with these City fellows. If you want capital, I'd rather pinch a bit and find it myself for you. I think I could do it, if it's a question of keeping you clear of that beggar. You can make the interest what you like—nothing, if it suits you. But don't put yourself under an obligation to an outsider."

Jimmy Leigh frowned slightly.

"Don't you worry about obligations, Colonel. I can pay Hubbard any debt I owe him without sponging on my friends."

The brusqueness of the reply set the Colonel thinking; but he understood that Jimmy had given him a broad hint not to continue the financial discussion. Fortunately a chance occurred to change the subject without difficulty. As they turned away from the green, a curious figure approached them.

'Sappy' Morton had an intellect considerably below par. Even the Colonel, with his affection for Fernhurst Parva, had to admit that one of its inhabitants was, as he gently put it, 'hardly normal.' The rest of the population, blunter in description, referred to Sappy as 'the village idiot.' Across that great moon-face there flitted a continual procession of expressions; but all that they revealed was emotion without a trace of intellect. And when the slack mouth opened, only the most rudimentary speech flowed out.

At the sight of Colonel Sanderstead, Sappy's countenance was overspread by a vacant grin which represented his highest expression of delight. He came down towards the players at an ungainly trot, pulled himself up, and gave a vague gesture which seemed to have some remote kinship with a military salute. The Colonel solemnly and punctiliously acknowledged the salute, much to Sappy's evident joy.

"Well, Sappy, been a good boy since I saw you last?"

"Good. Good," the idiot responded, eagerly.

"And what are you doing with yourself, these days?"

Sappy reflected for a few moments before he replied:

"Sappy looking for pretty things."

The Colonel exchanged a glance with Jimmy Leigh. To both of them, Sappy's peculiarities were a source of some astonishment. The search for 'pretty things' was the one passion of the idiot. He would sit for hours at a time intent on some flower that he had picked, turning it over and over to bring some fresh aspect into view. Butterflies he would chase for half an hour at a time, merely for the pleasure of watching them; and, curiously enough, he never attempted to catch them. There was no strain of cruelty in Sappy's disordered mind. So far as the Colonel had been able to fathom the shoals and channels of that vague intelligence, Sappy regarded all living things as his brothers. The creature was easily moved to emotion; and once Colonel Sanderstead had come upon him, intent upon the scarlet and gold of a sunset, with tears rolling unheeded down his cheeks.

"I'm afraid most of your pretty things will be going to sleep for the winter, soon, Sappy. Autumn's drawing on. No more butterflies or flowers for you then, you know. Never mind, perhaps we'll have snow and you'll see the trees covered with it."

"No more butterflies? No more flowers?"

Jimmy Leigh broke in:

"Mr. Hubbard's put all the butterflies to sleep in glass cases, Sappy."

The idiot gaped at him unintelligently, so Jimmy patiently amplified his explanation.

"Mr. Hubbard catches butterflies. He puts them to bed in a glass case. He shuts the case. No more butterflies till next summer, Sappy."

An expression of alarm flitted across the imbecile's great face.

"Hubbard bad, bad. Hurt Sappy."

"Eh, what's that?" demanded the Colonel, sharply. Sappy was a protégé of his; and he had put down with a heavy hand any attempts on the part of the village boys to torment the idiot.

But it was impossible to extract any information from Sappy. He repeated: "Hubbard bad, bad," several times; but beyond that nothing could be got out of him. The Colonel made a mental note that the matter was worth looking into. It was bad enough that this greasy beggar Hubbard should settle down in the district, without adding to his sins by tormenting a defenceless creature like Sappy; and clearly, from the idiot's bearing, there had been trouble of some sort. Colonel Sanderstead gave up the task of eliciting information from the simpleton and bethought him of a way to restore Sappy to good spirits:

"What's the time, Sappy?"

The imbecile's face broadened out into the vacant grin which was his sole expression of pleasure. He caught the Colonel's sleeve and pointed eagerly to where the church tower of Fernhurst Parva rose out of the trees.

"Ding-dong, ding-dong, ding-dong, ding-dong! Dong!"

He paused for a moment, and then completed his count:

"Ding-dong!"

"Quarter-past one, eh?"

The Colonel looked at his wrist-watch, which he had replaced after finishing his game:

"It's 1.25 p.m., Jimmy. He's right again. Wonderful how he remembers these chimes. I've never known him to make a mistake."

He turned back to the idiot and pointed towards the church tower.

"Another chime coming soon, Sappy. You listen for it. Good-day to you."

"Ta-ta, Sappy," said Jimmy Leigh, as he followed his host towards the house. "You listen well."

"Sappy listen," the idiot assured him, his attention strained on the distant tower among the trees.

"You were boasting of your reputation as a detective, Jimmy," the Colonel remarked, as they walked up the path. "I've often wondered how an ordinary man—say you or I—would get on, if he had to investigate a mystery. There's no saying: we might manage quite well."

"Or again we mightn't? It's always best to state a case in full, you know."

"Well, I shouldn't mind having a try," Colonel Sanderstead confessed. "But in the ordinary run one never finds any cases to try one's hand on. Our circle seems to be very free from murders and sudden deaths."

"Not so free as you'd think," corrected Jimmy Leigh, his face clouding over at some recollection. "It's not three months since young Campbell shot himself—Cyril's sub., you remember. Cyril was badly cut up about it. So was I, for that matter. Young Campbell pulled me out of a tight place, once upon a time. A friendly lad."

"You needn't try to pass it off as a joke, Jimmy. There's nothing to be ashamed of in emotion of that sort. Have you any notion of what was at the root of it. It seemed a queer affair."

"Cyril suspected the cub was blackmailed; but there was no certainty about it."

"Blackmail! That's a foul business. If I had my way, I'd make blackmail a capital offence and hang without scruple. Murderers are gentlemen in comparison to blackmailers."

Jimmy Leigh seemed to have recovered his normal spirits.

"All right, Colonel. If any blackmailer gets throttled in Fernhurst Parva, I'll know who's responsible. Don't be afraid. I shan't split on you. On with the good work, say I. I never was a sympathiser with vermin, myself. So you can count on me to keep it dark if I find the corpse of one of your victims lying about. Well, till next time; and thanks for the game."

He straddled his motor-cycle and pushed off.

2
THE LETHAL RAY

As COLONEL SANDERSTEAD passed the trim Vicarage on the following morning, the door opened and he paused for a moment to let the Vicar join him. The Reverend Peter Flitterwick was a shade older than the Colonel—a thin, clean-shaven man with a slight stoop, and spectacles which lent him an air of peering benevolence.

"Good morning, Flitterwick. Pleasant day."

"Good morning, Colonel. Indeed a most pleasant day and a pleasant place also. *Angulus ridet*, as Horace has it; this little corner of the world smiles to me each time I cross my door."

"Oh, yes, quite so."

The Colonel, somehow, never cared to hear Flitterwick's praises of his beloved village; for some obscure reason, he felt a suspicion that they arose more from toadyism than from any real appreciation of Fernhurst Parva. He glanced at his wrist-watch and struck into a smart walk.

"You're going to young Leigh's, aren't you, Flitterwick? We'll have to hurry up, then. It won't do to be late for our appointment."

The Vicar, who was not in good training, found that he had enough to do in keeping step with the Colonel; and conversation was broken off until they reached the Bungalow, which was precisely what Colonel Sanderstead desired. Somehow he never was quite sure of Flitterwick: he felt that the Vicar was too soapy, even if it were mere mannerism; and he disliked that habit of quoting Latin and then offering a translation in parenthesis. Colonel

Sanderstead had heard him astounding old Miss Meriden with a classical tag, once. Shocking bad taste, that.

At the Bungalow, the old housekeeper opened the door.

"Good morning, Mrs. Pickering," said the Colonel, with more heartiness than he had shown with Flitterwick. "All right again, I hope? Rheumatism quite gone? Good. But I'm afraid this place is a bit damp for you, too much down in the hollow, perhaps. Is Mr. Leigh disengaged?"

"If you'll step this way, sir."

She ushered them into Jimmy Leigh's work-room: a big low-ceilinged apartment at the back of the house, with a French window opening out on to a lawn. It seemed to be half-laboratory and half smoke-room, to judge by the furnishing. Big saddlebag arm-chairs were grouped about the fire, whilst round the walls were work-benches of the laboratory pattern.

As the Colonel entered, he became aware that there was to be a fourth in the party, and only politeness kept him from showing his distaste for the company into which he had been brought. He shook hands with Jimmy and nodded stiffly to the remaining occupant of the room.

Hubbard was not an attractive character. He was a big clumsy man, with an expression of watchful slyness which sat ill upon a person of his bulk. Somehow, with his little close-set eyes, his red face, his ugly hands with their vulgar display of rings, his large and slightly flat feet, he looked out of place between Jimmy and the Colonel. At their first meeting, Colonel Sanderstead had felt an instinctive antipathy for him. There was something about his manner, not furtiveness, exactly, but something akin to it, which had jarred on the Colonel's nerves. A nasty type, the Colonel had judged him: a man who would try to gain his ends by soap if he were dealing with a strong man, but would bully to the extreme if he got a weaker man into his power.

Hubbard seemed to have missed the cavalier touch in the Colonel's nod.

"Good morning, Colonel Thanderthead. Very pleathant weather to-day; but lookth a bit like rain, eh?"

The combination of the lisp with a naturally rough voice sub-consciously irritated the Colonel. He nodded again, as stiffly as before, and then, to avoid further conversation with his *bête noire*, he glanced round the room in search of something which would enable him to address Jimmy Leigh. His eye was caught by a long metal tube running out from the French window on to the lawn, an apparatus resembling the protector of the shooting galleries which occasionally appeared at the fairs of Fernhurst Parva.

"What's that thing?" he asked.

Jimmy Leigh grinned.

"That? That's the Lethal Ray Shooting Gallery—patent not yet applied for. Place a penny in the slot, press the button, and down comes a rat, rabbit, or guinea-pig. No aiming no ranging. A perfect toy for the youngest child. A novelty. Likewise a curiosity. Buy one to take home with you to-day."

The Colonel went forward and peered into the long metal chamber; but there was nothing which specially attracted his interest. The thing was simply an iron tube, about eighteen inches in diameter and built up in sections to a length of fifteen feet. The two ends were closed by means of glass plates; and the whole thing was supported on rough wooden trestles. As Colonel Sanderstead examined it, he was relieved to hear Hubbard engaging Flitterwick in conversation.

"You've never come acroth to thee my collecthion, parthon. Any morning you like, after ten o'clock. But perhapth you're not much interethted in butterflieth?"

The Colonel absent-mindedly noted Flitterwick's annoyance at Hubbard's form of address. Parson! What an outsider the fellow was. And what was Jimmy Leigh doing with a creature like that in his house? It wasn't like Jimmy. Usually he was careful in his choice of associates—more particular than most people.

"I shall be delighted to take an early opportunity, Mr. Hubbard, delighted." Flitterwick's voice hardly expressed the pleasure that his words implied. There was a sort of duty-to-be-gone-through tinge in his tone. "You may expect me on the first morning which

my duties leave unoccupied. I understand that your collection is a
wonderful one."

"Itth very fair, thertainly. Itth cotht me a lot o' trouble to put
together."

"Ah, quite so; you must be an enthusiast, Mr. Hubbard, a lover
of beauty, evidently. Alas! Beauty is frail ware. You remember the
verse in the *Ars Amatoria? Forma bonum fragile est*. A reprehen-
sible writer, Ovid, though full of beauty."

"I never read him, parthon. They didn't teach Greek in my
thcool. I gather he'th amuthing, from what you thay. Got the
goodth, eh? Hot thtuff? You fellowth know where to nothe it out."

He nudged Flitterwick meaningly in the ribs; then, growing
confidential, he put his arm round the Vicar's thin shoulder.

"There'th a nithe little butterfly I've got my eye on up in Upper
Greenthtead. I marked her down one day I wath pathing in the
car. I'd like to add her to my collecthion."

The Colonel winced, relaxed his lips as if to say something, then
thought better of it and continued his inspection of the apparatus.
Jimmy Leigh gave him an excuse by dragging forward a large trolly
loaded with some complicated machine, which evidently formed
part of the 'shooting gallery.' The Colonel helped him to place it in
position at the end of the iron tube. Meanwhile Flitterwick was
making efforts to steer the conversation on to other lines.

"Butterfly-collecting must be a most interesting recreation, Mr.
Hubbard. Could you give me some idea of the *modus operandi*,
the way you go about it? I fear that I am deeply ignorant of the
whole affair."

Unobtrusively he made a successful effort to free himself from
Hubbard's affectionate embrace.

"There'th really nothing in it, parthon. After you've caught a
butterfly with the net, you take it
out with your fingerth and put it into the killing-bottle. . . ."

"The killing-bottle? Really? And what is the killing-bottle?"

Flitterwick knew all the little tricks to suggest intense interest
in a conversation; but through continual use they had grown

slightly mechanical. His eager questions might seem verbally to imply a keen desire for further information; but the tone in which they were uttered could not conceal his boredom. Hubbard, however, was too obtuse to notice that.

"It'th a wide-mouthed bottle with thome crystalth of thyanide of potash at the bottom of it. The thyanide give-th off pruthic athid fume-th; and that killth the butterfly."

"I understand. Cyanide of potash in the bottle; and it gives off prussic acid; and that kills the butterfly. Really? Indeed? Most ingenious."

"That preventth the butterfly from damaging itth wing-scale-th in the death-thtruggle. Itth killed inthtantly."

"Ah, most ingenious, most ingenious. And then, Mr. Hubbard?"

"Then you have to mount the butterfly before it gets thtiff. Pin it on a thetting-board, you know, with a cork cover and a groove for the body and bitth of cardboard to fix the wingth in pothithion."

"Ah! very ingenious, Mr. Hubbard."

Hubbard seemed to take this tribute as a personal one. He made another endeavour to lay his hand on the Vicar's shoulder, and invited him to visit Swaythling Court as soon as possible so that he might see the actual apparatus.

By this time, however, Jimmy Leigh, with the Colonel's help, had got his apparatus arranged in the position which he desired. He was now busy connecting wires with terminals; and when this was finished, he drew the attention of the company to the complete machine.

"Pass on to the next caravan, gentlemen. Here you see the Lethal Ray Shooting Gallery or Painless Destructor. Supersedes all rifles, revolvers, automatic pistols, bludgeons and knuckle-dusters. Kills instantaneously and leaves absolutely no marks. A pocket edition will enable householders to eliminate a burglar without soiling the carpet. The full-size machine will kill anything from a flea to an elephant. Makes an enjoyable recreation for long winter evenings. You press the button; it does the rest."

"Suppose you tell us something about it, for a change," interrupted the Colonel, caustically.

Jimmy Leigh became serious.

"The trouble is, Colonel, that it's very difficult to make a complex thing like this clear to laymen. I really can't go into the whole affair, because it would probably take me until to-morrow if I did. You see, you people don't even know what a choke-coil is; you haven't the groggiest notion of the effect produced by changing the surface-area of a condenser. And this affair is a pretty complicated stunt depending upon the mutual influence of induced currents. Will it be enough if I give you the backbone and leave out the rest?"

"Quite enough," said the Colonel, who abhorred technicalities which he did not understand—as Jimmy Leigh already knew.

"Very well. First Steps in Murder, page one. Every time a muscle contracts in your body, there's a slight flow of electricity in one direction or another. Now a current of electricity in one direction can be neutralized by another, equal current, flowing through the same material in the opposite direction. They cancel each other out, as it were. Got that?"

The Colonel nodded. His other two hearers seemed to be paying little attention.

"Your heart, Colonel, is simply a mass of muscle; and with every beat of it, a slight current of electricity is generated. They use that in the electrocardiograph to determine whether the heart is normal or not. Suppose, now, you could interfere with that generation of electricity, stop it—to take an extreme case—you would knock the heart out of action; and your subject would suffer from something that would look like a bad attack of heart-disease. If your experiment was prolonged, you could throw the heart so much out of gear that the subject would find his vital machinery stopped completely. See that?"

"I'm not out of my depth yet," the Colonel admitted with some pride.

"Well, that's all there is in it. This machine here sends out a ray which I can direct to any point. That ray has the heart-interfering property; it disorganizes the electrical action of the heart-muscle. It affects all the muscles of the body, of course, but the heart-muscle is the only one we need bother about just now. Consequently, if the ray passes over an animal, the beast collapses. Don't take my word for it. I'm going to show you the thing actually at work. I've got a rat I trapped yesterday and you can touch it off yourself if you like. Just wait a jiffy till I get the beast."

"*Fiat experimentum in corpore vili*, by all means," interjected Flitterwick.

"Quite right. 'Try it on the dog,' as we used to say. I'll be back in half a mo'."

While Jimmy Leigh was absent from the room, the Colonel occupied himself with an examination of the apparatus which now stood opposite the glass-fronted end of the iron tube. It seemed an extremely complex affair. A huge bobbin of black ebonite occupied the lower floor of the trolly, along with something that looked like an electromotor of peculiar construction. The upper platform was crowded with coils of wire, glass tubes blown into peculiar shapes, apparently empty jars partly coated with tin-foil, things which the Colonel supposed to be switches, and one or two electric lamps with buffed glasses. Terminals held wires which were connected at the other end to binding-screws on the bench near at hand. The Colonel could make neither head nor tail of the machine; and his admiration for Jimmy Leigh's scientific attainments rose a few degrees higher than before. He must be a wonderful fellow if he could see his way through such a complicated affair, more wonderful still if he could invent a thing like that.

Hubbard put his hand on the Colonel's shoulder and leaned down to look at the apparatus. Colonel Sanderstead abruptly broke off his examination and retreated a few paces. Hubbard paid no attention to this; evidently he was quite accustomed to people resenting his familiarity. He stared for a few moments at the machine, then gave it up.

"I can't thay I care much for this thort of thtuff. All I'm interethted in is the finanthial thide of it. If Jimmy Leigh can do what he thays he can do, then itth a thound affair and I'm willing to put money into it, lotth of money."

"Damned dividend-hunter," was the Colonel's reflection. "I must persuade Jimmy to cold-shoulder this person. He's not the sort of fellow Jimmy should be mixed up with at all. Jimmy got his other patents marketed without any bother. Why should he want to encourage an outsider in this case?"

But his further meditations on this unwelcome topic were broken by Jimmy's return with a large wire cage in which a fair-sized rat was imprisoned.

"Now then, uncle," Jimmy addressed his captive, "we're just going to give you a whiff of chloroform to quieten you down a bit; and then we'll proceed to put you into a happier world where all the walls are cheese."

The Colonel pricked up his ears.

"Are you going to chloroform the brute? Won't the ray work on a normal animal?"

"Certainly it will. But it's better to give the beast a whiff, not more than a whiff, at the start. Otherwise you'd have it scampering about too much. I want you to be able to watch exactly how it behaves. Besides, to be quite frank with you, Colonel, the ray works best when the patient is not overexcited. If he's slightly narcotized, it seems to help the action; though it isn't absolutely necessary. I guarantee to kill a sheep with this machine, just as it stands."

"That's all right, Jimmy," said the Colonel, hastily. "I wasn't doubting you, of course. I only asked for information."

"Well, here goes."

Jimmy Leigh poured a few drops of chloroform on a clear space on one of the benches, placed the rat's cage over it, and covered it with a cloth for a few moments.

"That's about enough, I think."

He lifted the cloth, placed the cage in front of the tube of the 'shooting gallery,' withdrew both the glass slide and the sliding door of the cage, and bundled the rat into the iron cylinder, replacing the glass slide behind it.

"Now have a look at uncle; make sure there's no deception and that I haven't a dead rat up my sleeve."

The chloroform had evidently dazed the animal, for at first it sat still and paid no attention to movements on the part of the observers. Gradually, however, it seemed to recover and began to move about, though languidly. Jimmy Leigh clicked home a switch and immediately the rising whine of a motor contact-breaker sounded, which seemed to disturb the rat slightly. It retreated slowly down the steel tube, away from the nearer window. Jimmy Leigh busied himself with the manipulation of a series of further switches.

"Now, look out!"

A big tube in the apparatus suddenly shot out a flare of deep red light; there was a deafening report as a huge spark leapt between two electrodes. The rat gave a convulsive start, retreated an inch or two farther, and dropped dead on the floor of the tube.

"Stand clear till I switch off."

Jimmy Leigh went through some further manipulations; the angry glare died away in the glass tube; and the whine of the contact-breaker faded out into silence.

"All safe now. We'll hook him out for inspection. Perhaps you'll remove uncle's carcass yourself, Colonel, so that there can be no suspicion that I'm using a trained rat for the purpose of this experiment?"

With the help of a long rod furnished with a hook at the end, the Colonel succeeded in raking the rat out of the death-chamber. It was undeniably dead, struck down as if by a thunderbolt. The Colonel gingerly handed the little corpse to Hubbard, who examined it with interest.

"Itth thertainly ath dead ath mutton. Hath it any thpecial thymptoms, Leigh?"

Jimmy seemed to consider for a moment.

"It has. The eye-pupils are always widely dilated; and, funny thing, I've always found traces of cyanide—prussic acid anyway—in the stomach afterwards. Quite a big dose, too. Rum start, that. I can't explain it."

Hubbard seemed a trifle sceptical on one point.

"Thith arrangement here theemth a trifle elaborate. Are you thure you can direct the ray in any directhion you pleathe?"

Jimmy Leigh smiled indulgently at the query. "Doesn't it strike you that *unless* the ray had been directed last time, it wouldn't have been only the rat that went west? That machine would kill you just as easily as the rat; and yet you weren't touched when the shot was fired, so to speak. See this pointer?"

He indicated a slender brass needle screwed to the edge of the table, which in its present position was directed down the axis of the iron tube.

"That pointer gives you the danger-line. Everything else round about is quite safe."

"And what about the range of the machine? That'th a very important point."

Jimmy Leigh led them out into the garden, from which they had an open view of the country-side. He took his stand under a telephone wire which cut across the garden and extended away towards Micheldean Abbas.

"See old Swaffham's phone cable? Follow the line of that into the village. See the cottage on the hill right above? Two thousand—say two thousand two hundred. I could make the thing work over there just as easily as in this garden. Now look farther to the right. The church-tower; four o'clock; three finger-breadths; see that isolated oak? That's within range. Fernhurst Manor is just outside the radius. Now almost due north, Swaythling Court's well within the fatal radius. I could knock out anyone up there with this machine as easy as look at it. Your gate-lodge—ditto. High Thorne and Carisbrooke House are outside the range. That satisfy you?"

Hubbard seemed hardly to relish the information about his own house.

"There'th no chanth of that thing getting out of gear, ith there? I mean going off when you've got it pointed at thomething without meaning it?"

"You needn't worry," Jimmy replied, rather contemptuously. "If it hits you at Swaythling, it won't be an accident."

"I don't like that kind of joke," said Hubbard, rather viciously.

Flitterwick apparently made up his mind to change the conversation.

"A most surprising instrument, I think. Did it take you long to devise it, or was it just a flash of genius?"

Jimmy Leigh hardly suppressed his amusement over the latter suggestion.

"It certainly wasn't a flash of genius. You can put that down in your diary as a dead snick."

"Ah, *ad augusta per augusta*, then—through trial to triumph? It gives me the greatest pleasure to congratulate you upon a wonderful invention."

He glanced with evident distaste at the dead rat which Hubbard had dropped on the floor after his inspection. Hubbard, noting the direction of his look, gave the corpse a kick, as though to see if any life still remained.

"It theems a thound invethtment, Leigh. If you can apply it in war, there'th thure to be money in it:"

"It's a devilish invention," snapped the Colonel, who had never appreciated the methods of scientific warfare.

Flitterwick again provided a diversion. He looked at his watch; seemed perturbed; and picked up his hat:

"I must go, I fear. *Fugit irreparabile tempus*, as Virgil puts it so finely. Time flies, as we say so baldly in English. I have a great deal to do this morning. Many thanks, indeed, for the most interesting experience. Almost an historic occasion; certainly a memorable one. Good-bye, good-bye."

Flitterwick's withdrawal left an awkward situation; but Jimmy Leigh seemed determined to ignore any signs of strain between Hubbard and the Colonel. In fact, he deliberately went out of his way to exasperate the older man.

"Oh, by the way, Colonel, would you mind if Hubbard and I play over your links to-morrow morning? I'd rather like to take him on; and your place is the nearest, for both of us."

The Colonel fumed inwardly; but gave his consent with all the grace he could summon up.

"Thanks awfully, Colonel. Suppose we fix it up now, Hubbard. Ring up your office on my phone and say you won't be there to-morrow."

Hubbard agreed, went over to the telephone, which stood in one corner of the room, and rang up. Jimmy rather rudely left the Colonel to his own devices and became engaged in fiddling with some apparatus on one of the benches.

"Hubbard thpeaking. I won't be at the offith to-morrow. That'th all."

Jimmy Leigh stopped manipulating his apparatus and came forward as Hubbard turned away from the telephone. For some reason, he seemed anxious to be quit of his guests.

"Mind if I come across to dine with you on the day after to-morrow, Colonel? I've one or two things I'd like to talk over, if you don't mind."

"Very well," replied the Colonel. "I'll ask Cyril too, if you like."

"Cyril's playing bridge if I'm not mistaken."

He turned to Hubbard.

"See you at the first tee at ten o'clock, then?" And with very little ceremony he bowed them both out.

3
THE WARRANT

COLONEL SANDERSTEAD came down to breakfast in a dissatisfied frame of mind; and as his meal proceeded, he found that his feelings were not improving. Behind his quiet exterior he was acutely sensitive to any slight changes in the social atmosphere; and Jimmy Leigh's behaviour on the previous night had been unusual enough to set the Colonel thinking. He had been moody and erratic in his talk; and that had disturbed the Colonel vaguely, for although Jimmy was often whimsical, he seldom showed the morose kind of humour which he had displayed so freely on the night before. He had fidgeted and snapped all through dinner, looking at his watch again and again, as though he found the time dragging. His talk had been disconnected; and more than once the Colonel had found him so inattentive that he had had to repeat a sentence in order to make sure that Jimmy had followed his line of argument. And at twenty minutes past eight, Jimmy had put the finishing touch to his ill-manners by gulping down his coffee and departing abruptly, leaving the Colonel to spend the rest of the evening alone. The only excuse he had offered was that he had an appointment with that fellow Hubbard at the Bungalow at 8.30.

The more the Colonel thought over the matter, the less he liked it. He was fond of Jimmy Leigh; had watched him grow up from his perambulator days; and he felt dimly that Jimmy was in some trouble or other. He had meant to draw the boy out a little after dinner and try to get to the bottom of the thing. But Jimmy's abrupt departure had nipped that kindly scheme in the bud; and the

Colonel was left to puzzle over a mystery to which he had no key. What he did surmise about the affair was not encouraging. The association of Jimmy Leigh with a man like Hubbard was in itself astonishing; and Jimmy's moroseness was enough to hint that the relationship produced no agreeable feelings in him. In fact, as the Colonel thought over things, he recalled one or two phrases which Jimmy had used about Hubbard, phrases that implied anything but kindly feelings. The exact words had slipped out of his memory; but he had a general feeling that they suggested friction of some sort.

Still perturbed, the Colonel had risen from the table and was lighting a cigarette when someone knocked at the door:

"Constable Bolam wishes to speak to you, sir. He says he must see you at once; it's very important. He's waiting in your study."

For the moment, Colonel Sanderstead dismissed Jimmy Leigh's affairs from his mind. Bolam, the senior constable of Fernhurst Parva, had been an N.C.O. in the Colonel's command; and he had never shaken off the habits of discipline. Whenever he found himself out of his depth in his official duties, he referred the matter to the Colonel, who was a Justice of the Peace. Colonel and N.C.O.; J.P. and constable: only the names had changed so far as Bolam was concerned; the relative positions remained unaltered in his mind. He brought all his little difficulties up to the Manor for solution; and, to the best of his ability, the Colonel gave him help. Colonel Sanderstead's decisions were perhaps not always good law; but they were based on the theory that whatever was done must be the thing which would be best for everybody; and hitherto there had been no complaints against the results.

As the Colonel entered the study, the constable came sharply to attention. He was a man about forty, trained under the old Army system; and the Colonel regarded him as an ideal subordinate. "Bolam takes his orders; has enough brains to understand them; and carries them out to the letter," he used to say, in praise. Colonel Sanderstead, despite his later war experience, had never quite approved of independent thinking by anyone below commissioned rank.

"Well, Bolam, what's the trouble this morning? Something we can soon set right between us, I hope."

"Sir, at 8.35 a.m. the telephone rang in the office. I went to the instrument. Captain Norton was speaking from High Thorne. He requested that a warrant should be issued for the arrest of Mr. Hubbard of Swaythling Court on a charge of extorting money by menaces—blackmail, sir. I said that I would consult you on the matter. Captain Norton stated that he would come over here on his motorcycle immediately. He then rang off."

The Colonel nodded his approval. That was the proper way to make a report—no long-winded talk, no comments, just a plain statement of the facts. Bolam could be depended on to do things just as the Colonel liked them. Then Colonel Sanderstead allowed himself to reflect on the news. So *that* was how Hubbard made his money? Blackmail! The dirtiest trade of all. Just what one might have expected from a creature like that.

Then a further implication of the affair struck him. Cyril was applying for a warrant. That seemed strange. Cyril was the last person in the world that one would expect a blackmailer to tackle. The Colonel prided himself on his judgment of character; and he would have been prepared to go into the witness-box and swear that Cyril had never gone off the rails in the slightest degree. What on earth could have happened?

And then an even worse idea invaded his mind. A blackmail case always leaves some dirt sticking, no matter what course it takes; and here was one of the Manor family mixed up in the business. Worse still, the case would have to be tried locally; and the Colonel groaned inwardly when he thought of the effect it might have in Fernhurst Parva. Of course, the villagers would think nothing of it if they were left alone; the Colonel knew well enough that they would not hesitate for a moment in accepting Cyril's word against that of a stranger like Hubbard. The old territorial feeling was strong enough yet. But there was that miserable brute Simon to be reckoned with. The Colonel could imagine well enough what *he* would make of the story down at the 'Three Bees.' He would manage to twist it about and use it as a text to hang some of his modern notions on.

"We shall have to wait until Mr. Norton comes, Bolam. In the meantime, do you know anything about this fellow Hubbard? You must have picked up some information about him in the village from time to time."

"Sir, nobody likes him. On more than one occasion, sir, my attention has been drawn to his attempting to get familiar with girls. They resented it, sir. His behaviour was very improper. Some of the lads were very angry about it and more than once, sir, I have had difficulty in avoiding a breach of the peace. It was suggested that he should be taken out of his car and ducked in the pond."

The Colonel's face darkened. The Hubbard cup seemed to be filling up. Tampering with the girls of his village!

"Anything more, Bolam?"

"Yes, sir. Once I found him threatening Sappy Morton. It appears that they had had some disagreement over an insect that Hubbard was pursuing. Sappy said it was a friend of his; and Hubbard, not rightly understanding about Sappy's misfortune, was very rough with him."

"He seems to be very strong on taking it out of anybody weaker than himself, Bolam."

"It would appear so, sir."

The Colonel dismissed the subject. He had learned enough to confirm his conception of Hubbard; and he wished to hear no more.

"Anything new in the village, Bolam?"

"A lady came to the 'Three Bees' last night, sir. A Mrs. Vane. She seemed to be a friend of Mr. Hilton's. He came to see her on his motor-cycle."

The Colonel made a non-committal sound. He had no desire for gossip; but he shrank from snubbing Bolam, who, after all, was only answering a question. Bolam, however, misunderstood the Colonel's intention.

"Handsome lady, sir. Very showy."

"Indeed? Well, I think that's Mr. Norton's motor-cycle coming up the avenue. You might go round and let him know that I'm here, Bolam."

In a few moments, Cyril Norton came into the study, stripping off his driving gauntlets as he entered. Bolam brought up the rear, closing the door behind him. The Colonel looked his nephew over with approval; even in his clumsy motor-cycle overalls he carried himself well. His face betrayed no sign of nervousness; and the Colonel breathed a faint sigh of relief. Quite evidently Cyril was not much worried over the blackmail affair; he looked more like a judge than a culprit.

"'Morning, uncle. Sorry to trouble you so early; but I'm afraid I've bungled this affair; and there's not much time to lose if we're to catch the beggar. My fault entirely for not knowing my own mind better."

This confession surprised the Colonel. If there was one thing he felt sure about concerning his nephew, it was his tenacity. Once he embarked on a course, it was safe to assume that he would see the thing through to the end. Indecision was not one of his qualities.

Cyril Norton evidently read his uncle's expression.

"Unusual for me to have second thoughts? It is. But this isn't my own affair, so I had to look at it on all sides. A mistake, that. I ought to have stuck to my first idea. However, perhaps it may work out just as well in the end."

"Not your own affair?" queried the Colonel.

"No. Did you think anyone would blackmail me? He'd be a sorry man if he did!"

The Colonel felt an immense relief. Apparently the family of the Manor was not going to be mixed up in this sordid affair after all. At the worst, they would only come into it indirectly through whatever action Cyril proposed to take on behalf of some third party.

"Suppose we get to business," he suggested. "If there's any reason for hurry, the sooner things are started, the better. If it isn't yourself, then whom has Hubbard been blackmailing? And how do you come to be mixed up in the affair?"

A warning glance from Cyril turned the Colonel's eye to Bolam, standing rigidly at attention near the door. Colonel Sanderstead reflected for a moment. There was no need to bring the constable further into the matter than was absolutely essential.

DEATH AT SWAYTHLING COURT

"Bolam!"

"Sir!"

"I think perhaps you had better go into the winter-garden for a few minutes. I'll let you know when we need you again. You can smoke there, if you wish to."

"Very good, sir."

The constable made his exit; and they heard his steps receding down the corridor.

"Now what's all this about, Cyril?"

"Jimmy Leigh. I'm looking after his interests."

Colonel Sanderstead whistled faintly to himself. So that was why Jimmy Leigh had been so peculiar in his manner the night before. He had this business hanging over him. No wonder he seemed a bit down in the mouth. That would account, too, for Hubbard's familiarity with Jimmy the last time he had seen them together. And it would fit in, too, with the association of two such incongruous people. Jimmy was an erratic youngster; quite possibly he had, unintentionally, gone off the rails at some time or other. One never could tell, with these geniuses. And Hubbard had come across his trail; followed it up; and used his knowledge to squeeze Jimmy. That fitted with the talk about taking shares in the Lethal Ray machine; Hubbard probably meant to get the lion's share of the profits without having to pay a cent.

Cyril Norton unbuttoned his overall jacket and took a bundle of papers from an inner pocket.

"These are the documents in the case. It appears Hubbard got wind of something that Jimmy would rather hush up. Jimmy volunteered no information to me about it; and I didn't ask. No business of mine, it seemed to me."

"I quite agree."

"Evidently it got a bit on Jimmy's nerves; and he consulted me about it. He mistrusted his own handling of the business. You know what an erratic devil he is. So far as I could gather, he felt one minute that he had better pay and shut Hubbard's mouth; and the next minute he was worked up almost to the pitch of cutting Hubbard's throat. A man in that state isn't fit to tackle a blackmailer—

sure to give himself away. So I persuaded him to let me take over the business; got him to empower me to deal with Hubbard on his behalf. I don't suffer from nerves much myself; and I thought I could out-manoeuvre a swine like Hubbard easy enough."

"And how did you go about it?"

"Counter-attack, of course. No use trying defence with that sort of thing. The weak point in Hubbard's case was that we might cut up rusty; give him away and stand the racket ourselves. Then he would be in the soup instanter, and in quod very soon."

"And so?"

"As it struck me, the proper game was to give Hubbard the scare of his life; try to frighten him into a bolt, you know. That was the only way I could see which would clear Jimmy and yet let us burke the business, whatever it is. So I set about it on that basis."

He paused for a moment; and his eye caught the papers which he had laid on the table.

"I'm getting along too fast, perhaps. You'd better have a look at these and see what you think of them."

The Colonel picked up the packet and unfolded a few sheets of typewritten paper. There was no heading to any of them nor was there any written signature at the foot of the pages. Cyril leaned over and took the last one from the Colonel's hand, leaving him to read the rest at his leisure. It took only a few minutes for the Colonel to master the contents.

"Well, that's a pretty collection," he commented, as he finished his perusal.

"Hubbard was clever enough to draft most of the stuff so that it would be pretty hard to prove what he was really after. If one had a sharp lawyer to help, one could construe almost the whole of it quite innocently. This isn't Master Hubbard's first step in blackmail, I'm pretty sure.

"Now when I looked over the stuff, I advised Jimmy to see Hubbard and pretend to have the wind up completely, but to avoid closing the deal and to go away as if he needed just a last touch to bring him to heel. I thought that would draw Master Hubbard's fire; he'd think it safe to go in for more direct methods. And he did."

Cyril Norton handed the Colonel the last sheet.

My Dear Sir,

In view of the considerations which were touched upon during our conversations as to the transfer of the rights in your Lethal Ray invention to me, I must demand a deposit of £500 (five hundred pounds) as a guarantee that you will complete the patent formalities. I may say that this offer is open for three days only; and if you fail to close with it you must take the consequences, which I feel sure will be very serious to you.

A Well-Wisher.

"That's hooked him, I think, uncle. Threat in the last sentence; demand for £500 in the one before it. He calls it a deposit; but it's a demand for money, all right; at least, I read it so."

"So do I," said the Colonel. "The thing's clear enough to any reasonable intellect."

"Jimmy brought me that yesterday, as soon as he got it. It's just as well he put me in charge; for to tell the truth that letter seems to have been the last straw. He was in a mood for throat-cutting, all right. I'd have been almost sorry for Hubbard if he'd run across Jimmy just then.

"I calmed him down and sent him off home. I knew he was coming to dine with you last night; so I guessed there was no chance of trouble. . . ."

"But there was," interrupted the Colonel, a sudden illumination making him put two and two together. "He left me immediately after dinner, saying he had an appointment with Hubbard at the Bungalow."

Cyril seemed slightly taken aback, but not so much as his uncle had expected.

"H'm! This thing's getting a bit complicated for me. . . . Never mind. It'll straighten out."

He seemed to reflect for a moment, then continued his narrative:

"I went over the whole affair again; and then sat down and wrote Hubbard a letter. I told him a warrant would be applied for this morning without fail. I trundled over and dropped that into his letter-box yesterday. And I calculated that that would make him cast off his moorings and sail for ports unknown at no small speed. . . . And now it seems he determined to try one last throw; chance terrorizing Jimmy at the last moment and so getting through. That must have been the appointment that you say Jimmy went to keep. This is really a bit beyond me."

He pondered for a moment or two, then apparently took a decision.

"Well, anyway, you must make out that warrant and we must go through with it. It's the last trump in the game; and when he sees it coming he may make a break-away. If he does, you needn't raise too much of a hue-and-cry, you know."

Colonel Sanderstead was no loiterer when action was needed.

"Let's get on with it, Cyril. You know that if the fellow once gets out of my jurisdiction, my warrant's no good until it's backed by the local magistrate. I'll sign the thing now. But you'll need to swear an information, you know. Can't issue a warrant without that."

"Bring out your Bible, uncle. That won't take long."

"Another thing," the Colonel added as an afterthought, "perhaps it would be as well to bring in Bolam as a witness. We're relations, you know; and it might look a bit fishy if we had no third party present—rather too much of a family affair."

"Yes," conceded Cyril, reluctantly. "But in that case I'm not going to mention Jimmy's name. I'll swear to Hubbard having tried blackmail. I suppose that's enough?"

Bolam was recalled to the room; the Colonel procured a Testament and handed it to Cyril Norton.

"You're a witness, Bolam. Pay attention."

"I swear that the person known to me as William Blayre Hubbard, residing at Swaythling Court in this county, has attempted to extort money by means of menaces, so help me God."

"You heard that, Bolam?" inquired the Colonel.

"Yes, sir."

The Colonel searched in his desk, produced a paper, filled in the blanks, and signed it.

"There's your warrant, Bolam. It's to be executed at once."

"Very good, sir."

While Bolam was stowing the paper in his pocket, the Colonel had a fresh thought.

"I think we'll go over in the car, Bolam, it'll save you a trudge; and I have a sort of fancy to see this arrest made. Just in case the fellow makes a statement, or anything of that sort, you know."

He rang the bell and ordered the car to be brought round. Cyril Norton pulled on his gloves. As he did so, he threw a glance at his uncle which seemed to suggest a doubt as to the propriety of this procedure. The Colonel caught it and evidently felt that an explanation was required.

"Wait for us in the car, Bolam."

"Very good, sir."

When Bolam wag out of earshot, the Colonel turned to Cyril.

"I think it would be just as well that I should be there when the arrest's made. Bolam's a sound fellow; but this creature Hubbard will be like a rat in a trap—fit to bite out of sheer panic. And he might have arms, for all one can tell. I can't let Bolam take a risk that I wouldn't take myself, you see?"

"That's an idea," Cyril admitted. "Not that I think much of Hubbard as a gunman. Still, one never knows. I think I'll tack myself on to the party, on that basis, if you don't mind. Three ought to be enough to take him on, even at the worst. And I'd rather like to see the result of my efforts."

He smiled grimly and buttoned up his overalls as he spoke. The jest was lost on the Colonel, who was thinking of something else.

"Won't you come in the car with us?"

"No. I've got my bike here; and I can get home on it after we've nabbed the swine—if he's waited for that. I'll just dog along behind you. Hadn't we better be moving? Time's getting on."

Together they went down to the car, in which Bolam was sitting beside the chauffeur.

"Swaythling Court," the Colonel ordered.

4
WHAT THEY FOUND

LOOKING BETWEEN the shoulders of Bolam and the chauffeur as his car drove up the avenue from the Swaythling lodge-gate, Colonel Sanderstead incuriously noted that there had been rain on the previous evening; for the surface of the road seemed to be moist without being actually muddy. Then, with a sudden quickening of attention, he perceived something of more immediate interest: the wheel-tracks of a car which had left its trace along the whole length of the avenue.

"We've missed him," reflected the Colonel, not without a certain satisfaction. After all, if Hubbard had taken the hint and decamped in time to evade arrest, matters would be considerably simplified. There would be none of the washing of dirty linen which the Colonel dreaded. Certainly, if the blackmailer had learned his lesson and taken to flight, there would be no need for a hue-and-cry. Hubbard's teeth would be drawn; and that was the main thing.

"Pity that he's got off scot-free, though," was the Colonel's after-thought. "Hanging's too good for a crime of that sort."

The car swung round a turn in the avenue and drew up before the perron of the front entrance to Swaythling Court. Bolam jumped down from his place and opened the tonneau door for the Colonel, whilst almost immediately Cyril's motor-cycle drew up behind the car.

"Just wait here, Kearney," the Colonel ordered; then, followed by Cyril and the constable, he began to ascend the steps.

"Hullo! Here's a dog."

Colonel Sanderstead had a way with dogs; they seemed instantly to recognize a friend in him; and this beast was no exception. The Colonel stooped and patted it kindly.

"Cyril, this poor brute's half-dead with cold. It's nearly shivering itself off its feet. They must have left it outside all night—careless sweeps! No wonder it's half-frozen with a temperature like this."

He fondled the dog for a moment and then turned back to the business in hand. But as he rose from caressing the beast, his eye caught something lying on the step beside the jamb of the door; and he stooped again to pick it up.

"What's that you've got?" asked Cyril Norton, who had seen the movement.

The Colonel straightened himself up and looked at his find.

"It seems to be a Yale key."

He glanced at the door and noted the brass disk of the lock.

"It may be a latch-key of this door. That's a rum affair."

Keeping the key in his hand, he rang the bell loudly and they waited for the opening of the door. A minute passed; and nothing moved in the house.

The Colonel rang a second time, with the same result.

"No reply! Surely somebody must be awake in the place. Let's have another try."

But the third attempt was equally unsuccessful in eliciting any sign of life within the house. The constable put his ear to the door for a time while the Colonel rang a fourth peal on the bell.

"Nobody there, sir. Shall I go round to the back and try at the tradesman's entrance?"

The Colonel reflected for a moment or two, then came to a decision. He tried the key in the lock and it turned without difficulty.

"I'm rather rusty in the law about entering a man's house; but I think we ought to look further into this affair. Come along, Bolam. I'll take the responsibility, if we do happen to be exceeding our powers."

"Very good, sir."

Pushing the door open, the Colonel entered the house and then, motioning for silence, he listened intently. Not a sound came from the interior. In his parade voice, Colonel Sanderstead inquired: "Is there anybody here?" There was no response.

"Very rum."

"Sir, they've left the electric light burning in broad daylight."

The Colonel, following the constable's outstretched arm, perceived the glow of the hall lamps which the daylight had dimmed.

"Well, we'll go further into it. Come along, Bolam."

They moved down the hall, the Colonel in advance; but suddenly he halted and picked something off a rug. Holding the object gingerly between two fingers, he turned round and showed it to them: a tiny automatic pistol.

"A 0.22 calibre," he commented. "Now who would carry a toy like that? Only a crack shot or a fool."

"What the devil's this?" Cyril Norton broke out in genuine astonishment. "We seem to have blundered into the first chapter of a dime novel. Very rum, as you say, uncle. Damned rum, if you ask me. I don't half like it."

The Colonel looked for a moment at the puzzled faces of his companions, as though hoping to find a solution of the mystery there; then he carefully placed the pistol on one of the chairs.

"It might have finger-marks on it, you know."

Cyril Norton stooped and examined the tiny weapon, pushing a twisted corner of his handkerchief into the muzzle. When he stood up again, they could see that he was completely mystified.

"It hasn't been fired, anyway," he intimated, looking at the screwed-up handkerchief.

He stared again at the pistol, evidently thinking hard.

"There must have been some damned rum goings-on here last night. I can make neither head nor tail of it."

"Well, let's be getting on with it," suggested the Colonel, whose temperament inclined to action when action was possible. He wanted to get to the root of the mystery as soon as he could. "Let's try this room here. We've got begin somewhere."

Impatiently he flung open the nearest door, motioning the others to be ready. A gust of heated air blew across his face as he stood on the threshold.

"Phew! Hubbard's no fresh-air fiend, evidently. Open the windows, Bolam."

Then, as he stepped into the room, they heard his voice change: "Good God! What's this?"

Almost pushing him aside in their haste, Cyril Norton and the constable came in sight of the thing at which the Colonel was pointing. A low, broad desk stood in the centre of the room, the desk chair having its back to the fire-place. Half in the chair, half sprawling on the desk, they saw a bulky thing, its outlines partly concealed by a green baize cloth which had been clumsily thrown over it. Jutting out from under one side of the cloth, a limp hand lay on the polished surface of the desk.

Half a dozen strides took the Colonel to the muffled body. Stripping off the cloth, he flung it on the floor beside the chair; and the three invaders gathered around the desk.

"Hubbard!"

The Colonel's exclamation was unnecessary. The blackmailer's face was concealed, for the head of the corpse was buried in the arms which rested on the desk; but Hubbard's identity was clear enough. Colonel Sanderstead slowly removed his hat; Cyril and the constable followed his example: and for a few moments there was silence. Cyril Norton was the first to speak.

"Apoplexy? He was one of these fat-necked beggars; and he must have found last night a strain."

The Colonel found something unwelcome in the speculation, made thus in the presence of death. He put down his hat and turned back to examine the body again, without replying. Without seeming to notice his uncle's attitude, Cyril Norton continued his reflections.

"Suicide, possibly. Or a weak heart, perhaps. But if it was either of these, then who put that cloth over him? There's nobody in the house, apparently, I wonder, now . . ."

He broke off for a moment; then, with a flash of irritation, he added:

"It beats me!"

And after a more prolonged meditation he repeated his earlier verdict:

"There must have been some damned rum goings-on here last night."

Colonel Sanderstead had been stooping over the body.

"I can put a name to one of them, Cyril. Murder! This was how it was done."

Cyril Norton went forward and, with the Colonel's finger to guide him, saw clearly what he had missed in his first glance at the body. Hubbard's coat had been ruffled by the attitude into which he had fallen; and the folds of the cloth had concealed something which was now plain enough to Cyril. Colonel Sanderstead felt a certain discoverer's pride as his nephew bent over the corpse. He began to think that possibly he had a distinct turn for detective work.

"Do you see it, Cyril? It seems a curious sort of wound. There's very little blood from it, or we'd have seen it right away. Perhaps he bled internally; I believe some wounds do."

"Not much blood, certainly," his nephew concurred, looking up with an expression of bewilderment which seemed to become tinged with something akin to apprehension as he bent down once more to examine the body. The Colonel noticed that flicker of un-easiness, but he had other things to think about.

"That wound—have a good look at it—seems to me as if it had been made with a stiletto."

"Or the large blade of a pen-knife; that would be about the right size and shape," Cyril Norton commented.

"Something of the sort," conceded the Colonel. "Don't touch the folds of the clothes. We'll need to get a doctor on to this thing."

He sniffed once or twice, as though trying to recognize a perfume.

"That fellow must have used scent, surely. It's pretty strong, too. The whole room smells of it; and it comes from him. Hair-oil, perhaps. Do you smell almond-oil?"

"Yes. He was the sort of fellow who would use that kind of thing."

"Bolam! Open all the windows, wide. This place is like an oven."

The constable threw open the two big sashes; and a chill draught blew through the room to the open door.

Suddenly, across the solemnity of the death-chamber, there burst a torrent of vile profanity. It flowed out without a pause, as though some verbal sewer had been flushed. It was directed at no one in particular and seemed merely the liberation of some foul and angry mind at odds with the Universe.

The Colonel was the first to recover from his surprise.

"Cover up that parrot," he jerked to Bolam. The constable, following the Colonel's gesture, discovered a large gilded cage standing in a recess opposite the table. He stooped down, picked up the baize cloth from the floor and threw it over the cage. The obscene current broke off abruptly; and they heard the parrot moving uneasily on its perch.

"Nice funeral oration, that. It gave me a bit of a start," Cyril admitted with a faint smile. Then his face changed, as he saw that the constable's back was turned. He caught the Colonel's eye; glanced down at the corpse beside him; and then, with a grave face met the Colonel's look again. Colonel Sanderstead was by no means dull. He picked up the meaning of the by-play instantly, as if his nephew had put the thing into words. The blackmail; the murder; and—Jimmy Leigh! "What are you going to do about it?" Cyril Norton's mute question was as plain as print. Now the Colonel understood why his nephew had been worried. He knew, better than the Colonel, the state of Jimmy Leigh's mind; and perhaps, from the opening of the mystery, he had been afraid of finding the very thing they had discovered. He had concealed his anxiety under a guise of bewilderment—a clever touch, that.

But, on further reflection, the Colonel had to admit that Cyril's surprise had been real enough; it was not mere acting. Like the Colonel himself, Cyril Norton had been all at sea. His summing-up: "There must have been some damned rum goings-on here," was a genuine statement. And, as the Colonel was to discover at a later stage, these second thoughts were nearer the truth than his first impressions. His nephew was in reality quite as puzzled as he had appeared.

Cyril Norton was still gazing intently at his uncle's face, awaiting the answer to that unspoken question, when Bolam turned round again; and the opportunity had passed. Colonel Sanderstead became suddenly businesslike.

"We must see if the murderer left any clues behind him. Bolam!"

"Sir?"

"Take your note-book and jot down anything I tell you. We're going to examine the premises, and a record ought to be made at the time."

"Very good, sir."

"We'd better have everything from the start. Put down first of all the time when we reached the house—about ten minutes ago; that will be near enough. Then the finding of that latch-key; the fact that we got no answer when I rang the bell; the 0.22 pistol in the hall. . . . Am I going too fast for you?"

"I'm taking it down in shorthand, sir."

"Good man, Bolam. Give me a longhand copy when you've had time to transcribe it. . . . Next, the fact that the electric light was still burning in the hall."

"And in this room, too, sir?"

Cyril Norton looked up to where the spray of electric lamps glowed palely over the desk. The Colonel caught his look and hurried to offer an explanation before either of the others could supply one.

"Hubbard must have fallen asleep, lying forward on the desk as he is now. Of course the lights would be on. Then the murderer must have stolen in and knifed him from behind. You don't imagine that wound would have been inflicted in the dark? Then the murderer must have slipped out and forgotten to switch off the lights. Or he may have left them on deliberately."

"That sounds all right," Cyril Norton acquiesced. "But that looks as if the murderer, whoever he was, had got rattled. Why leave the lights on, burning there all night? Rather apt to attract attention, I'd have thought. Someone might have come in to turn them off, thinking they'd been left on by accident. I think if I'd been in charge of this business I'd have switched them out."

"Well, let's go on," suggested the Colonel, who was beginning to enjoy the role of detective. "Put that down about the lights, Bolam. Now we'll take the desk as a starting-point."

He walked round it, examining the articles on it carefully.

"Ah! Here's your letter, Cyril, I think.

> Sir,
> I wish to inform you that to-morrow morning I in-tend to apply for a warrant for your arrest on a charge of blackmail.
>
> Yours faithfully,
Cyril Norton.

You needn't take that down, Bolam; the document itself's there if we want it. H'm! You didn't waste words over him, Cyril."

"Why should I?"

"True. Well, let's get on with it. Now, here's a queer thing!"

The Colonel's discovery was a flat plate of wax out of which protruded a fragment of wick, evidently the remains of a candle which had been burning on the desk-top until it finally guttered out. The three of them looked at it with astonishment. Cyril Norton was the first to break the silence.

"Now, what the devil does a man want with a candle alight in a room where the electric light is burning? This thing leaves me standing! How do you account for it, Uncle Sherlock?"

The Colonel was not over-pleased by the sarcastic tribute to his detective powers. He looked at the candle-stub with a frown for a full minute, revolving possible explanations in his mind.

"He didn't need it for light, that's evident. But he might have been sealing a letter with sealing-wax and lighted the candle to heat the sealing-wax. That's a possible explanation."

"Oh, it's possible, all right," Cyril admitted. His expression, however, indicated that it did not satisfy him. "But I see no letter. And I don't see any sealing-wax, either."

"He may have dispatched the letter and put the sealing-wax back into a drawer. We'll see later."

"It won't wash, uncle. Point No. 1: Anyone would blow out a candle at once after using it. Point No. 2: Anyone who was in the habit of using a candle for sealing-wax would use one of the small kind, not an ordinary cheap thing like this. And Point No. 3: In a house of this kind there would be candlesticks, and no man in his senses would stick his candle to the surface of a polished desk like this."

The Colonel was rather vexed by this cavalier demolishing of his hypothesis.

"Do you happen to have any better idea of your own, Cyril?"

"No. The thing's beyond me altogether."

"Well, let's get on. Have you got the candle down in your notes, Bolam?"

"Yes, sir."

Cyril Norton was still looking absent-mindedly at the pool of wax on the surface of the desk. Suddenly his eye wandered to the carpet.

"Point No. 4: the clincher, I think. There's a trail of grease across the floor from the desk to the door. You don't suggest that Hubbard went wandering around with that candle in his hand all over the room?"

The Colonel went down on hands and knees and made a long inspection of the grease-spots on the carpet.

"We'll follow up that trail by and by," he intimated, as he rose to his feet again. "In the meantime, we'd better finish with this room. We must be systematic."

He returned to the desk.

"Not much else here, I think. Note this down, Bolam. A whisky decanter, stoppered, about half-full. A soda syphon; about a quarter of the soda left in it. And what's this?"

He held up a squat, wide-mouthed stoppered bottle containing some lumps of a crystalline material.

"Sir, I believe that is the bottle, that the . . . the deceased used for killing his insects."

"Oh, is that so, Bolam? I wondered what it was. Well, put it down on the list. Then there's this tumbler; it's got about a dessert-spoonful of whisky and soda left in it. Nothing else on the desk except a stationery cabinet with some blank notepaper and envelopes and a blotting-pad with a clean sheet on top. That finishes the desk; now for the rest of the room."

Cyril Norton appeared to pay no attention to his uncle's enumeration of the articles on the desk. His eyes were still fixed on the remains of the guttered-out candle; and his expression suggested intense concentration upon a baffling problem.

"Some of it fits," he said, as if thinking aloud, "but the rest of it simply won't. What the devil does a man want with a candle in a lighted room? I can make neither head nor tail of it."

He broke off in obvious irritation and transferred his attention to the Colonel, who was now extending the circle of his investigations.

"Why, here are his keys sticking in the keyhole of his safe. It's not even locked. Let's look into this."

The Colonel swung the door of the big safe open and stared in surprise at the array of empty shelves which confronted him.

"Not a solitary paper left in the thing. That's funny."

He glanced round the room, and his eye was caught by a mass of fine ashes in the fire-place. Going across to the hearth he knelt down and examined the huge grate with interest. Then cautiously he touched some of the metal-work.

"Still hot! There must have been a devil of a fire in this last night. And a lot of the ash here is obviously paper-ash. I can see fragments of writing on some of it. He must have been destroying documents on a big scale—compromising stuff that he couldn't afford to leave about."

Cyril stepped over to the hearth-rug and looked at the mass of ash and cinders which choked the grate and lay piled high up in the fire-place.

"Hubbard didn't necessarily do that himself. It may have been the murderer. Most likely it was the murderer. Anyway, the work's

been done thoroughly. There doesn't seem to be anything but fragments; he must have stirred the stuff up while it was burning and
then heaped any amount of coals on top. What a furnace! It's no
wonder the place was like an oven when we came into it. Pure luck
that a blaze of that size didn't set fire to the whole house."

The Colonel looked gloomily at the mass of embers which probably represented all that remained of a clue to the mystery. All at
once he bent forward, looked keenly down amongst the interstices
of the pile; then, very delicately he introduced his hand and extracted something which had caught his eye.

"*There's* a find, anyway," he said, with a certain pride, as he
drew from among the ashes a long, slender metallic object. "Here's
the weapon."

Under his directions, Bolam spread some sheets of clean paper
on a small table which stood near the window. The Colonel blew
the ash carefully from his find and then deposited the thing on the
paper.

"I'll describe it, Bolam. Take this down, word for word."

The Colonel was recovering his detective enthusiasm. He felt
that the discovery of this object re-established his credit, which
had been slightly shaken by Cyril's dismissal of the sealing-wax
theory of the candle.

"Length of object over all, about twelve or fourteen inches.
Made up of two parts. A steel blade, about nine inches long by
three-quarters of an inch broad at its base and tapering to a sharp
point. The blade's almost flat—not more than a quarter of an inch
thick where it enters the handle. Steel handle, with slight orna-
mentation, about four inches long—just a comfortable size for a
hand-grip. No fingermarks, of course, and no blood-stains. One
couldn't expect anything of that sort after it had been lying in that
fire. Now, just to make sure, we'll compare its size with the cut in
Hubbard's coat."

Tearing a strip from a stiff sheet of notepaper, the Colonel
wrapped it round the blade where it entered the handle and pinched
it until it took the shape of the steel, after which he slipped it off,
still retaining the mould.

"I don't want to bring the dagger near the wound itself. Much better to be able to say that they were never in contact. Now we'll fit the paper to the cut in the cloth."

Going across to Hubbard's body, he brought the

paper ring down on the top of the slit in the coat and adjusted it until they were exactly in register.

"They fit precisely," he announced in mild triumph; and took a step aside so that the others might see clearly. "Now that clears up part of the business. We know what he was killed with, anyway; there can be no dispute about that. Let's have another look at the weapon and see what it has to tell us."

He went back to the table again and pondered for a while over the wicked-looking steel fang.

"Don't take this down, Bolam. I'm just thinking the matter out; and it isn't evidence. Now I was sure when I saw the wound that it was made with a stiletto; and here's the very instrument I predicted. One naturally asks: 'What sort of person would use a weapon of that sort?' It isn't the sort of thing the ordinary person carries in the pocket. It won't fold up; it's a clumsy length. Then again, you can't buy a stiletto at the first cutlery-shop. They aren't used in this country. What does that point to? I think I can tell you. It means one of two things. Either this murder was committed by a foreigner who could buy a stiletto in his own country; or else the murderer had access to some collection of old arms and picked out the stiletto as being the thing he needed for this affair. Now that narrows down our search very considerably. See that, Bolam?"

"Yes, sir."

Bolam was evidently deeply impressed by the rapidity and sureness of the Colonel's reasoning. Cyril, however, had listened to his uncle's exposition with a faintly sardonic expression; and he now broke in.

"You'll have to extend your search to another class—the people who use paper-knives. That's just an ordinary steel paper-cutter. You can buy them anywhere. I shouldn't wonder if it belonged to Hubbard himself and was lying on the table."

The Colonel looked crestfallen.

"Perhaps you're right, Cyril. I hadn't thought of that. We can easily test it by questioning the servants. But where are the servants?"

He stepped across to the bell and rang a prolonged peal which they could hear thrilling through the silent house. There was no response.

"There's nobody on the premises, it seems," the Colonel said tentatively, as if he almost expected that Cyril would find a flaw in the statement. "I wonder what's happened to them. It looks a bit fishy finding a murdered man in an empty house; and Hubbard must have kept a staff of sorts."

"Sir," volunteered the constable, "he had one man—a sort of butler—and another man—the chauffeur—and two maid-servants."

"Four servants? Surely they can't all be in it. This is a rum affair, very rum. What are you looking at, Cyril?"

Cyril Norton pointed to an open typewriter which stood on the table beside the paper-knife.

"There's his typewriter, evidently. A Hammond. Hadn't we better compare its type with the typing of these letters I showed you? Nothing like making sure of one's ground."

The Colonel seemed less interested in this point than he had been in the other discoveries. The blackmail case had been overlaid in his mind by the excitement of the murder; and he saw little advantage in recurring to it. However, he consented to satisfy Cyril; and bent over the machine.

"Hulloa! There's the beginning of a letter on this sheet. It reads: *'My dear Sir, If you don't pay the money down to-morrow . . .'*"

Cyril unbuttoned his overall and drew out the packet of letters which he had shown to his uncle at Fernhurst Manor. Unfolding one of them, he scrutinized alternately the paper in his hand and the sheet clamped in the machine. At last he turned to the Colonel again.

"That's clear enough. Look at the 'd' in 'don't' and this other 'd' in 'down.' In both cases there's a defect in the type: the ring of the 'd' is clear enough, but the upright stroke and the tenon at the top are both defective. The shuttle's been chipped slightly. Now compare that with the 'Well-wisher' letter. Look at the two 'd's' in 'demand,' and the other 'd's' in 'during' and 'considerations.' Same defect running right through. Both letters were written with the same shuttle. What a damned idiot Hubbard must have been to use a traceable thing like that when he could have bought a split-new shuttle for a quid. They're interchangeable on the Hammond machine. Anyway, I think that's clinched the matter. We could have brought the blackmail home to him easily enough merely on the strength of his typing."

"I don't see that it matters much now," commented the Colonel, who had been slightly rasped by Cyril's dismissal of his own discoveries.

"True enough," his nephew admitted. "But I like to be thorough."

To change the subject, the Colonel suggested that they might resume the examination of the room. His eye, ranging round the walls, was suddenly caught by something which he had missed in his earlier investigations.

"Here's another funny thing. Look at that glass case on the wall alongside the parrot-cage in the recess. Somebody's smashed the glass front."

They went over to where the object hung, a large wooden case suspended from the wall. The lower edge was about three feet from the ground; and the case itself was about a yard high. The thing was simply an exhibition case such as is found in museums; and it contained a number of brilliantly tinted butterflies pinned down in rows.

The Colonel inspected it carefully, looked at the fragments of glass scattered on the carpet below it, and then hesitated before speaking. He had been proved wrong several times, and he was afraid to risk another mistake.

"That glass might have been broken, in a struggle, by someone's elbow," he suggested. Then, seeing something in Cyril's expression, he added hurriedly, "But there doesn't seem to have been any struggle."

He inspected the case again, and detected a fresh point.

"Look here. At least one specimen has been removed from its place—the centre-piece of the whole collection. What do you make of that?"

Cyril Norton looked up sharply and again his face took on the expression of bafflement which the Colonel had noticed before.

"This dime novel's far beyond me, uncle. I simply can't make head or tail of it. One could fake up half a dozen explanations that will fit fifty per cent. of the facts; but what I can't see is any reasonable theory that will fit the whole of the evidence. There's no logic in the thing."

"It seems to me hard enough to find one hypothesis that will fit even a part of the facts," the Colonel confessed. "I'd like to hear one of your half-dozen."

Cyril Norton took up the challenge without hesitation.

"Well, I'll have a dash at it. How would this fit the facts? Suppose Hubbard, being a trifle overwrought after getting my letter, primed himself with Dutch courage from the decanter there. Then, while he is destroying compromising documents preparatory to a bolt, the main fuse of the house gets blown, and the light goes out. He fishes out a candle from somewhere or other and sets about replacing the fuse. Then he wanders up here again; and, being rather canned, he sticks the candle on the table and forgets all about it. He sits down, a bit muzzy, and drops asleep.

"A burglar then arrives; finds Hubbard has carelessly left his latch-key in the door—a thing that might happen to any of us; comes into the house that way; finds Hubbard here asleep with the safe-door open. The burglar helps himself to a few valuables from the safe—we haven't an inventory, and for all we know there may have been something in it besides documents. Just as the burglar has got his claws on the loot, Hubbard wakes up—still muzzy. The burglar, on the spur of the moment, snatches the paper-knife from the table and does Hubbard in. Then he decamps via the front door, jolting out the Yale key as he slams it behind him.

"That covers everything except the 0.22 automatic on the mat and the broken show-case. And there's nothing against that theory if you assume that Hubbard was drunk enough to stick the candle down and forget about it. Oh, it's easy enough to fake up a yarn to fit parts of the evidence. It's when one tries to make the whole hundred per cent. fit that one falls down."

"We can test your hypothesis, anyway." The Colonel was not sorry to take the opportunity of playing critic in his turn. "All we need do is to follow up the grease-trail and see if it leads to the fuse-box."

"It won't," Cyril Norton admitted amiably. "The fuse-box is about the last place in the world I'd expect that trail to lead to. But we needn't waste time in talk. Suppose we get on the track now and see where it does lead?"

The Colonel nodded; and they moved towards the open door. As they did so, the sputter of a motor-cycle engine sounded under the window, passed on, and ceased abruptly. Someone ascended the perron; a latch-key clicked in the Yale lock; and as they stepped out into the hall, the front door opened to admit a man in motor-cycle overalls.

5
THE BUTLER

"CURIOUSER AND CURIOUSER!" quoted Cyril Norton, as he saw the incoming figure. "Is this the First Murderer, or a master-sleuth sprung from nowhere with a solution in his hip-pocket, or a friend of the family, or a mere casual caller? It seems to be Visiting Day at Swaythling Court."

"Sir, it's the butler," whispered Bolam, after a glance at the approaching figure, "I didn't recognize him at first, in his overalls."

The Colonel caught the whispered identification and looked keenly at the man who was coming rather hesitatingly towards them. What he saw did not impress him favourably.

"Rat-faced creature," he murmured to himself.

There was a certain justification for the unkindly comment. The butler's sharp nose jutted out over a long, thin-lipped mouth and receding chin, giving the whole countenance a pronounced rodent-like character. The Colonel got the impression of a personality stamped with a combination of weakness, predaceousness and cowardice in almost equal proportions; and even at the first glance he disliked the man before him.

"Who are you?" demanded the butler, looking uneasily from one to the other. The tone of his voice expressed only a natural surprise; but the Colonel, watching closely, saw that the newcomer's lower lip quivered as though the butler's nerves were slightly out of control. Still keeping his attention fixed on the butler's face, the Colonel broke his news:

70

"Your master was murdered during the night. Do you know anything about it?"

What the Colonel had expected to see, he could hardly have defined. Of course, when a servant learns abruptly that his master has come by a violent end, it is natural to count upon some change in his facial expression; but what precise shade of emotion one could anticipate was not very clear in the Colonel's mind. He had shot out his statement sharply with a half-defined hope that from its effect on the butler he might learn something of value; but in practice he found that he had gained nothing. Surprise, he seemed to see, and something that might almost have been called relief; but he had to admit to himself that for all practical purposes the face of the butler had shown nothing which gave a clue to the mystery. Colonel Sanderstead could not even make up his mind whether the man was acting or not. He contented himself with a mental comment:

"Hang-dog fellow. A very furtive look about him, somehow."

The butler's first surprise seemed to pass off. He ran his tongue swiftly over his lips, as though he had felt unable to speak clearly; then, quite firmly, he denied all knowledge of the mystery. Rather to the Colonel's surprise, he did not protest overmuch.

"You've no objection to answering a few questions, I suppose?" demanded the Colonel.

"None at all, sir. I'm perfectly ready to give any information that I can."

Despite his prejudice, Colonel Sanderstead had to admit to himself that the man seemed to have no hesitation in the matter. The butler appeared simply a naturally nervous man who had suddenly been placed in an unexpected position. He pulled off his gloves and played with them, straightening them out and then rolling them up; and he kept his eyes averted from the faces of the three inquisitors; but though he looked like a rat, the Colonel could not honestly say that he had the air of a trapped rat.

"Very well, Bolam! Take all this down. Now, what's your name, first of all?"

"Thomas Leake, sir."

"How long have you been Mr. Hubbard's butler?"

"He engaged me shortly before he came to Swaythling Court, sir."

"Now, how did it come that you—and the other servants—were not here this morning when we came to the house?"

"Mr. Hubbard had given us all permission to go to a dance in Micheldean Abbas, sir. He very kindly paid for our tickets."

"Ah, indeed. Will you give me some information about what happened before you left the house?"

"At half-past six, the two maids and the chauffeur left here in the car, sir. Mr. Hubbard made rather a point that they should get away in plenty of time."

"Half past six?" interrupted Cyril Norton. "And now it's well on in the forenoon. Did your dance last round the clock? You must be a stout lot of fellows!"

The butler seemed in no way put out by the question.

"The dance was a Cinderella, sir. It stopped shortly after midnight. But Mr. Hubbard had made a point that we were not to come back here in the small hours and disturb him. He insisted that we should stay the rest of the night at Micheldean Abbas, and not return here before half-past ten in the morning. We put up at the 'Cat and Fiddle,' sir."

The Colonel was faintly vexed by this interruption of his systematic investigation. His next question brought them back to the original line:

"What happened after the rest of the servants left? You were alone in the house with Mr. Hubbard?"

"Yes, sir. At seven o'clock I served dinner. Mr. Hubbard took some cold roast in order to let the cook get away earlier. After that, I looked to see if the breakfast-tray had been prepared and placed in the pantry, as Mr. Hubbard had directed. I then took some whisky and a syphon into his study: After that I left the house— about half-past seven, I think. Before going, I went round to see that all the fastenings were secure; and on leaving the house I dropped the lever of the Yale lock on the front door, as Mr. Hubbard had directed me to do. No one could have got into the house by any of the doors."

"Do you recognize this key?" The Colonel produced the latch-key which he had found on the doorstep.

"That's Mr. Hubbard's key, sir. I have another one. His is slightly twisted in the handle, as you see. It met with an accident once."

Colonel Sanderstead endeavoured to think of more questions which he could put to the butler; but nothing further suggested itself. He was about to lead the inquiry on to the paper-knife, when Cyril Norton interposed.

"After you left the house at half-past seven, Leake, you were not inside it again until we saw you return a few minutes ago?"

"No, sir."

Cyril Norton appeared to be satisfied with this. He effaced himself to allow the Colonel to proceed.

"Come into the study, Leake. We wish to know one or two other things."

If the Colonel hoped to secure anything of interest by confronting the butler with his master's body, he certainly failed. Apart from a glance of curiosity at the corpse, Leake betrayed no visible emotion. He seemed to have got his nerves under better control, now that his first surprise was over; and although his lower lip still trembled spasmodically, he showed no marked symptoms of perturbation.

Colonel Sanderstead pointed to the table on which the weapon rested; and the butler obediently crossed the room and examined the steel blade.

"This is Mr. Hubbard's paper-knife, sir. It seems to have got into the fire by the look of it. The last time I saw it was when I brought in the whisky and syphon. It was lying on the desk close to where I put down the tray."

Cyril Norton showed a faint amusement at this confirmation of his hypothesis about the weapon. The "stiletto" theory was out of court completely, after this evidence. He was careful to spare the Colonel's feelings, however; and his uncle, who was pondering over his next question, failed to notice Cyril's smile.

"Have you ever seen this safe open before, Leake?" he demanded. "Did it, to your knowledge, contain anything of value except papers?"

At the mention of papers, the butler looked eagerly towards the empty shelves; and then, seeing nothing, he glanced rapidly round the room. The mass of ash in the fire-place appeared to draw his attention and, in some way, to relieve his mind.

"No, sir. Mr. Hubbard never opened the safe in my presence. He kept his keys very carefully."

Colonel Sanderstead paused in his examination, turning over in his mind the points he had elicited, in the hope that they might suggest further questions. But nothing occurred to him; and he was about to close the inquiry when Cyril Norton spoke again.

"Look round the room, Leake. Do you see anything out of the ordinary? Anything displaced from its normal position or anything missing?"

The butler's eye travelled again round the room, paused for a moment at the fire-place, and then fixed itself on the showcase of butterflies.

"That glass case, sir. When I left at half-past seven, the front of it was intact; I see that it is broken now. And something has been taken out of it, too. There was a very large butterfly in the very centre, a thing with very highly coloured wings, sir, each wing about as big as my hand. Mr. Hubbard was very proud of that specimen. He often used to tell me that it had cost him more than all the rest of the collection put together. He once told me the name of it, but I have forgotten it. It was a South American butterfly, I think; a very brilliant one. When light fell on it, the wings used to glitter like polished metal. I often used to look at it, sir; that's how I can be so sure about it."

"Ah!" interrupted the Colonel. "You're sure that it was valuable?"

"Mr. Hubbard told me so, sir, several times."

The Colonel dismissed the butterfly from further consideration and returned to Cyril Norton's line of inquiry.

"Do you see anything else in this room that strikes you, Leake?"

"This candle-end on the table, sir. There was no candle in the room when I left the house."

"Anything more?"

The butler examined the room minutely for a time, then shook his head:

"I see nothing that strikes me particularly, sir. As far as I can see, everything else is quite ordinary."

"Very good, Leake. Now can you tell me if Mr. Hubbard had any callers during the day?"

"Apart from tradesmen, sir, only one person came to the house yesterday. In the afternoon, Mr. Hubbard was busy rearranging some of his butterflies in their cases, as he sometimes did. About three o'clock, the front door bell rang and Mr. Hilton, the gentleman who used to live at Carisbrooke House, sir, asked to see Mr. Hubbard. Mr. Hubbard had given no instructions about Mr. Hilton, but he did not seem surprised to see him. I showed Mr. Hilton into this room."

Cyril Norton's face had shown an expression of keen interest when Hilton's name was mentioned. It almost seemed as though the introduction of this fresh character into the Hubbard drama had cleared up part of the difficulties in his mind.

"Well, what happened then?" he demanded. The butler walked across the room to the door and twisted the handle gently.

"This door, sir, has a very bad latch. Unless one takes particular pains in closing it, it is apt to miss the catch and fall slightly open."

He illustrated the defect, opening and closing the door once or twice. Then he continued:

"Yesterday afternoon, when I admitted Mr. Hilton into the room, the door behaved in this way; it sprang open after I had closed it behind him. My duties kept me in the hall for a time; and I could not help overhearing fragments of the conversation."

The Colonel's face betrayed total incredulity of the butler's explanation. Quite obviously, he thought, the rat-faced fellow had been at the keyhole, listening for what he could pick up.

"Well, go on."

"I heard only snatches of the conversation, sir; but from what I did hear, it was quite evident that Mr. Hubbard and Mr. Hilton had a disagreement. They did not speak loudly; but the tones of both voices were very angry. They used strong language. It seemed to me, from what I heard, that they were bargaining about something."

Cyril Norton had dropped his pretence of incuriosity. He seemed to have come at last upon the crux of the problem which had given him so much trouble.

"Did you gather what the upshot was, Leake? Did they come to an agreement or did the bargain fall through?"

"I could not be certain, sir."

Cyril Norton's face fell; he seemed to be completely taken aback by this information.

"But I should imagine, sir," the butler continued, "that they continued to disagree. I happened to be in the hall when Mr. Hilton came out. He was very angry; his face showed it. He brushed past me, opened the door himself and slammed it behind him. I have seldom seen a gentleman so angry."

Cyril Norton appeared to be slightly relieved by this interpretation of the events. His face resumed its normal expression. The Colonel, who had been watching him, found no difficulty in guessing the trend of his thoughts. He himself had seen the possibilities which lay behind the butler's narrative. At last, in the depths of this apparently inextricable tangle, they had come across something definite—somebody who had shown ill blood against Hubbard. And this new factor was the person against whom Cyril himself had the deepest grudge that a man could have. No wonder he had seemed eager about it when that evidence turned up.

With a certain feeling of wonder, the Colonel retraced in his mind the events of the morning. The blackmail case, which had seemed so important less than a couple of hours before, had now retreated so far into obscurity that he had almost forgotten Jimmy Leigh's troubles. And, in fact, Jimmy Leigh was out of his difficulties by now. Whoever it was that murdered Hubbard had made a thorough job of the thing; all the papers in the safe were gone, reduced to indecipherable ash in the fire-place. Any secrets which Hubbard's brain might have held would never be disclosed now. A good many people beside Jimmy Leigh would sleep better o' nights when the news came out. The Colonel let his eyes rest on the hunched-up body which sprawled across the desk; and all his clean nature rejoiced that the blackmailer's career had been cut short. He turned away, with a faint disgust, and his mind carried him unconsciously on to the next stage. Who was the murderer? Hilton? It seemed that again the thing was swinging round in a direction which he did not like. Through Hilton—if he were guilty—through Stella, through Cyril Norton, the business was threatening to touch the fringe of the Manor family; and it would be a nastier affair than a blackmail case.

Colonel Sanderstead's gaze encountered the figure of the butler, who was standing beside the doorway. Leake met his eye for a second and then, looking away again, put a question:

"Is there any further information I can give, sir?"

The Colonel reflected for a moment or two, but he could think of nothing that he wished to ask. "I think that's all, Leake."

"Then, sir, if you have no objection, I will take the parrot. I clean out its cage every morning, sir. Very dirty birds, parrots."

He stepped across the room, lifted the bird, and was retreating to the door when Colonel Sanderstead noticed the green baize cloth which still draped the cage.

"Just leave that cloth, Leake."

A flicker of astonishment passed over the butler's face as he obeyed the order; then, carrying the parrot, he left the room.

The Colonel eyed his retiring back in some perplexity. A cool hand, evidently, that butler! In the midst of all this upturn, he could find time to think of cleaning out a bird-cage. Though loath to change his views, the Colonel began to revise the opinion which he had formed of Leake on the strength of a first impression. The fellow might look nervous enough on the surface; but underneath his skin he was obviously a cold-blooded character. He had given his evidence clearly, without any sign of hesitation or shuffling; and he had seemed perfectly frank about it. Distinctly a personality, Mr. Thomas Leake. And yet the Colonel was very far from liking the man. He looked furtive; and that tremulous under-lip made a bad impression.

Seeking for something to bolster up his instinctive dislike, Colonel Sanderstead turned the interview over in his mind; and suddenly it struck him that Leake himself had put no questions. Was that quite a natural state of affairs? It certainly seemed strange that a butler should display such apparent incuriosity in the circumstances. But as the Colonel pondered over the problem, his eye caught the figure of Bolam standing patiently there, notebook in hand; and that glance suggested to his mind a possible explanation. Suppose that Bolam had been in Leake's place, would he not have behaved in precisely the same manner? Would not he also have refrained from putting questions to his superiors? Colonel Sanderstead had to admit that it was very likely. But Leake and Bolam were two very different types; what Bolam might do in certain circumstances was probably no guide to Leake's actions.

The Colonel's eye came round once more to the constable; and, catching his glance, Bolam ventured to bring forward something which he thought of interest:

"Sir, at about half-past nine last night I was patrolling the Bishop's Vernon road in the vicinity of the Swaythling Court lodge. As I came up, Mr. Hilton and a lady were standing about fifty yards south of the lodge in the middle of the road. Mr. Hilton had his motor-cycle with him and seemed to have caught up the lady, who was walking. When I came near them, I recognized the lady as Mrs. Vane, the lady who is staying at the 'Three Bees.' They were talking together; and it appeared to me that they were having words—disagreeing, I should say, sir. As I passed them, I heard Mr. Hilton say: 'You shan't go there to-night'; and he nodded towards the Court. After I had gone a short distance farther—I could just make out their figures in the dark—I saw the lady turn back towards Fernhurst. Almost at once I heard Mr. Hilton's engine start; and as he did not pass me, he must have gone after her."

Cyril Norton had pricked up his ears at the mention of Hilton's name; but he put no question to Bolam. For once, the Colonel felt that there was a certain drawback in Bolam's reportorial method.

"And what do you infer from that, Bolam?" he demanded.

Bolam looked slightly confused, as though he felt that he had perhaps gone too far in making his statement; but Cyril Norton stepped in to save the constable's face:

"It's pretty evident what Bolam thinks, although he's not sure enough of his ground to say it. Here's Hilton turning up in the business again; and determined to prevent at all costs an interview between this Mrs. Vane, whoever she may be, and Hubbard. Bolam connects that with the quarrel in the afternoon between Hilton and Hubbard: two facets of the same jewel, perhaps. That's what you meant, isn't it, Bolam? But you felt a bit diffident about it, because you weren't sure, eh?"

"That's just how I felt about it, sir."

"Quite right to bring it out, then," Cyril commended him. "It's another bit of the jig-saw, though I don't see yet where it fits in. It'll drop into its place by and by when we know a bit more. We seem to be on the road towards a motive for this business; and that's always helpful."

He paused for a moment; and a different thought seemed to occur to him:

"By the way, uncle, isn't it time we had a doctor on to this affair? What do you say to sending for young Mickleby at once?"

The Colonel concurred; but when he suggested dispatching Bolam as a messenger, Cyril objected.

"Young Mickleby may be out on his rounds just now; and Bolam would never be able to catch up the Ford. Besides, Bolam's too useful to us, with his shorthand. I'd go myself; but I'm too interested in the business to miss anything. I want to see the trail while it's fresh. Leake's got a motor-bike. Suppose we send him?"

"Very well."

"I'll get hold of him," volunteered Cyril Norton. "I'll tell him to bring his machine round to the front door and you can give him your instructions there. I've no *locus standi* in this affair, you know. It's for you to give directions."

In a minute or two the butler had got his motorcycle at the foot of the steps; and Colonel Sanderstead went down to give his orders.

"Get Dr. Mickleby at once, Leake. If he isn't at the house, find out where he is and follow him up. Bring him here immediately. Tell him there's no time to lose. Explain to him what he's wanted for. Now get off, at once."

As he watched the butler's cycle move off down the avenue, the Colonel's eye was caught by the marks of various tyres which stretched away from the sweep in front of the house; and the sight of them recalled to his mind the track which had caught his attention as he approached the Court earlier in the morning.

"There might be something there," he reflected; and he moved slowly down the avenue, examining the surface of the road as he went.

"Let's get the two motor-cycles eliminated first of all," he said to himself. That task presented no difficulty. The trail of Cyril's tyres ran back, clean-cut, from where his cycle stood on its stand behind the Colonel's own car. Two other tracks he put down to the butler's machine.

"But surely there ought to be three of his trails?" the Colonel speculated. "First of all, he went off to that dance: one track. Then he came back this morning: a second track. And finally, he went off again after Mickleby."

Very little consideration, however, served to clear up the matter.

"Of course! The only tracks here were made after the shower last night; and that was about ten o'clock. So on his way to the dance his tyres made no impression. That leaves only two sets of marks: just what I found. And what's more, when the Court car went off with the chauffeur and the maids, it would leave no traces either. So we can eliminate it from the problem. That's all right. Now for the car tracks."

He attacked the business with increasing satisfaction. Really, he felt, he was getting into his stride. Now that Cyril's half-ironical eye was removed, he was able to give his whole attention to the affair; and he thought that so far he had done very well indeed.

The car trails strengthened his self-confidence, for the problem presented by them turned out to be very simple. Once he had identified his own car's traces, only a double trail was left unexplained. There was no possible mistake about it; for his own car carried ordinary rubber treads, whereas this unidentified motor had been shod with steel-studded, non-skid tyres.

"So some time between ten o'clock last night and the time we arrived this morning, a car's been at the front door: made the journey up from the lodge and down to the road again, as the double track shows. And the man who drove it represents yet another factor in this infernal tangle!"

Colonel Sanderstead knelt down and scrutinized the ribbon of circular pittings imprinted on the road surface; and as he did so, his eye was caught by an irregularity in the pattern. An examination of some yards of the track satisfied him:

"One of those tyres has lost a steel stud. Now that's always a possible clue to the car. It would identify the track well enough if one could come across it."

As he turned up the avenue again, he saw Cyril Norton coming down the steps of the house. At the sight of his nephew, a certain innocent craftiness crept into the Colonel's expression.

"I'll keep this to myself," he decided. "Cyril's been trying to pull my leg all the time; and I think I'm justified in keeping my own discoveries for my own use. Let him find it out for himself. I don't mind telling him that there's an extra car to be accounted for; but we'll see if he spots the way of identifying it."

With this resolution, the Colonel approached his nephew.

6
THE MAP AND THE COMPASS

As it happened, Colonel Sanderstead failed to secure an opportunity to make even the incomplete revelation which he had projected. Cyril, it seemed, was not troubling his head about his uncle. In fact, as the Colonel came up, his nephew looked past him with a gathering scowl on his face, intent upon something which he saw further down the avenue.

"Here's that damned ass Flitterwick coming up on his push-bike," he announced, when the Colonel was near enough for conversation. "*He's* likely to be a lot of use to us this morning, getting in everybody's road and chattering drivel when one wants peace to think this affair out quietly. What the devil brings him here now, of all times?"

"Well, I suppose we've got to put up with it," commented Colonel Sanderstead gloomily. He quite agreed with Cyril as to the state of the case. Both of them stood watching the approaching Flitterwick with the air of men awaiting a guest to whom they cannot, with politeness, close their door.

"We needn't precisely gush with information," Cyril pointed out; and his uncle glumly acquiesced in the implied policy. He knew only too well that anything Flitterwick gleaned would soon become common property in the village. The vicar would surpass himself on this occasion. What a chance for gossip! He would take a special pride in having been on the very scene of the murder long before anyone in the village had any idea that a crime had been committed.

Flitterwick laboriously pedalled up to where. Cyril and his uncle were standing; and his first words, as he dismounted, reminded them that as yet no news of Hubbard's death had got abroad.

"Good morning, Colonel. Good morning, Captain Norton. It promises to be a most beautiful day; and I took advantage of a leisured forenoon to avail myself of our good friend Hubbard's invitation to inspect his entomological collection. You seem to have been tempted to do the same. But where is our host?"

"His body's inside," said Cyril grimly, before the Colonel could speak, "but where the rest of him is I've no idea. It's a point that lies in your province, perhaps."

Flitterwick's inquisitive eyes brightened as he glanced from one face to the other, scenting a mystery.

"*Davos sum, non Oedipus*; I am no worthy disciple of Sherlock Holmes: and you speak in riddles. What has happened to our good friend Hubbard? Nothing serious, I trust?"

"Nothing out of the common," snapped Cyril Norton, impatiently. "He's dead. It might happen to anyone."

Flitterwick's face betrayed complete astonishment blended with a rising curiosity; but in a moment he recovered himself and assumed his professional air of condolence.

"Dead, you say? Strange, very strange, indeed. He seemed good for many years of life when I saw him the other day. Ah, well, *debemur morti, nos nostraque*, as Horace has it; we, and all that is ours, are given over unto Death. By the way, is it infectious?"

"Is what infectious?"

"I mean," explained Flitterwick, "did our good friend pass away in consequence of some infectious disease? Is it safe to approach the house?"

"Unless you call a knife in the back infectious, I should say that it was perfectly safe."

Flitterwick's eyes grew round.

"You don't mean to say he's been murdered?"

Cyril Norton's method of conveying information had jarred on the Colonel. He decided to intervene himself.

"The fact is, Flitterwick, someone—we have as yet no clue to his identity—someone evidently had a grudge against Hubbard and some time last night he seems to have got into the house and stabbed him. We came here this morning on business and discovered Hubbard's body. But remember, it's inadvisable to say much about it down in Fernhurst Parva just now. The less information leaks out, the bigger chance there is of getting hold of the murderer. So please be as reticent as you can about the business."

"I think you may rely upon my discretion, Colonel. I agree with you that nothing should interfere with the course of justice. But are you sure that it was not a case of suicide?"

The Colonel thought for a moment or two as if struck by an unexpected idea. He bent his right arm behind his back and tapped himself below the left shoulder-blade, much to Flitterwick's astonishment. Then he communicated the results of his experiment.

"Hubbard might have stabbed himself in the back, certainly; but the weapon that made the wound was not in his hand or anywhere near him; and there were other points that seem to negative any suggestion of suicide. On all counts, murder seems to be the only possible explanation of the affair."

Flitterwick was evidently preparing to push his curiosity further; but the Colonel, fearing that he might be led into indiscreet revelations, proposed that they should go into the house.

"We have a few further investigations to make on the scene of the crime, Flitterwick; and time is getting on. Perhaps you would care to go into the study for a few moments—you may find something in your own line to do, while we are busy with our affairs."

A gleam of morbid curiosity passed over Flitterwick's face at this suggestion. He assented eagerly; and they made their way to the chamber of death. The Colonel passed in first, and as he did so, his foot came into contact with some small object on the carpet which had escaped him in the previous search. Stooping, he picked up the thing his boot had touched and took it to the window to examine it.

"I wonder what this is: two bits of metal hinged together with a couple of small nutted bolts let into it."

Cyril Norton stepped across the room and glanced at the little contrivance.

"That's a belt-fastener for a motor-cycle belt. Just the ordinary pattern; nothing distinctive about it. They're turned out by the thousand. Everyone who rides a belt-driven machine carries one or two as spares. It may have fallen out of the butler's pocket or it might even have dropped out of mine when we were stooping about in our search this morning. If it belongs to the butler, it may have been here for days—since the carpet was swept last, anyway. It may fit into the jig-saw eventually, of course, but so far there's nothing to connect it with anything, since we don't know that it was actually dropped since last night."

The Colonel felt a return of his faint resentment at Cyril's critical attitude. Whenever anything was discovered, his nephew seemed interested only in destructive reasoning; and he took care never to offer a serious constructive suggestion which the Colonel in his turn might attack. There was a certain irritating air of superiority about his methods, as though he himself were fitting everything together in his own mind and deliberately refraining from offering any help to his fellow-investigator.

"Well, we needn't trouble about it just now." He slipped the fastener into his pocket. "Let's get on with our investigations. We'll leave you here, Flitterwick," he added, seeing that the vicar was preparing to follow them.

At the study door, they had no difficulty in taking up the trail. Spot after spot of grease showed up clearly in a line across the floor of the hall; and they followed the direction of the track as it led towards the back premises of the house.

"Now for your fuse-box," said the Colonel, ironically. But his faint sarcasm missed fire.

"I said the fuse-box was the last place I expected it to lead to," Cyril reminded him.

The trail led them along a tiled passage and eventually reached a closed door, which the Colonel opened. Cyril Norton glanced round the room.

"The butler's pantry, evidently. And the whole window's smashed in. Somebody seems to have burgled the place last night."

The Colonel's attention had been attracted by something nearer at hand.

"Look here, Cyril! This is evidently the breakfast-tray that Leake spoke about. But look at the state it's in. See the bits of cold chicken strewed all about the floor? The sugar-basin's upset too. What a mess!"

Cyril Norton examined the debris carefully without touching anything.

"Another bit of insanity thrown into the business! One would think the whole affair had been specially devised so as to be incomprehensible. It beats me. Do you notice that these bones have been gnawed? And that breast part had been torn away. Look, neither the knife nor fork has been touched. It looks as if the visitor, whoever he was, had taken the thing up in his hands and worried the meat off the bird. . . . Worried . . . By Jove, that's a possible explanation!"

Without paying any attention to the mystified Colonel, Cyril went over to the broken window and looked out.

"That's probably what happened," he commented. "You remember that dog we found outside the front door this morning? It's the key to this part of the business, possibly."

In his turn the Colonel approached the window and, glancing out, he found it overlooked a stone-paved walk which passed along the side of the house, the broad window-sill being only a couple of feet above the ground level.

"Now," Cyril went on, "suppose our friend with the candle broke into the house through this window, went on to the front, shutting this door behind him as he passed. Then, later on, that dog roams round the building, trying to get in. It sees the broken window—the whole lower pane's smashed clean out—and it jumps up on the sill and gets inside. It's probably hungry; and it smells the chicken on the tray. It jumps up, upsets everything; pulls down the fowl and gnaws most of the meat off it. Then it gets a scare in some way, or else it suffers from its conscience; and off it goes through the window again. That fits well enough."

"It fits, certainly," the Colonel admitted, "but it doesn't seem to matter a rap when it does fit."

He was not sorry to be able to minimize Cyril's contribution; so he took the opportunity of playing critic.

"It doesn't explain several things; and they happen to be the really important bits. First of all, it doesn't explain why the burglar knocked in the whole of the glass instead of cutting out a bit and lifting the catch of the window by putting his hand through the hole."

He looked through the window again for a moment:

"There's the very stone he did the thing with, lying on the paved path there. Then again, your theory doesn't explain why Hubbard wasn't roused up by the noise; for that whole pane falling in must have made the deuce-and-all of a clatter. And, finally, it doesn't help us to identify the burglar. I don't say you aren't right. I think you are. But so far as solving this puzzle goes, I think I can make you a present of your dog and not lose much by doing it."

Cyril Norton took the Colonel's comments in good part.

"Well, let's crawl through this window and see if we can find anything on the outside," he suggested, setting the example.

But the most careful examination revealed nothing except the burnt end of a match lying on the paved path, evidently the remains of the match with which the burglar had lighted his candle. Foot-marks of any kind were not to be found; the stone flags had allowed the housebreaker to approach the window without leaving a trace.

Just as they had completed their inspection of the ground, a car ran slowly round the corner of the house and made its way to the garage.

"That must be the house car coming back with the maids and the chauffeur," the Colonel suggested. "Suppose we go over to the garage and put a few questions to them before they get to know anything about the state of affairs."

Cyril agreed; and together they made their way to the garage in time to intercept the servants before they entered the house. So far as verbal inquiries went, they elicited nothing new. The stories of the two maids and the chauffeur tallied completely with the evidence already given by the butler. But Colonel Sanderstead, though he said nothing about it to Cyril Norton, acquired a fresh piece of information. A glance at the car showed that it, like his own, carried rubber tyres; so the extra tracks of armoured wheels must undoubtedly have been made by a third motor, which was still unidentified.

"Mickleby ought to be putting in an appearance soon, if Leake managed to get hold of him," said the Colonel, as he and Cyril walked round to the front of the house after leaving the garage. "Ah, there he comes in the Ford. We'd better wait for him here."

Almost immediately the doctor drove up, followed by Leake on his motor-cycle. Colonel Sanderstead went forward.

"'Morning, Mickleby. Nasty business for you here, I'm sorry to say. Hubbard's been murdered, apparently; and we want you to look into the matter from the medical point of view. There'll have to be an inquest, of course, and they're sure to want expert evidence."

Dr. Mickleby was a taciturn young man with a faint air of pomposity which impressed his village patients. He nodded gravely at intervals during the Colonel's exposition of the affair; but refrained from any comments. When he had gathered all the information which he considered necessary, he took a leather bag from his car and asked to be shown the body. Cyril Norton led him to the study and left him there, in company with Flitterwick, who seemed intensely interested in the proceedings.

When he rejoined his uncle, Cyril Norton's face showed that he was pondering over something which was giving him trouble. With a vague gesture, he invited the Colonel to walk with him down the avenue for a short distance; and as soon as they were out of earshot of the Colonel's chauffeur, who was still waiting beside his car, Cyril apparently decided to bring out what was on his mind.

"Black affair, this, uncle. Complicated business. I don't understand anything like the whole of it. But I prefer to play fair with you. No use being anything but straightforward among the family, I think. I've seen enough to make me anxious; and I expect you've seen about as much."

The Colonel was somewhat taken aback by his nephew's earnestness; and he failed to see the line of thought which suggested it. Cyril, examining his face closely, saw his bewilderment; and decided to be quite frank in his language:

"*You* don't know what's at the back of all this; and *I* don't know, either. But I can see awkward possibilities ahead if people begin muck-raking and putting two and two together. And there's one thing I can tell you. If Jimmy Leigh's name is brought into this affair, you needn't expect me to testify against him."

The last sentence switched the Colonel back to a line of thought which had been overlaid during the later steps in the investigation. He had almost forgotten about the blackmail case which had been the origin of the discovery of the murder. Somehow, step by step, he had edged away from it in his mind, until it had passed out of immediate consideration. But Cyril's words, with their ugly underlying suggestion, brought the whole thing back into the foreground. After all, the only person definitely known to have good reasons for removing Hubbard was—Jimmy Leigh. Hubbard had blackmailed him; and as Cyril had let slip, Jimmy Leigh was wrought up to a pitch that might well have led him into violent action. There had been that mysterious interview after dinner on the previous evening, an interview to which Jimmy had gone—as the Colonel knew—in a very abnormal frame of mind. What had taken place between the blackmailer and his victim only one living soul knew now.

The Colonel was by no means a dull man; and he could see quite well how dangerous a case might be built up against Jimmy if everything came out. The trouble in a murder case was to establish a motive; and here was a motive ready-made. It might be that Jimmy's peccadillo had been slight; but what really mattered was how Jimmy had looked at it. He might have thought it serious enough to make murder worth while if the blackmailer could be silenced. If only one knew what had happened!

Cyril Norton, scrutinizing his uncle's face, could gauge what was going on in the brain behind it; and he left the Colonel to think out his problem without interference. They took several turns up and down the road before Colonel Sanderstead broke the silence.

"I never was a good hand at intricate moral problems," he said, despondently. "I dare say there's a lot to be said on all sides of the thing; and there's no evidence to go on as far as I can see. One just has to make up one's mind on general principles. Mind you, I don't admit that there's a case against Jimmy Leigh—"

"No more do I," interjected Cyril, with emphasis.

"But," continued the Colonel, "even if there were a case, I think I'd settle the thing in my own mind on broad principles. I'm no refined moralist, able to split hairs. I'm just a plain practical man with a leaning towards honesty and the right."

Even this very vague expression of his moral ideas made the Colonel desperately uncomfortable. Principles, he felt, were things one acted on; one didn't discuss them: in fact one could hardly formulate them on the spur of the moment. He switched off and began afresh.

"The way I look at it, Cyril, is this. There's no 'case' against Jimmy Leigh at present; I've seen no evidence whatever in that house which would suggest to anyone that he was mixed up in the business. You and I happen to know some facts which might, if one twisted them, bring his name into the affair. But even these facts could go no further than the raising of unconfirmed suspicions. In themselves they prove nothing. Therefore unless something further comes to light, I agree with you that we aren't bound to divulge what we know about his relations with Hubbard."

He paused for a moment or two, making a further attempt to find expression for his principles.

"In a case like Hubbard's, I'm not sure that Law and Justice come to the same thing. A man who eliminates a blackmailer, to my mind, is doing a public service, whatever the Law may say about it. Legally, of course, it's murder; but if I were settling the case on first principles, unhampered by the Law, I think I'd be rather inclined to shake hands with the man who did it, if he had suffered by Hubbard's doings."

Cyril Norton's face betrayed his satisfaction at this rather confused account of the Colonel's views.

"That's pretty nearly how I look at it myself."

Then a fresh thought seemed to strike him.

"Why don't you drop in at the Bungalow on your way home and tackle Jimmy himself? It's quite possible that he may have facts that would clear him of any suspicion whatever—an alibi, say—and it would be just as well to get that straight. You're in a better position than I am in the matter; you're not so closely connected with him as I am, through Stella."

He appeared to meditate for a time before closing the subject:

"There's one thing I would take my oath on: Jimmy Leigh would never stab a man in the back."

The Colonel nodded his assent to this. From what he himself knew of Jimmy's character, he could hardly believe him capable of that action. He could imagine Jimmy wrought up to the pitch of murder; but it would not be that particular kind of murder.

As they turned and walked back in silence towards the house, Colonel Sanderstead saw the Vicar standing at the front door with the butler, evidently deep in conversation.

"Picking up all he can," was the Colonel's reflection; and he made up his mind to cut short Flitterwick's unofficial investigations. The less that chatterbox knew about it, the better. Anything he learned would be scattered over the whole village in a couple of days: a titbit here, another morsel for a second ear, and so on, until the affair was public property in its last detail.

Ascending the steps, Colonel Sanderstead remembered that he ought to see Mickleby before leaving the house; and brushing past the Vicar he went on into the study.

"Well, doctor, what do you make of it?"

Mickleby had assumed his most pompous air; and it was clear that he did not propose to be drawn.

"I shall have to carry out a post-mortem before I can say anything definite, Colonel."

"Ah, of course. You want to trace the character of the wound, and so forth. See where the blade went inside, I suppose."

Mickleby nodded without adding anything further.

"There'll have to be an inquest," the Colonel reminded him.

"I'll notify the coroner."

"Good. Nothing more I can do, is there? Any help I can give you?"

Mickleby again nodded, this time in dissent.

"Very good. I needn't stay here and get in your way. Good morning, doctor."

For the third time, Mickleby nodded, this time in dismissal; and he turned at once to continue his examination of the body.

On his way out, the Colonel annexed the Vicar in passing.

"Oh, Flitterwick, I'd like to hear your views on this affair. I'll send my car home; and you and I can walk down the avenue together, if you don't mind leading your bicycle. I want to drop into the Bungalow and ask young Leigh to play a round with me."

Flitterwick reluctantly parted from the butler and joined Colonel Sanderstead.

"Well, what do you think about it?" inquired the Colonel after they had walked out of earshot of the house. Cyril Norton had already departed on his motor-cycle; and the Colonel's chauffeur had just passed them in the car.

"*Adhuc sub judice lis est*, as we learned in our Horace at school: the case is still in progress, and it seems to me a difficult one. Life, Colonel, is full of mysteries and coincidences. Here this morning, I set out in answer to poor Hubbard's invitation, and as I pedalled up the avenue my thoughts were full of butterflies, of this wonderful collection in which the poor fellow took such a pride. I thought of that American specimen which he regarded, justly I believe, as the star of his museum. And, suddenly, I was plunged into this terrible tragedy, in which that very butterfly, that infinitely fragile thing of beauty, forms the central feature."

"What's that you say?" demanded the Colonel, startled out of good manners by this unexpected suggestion.

Flitterwick appeared to be gratified by having produced such a marked impression.

"Surely this case is simple in the extreme, Colonel. I penetrated to the heart of it almost immediately from the few words I had with Hubbard's butler. A most intelligent man, most intelligent."

"Well, what's your theory?"

"As one who has had in the course of his vocation to study the depths of the human soul, I can affirm, Colonel, that of all the passions, that of envy is the most widely disseminated. Now in the case of collectors, that passion reaches its maximum. It becomes in some cases a positive fury. Now we have poor Hubbard foully done to death last night; and when we examine the very room in which he was slain, we find missing from his cabinet the gem of his collection, the great American butterfly. Is it stretching our imagination too much if we see a connection, a very intimate connection, between those two facts? I think not. To my mind, it seems clear that the unfortunate Hubbard had aroused the envy of some rival collector who, carried away by his envy and covetousness, had decided to secure that marvellous specimen for his own, cost what it might. In some collectors the passion attains almost to the pitch of monomania; and it seems quite possible that some crazed enthusiast may have crept in, meaning to steal away that particular wonder. Grant that, and all the rest falls into place. There is a clear motive for the tragedy."

The Colonel turned a pair of expressionless eyes upon the Vicar's face: "That's an idea, certainly," he admitted.

He refrained from adding that it was an idiotic idea, though the adjective completed his thought on the subject. He was quite content to find Flitterwick following up that particular trail; for so long as the Vicar was on a wild-goose chase he was unlikely to do much harm by his gossiping. They walked on in silence until they reached the lodge.

"Excuse me for a moment, Flitterwick; I have a message to leave here."

The Colonel stepped up to the door, while Flitterwick walked slowly out of the gates on to the road. The lodge-keeper appeared in answer to the Colonel's knock; and very briefly Colonel Sanderstead gave him as much of the news as seemed necessary.

"By the way," he added, as though struck by an after-thought of no great importance, "did anybody visit Mr. Hubbard yesterday? Did you notice anyone passing the lodge?"

The lodge-keeper considered the question for a time.

"Mr. Hilton came in the afternoon, sir. I couldn't, say exactly what time it was. I didn't see him go out again; but I was working round at the back, part of the time; and I may have missed him."

"Anybody else?"

"No, sir, not so far as I can remember."

"When do you go to bed at night?"

"We're always in bed by half-past ten, sir. We're very regular people."

"So last night, I suppose, you would be asleep before, say, eleven o'clock?"

"Oh, yes. I doze off almost as soon as my head touches the pillow, sir; and when I fall asleep, I sleep sound."

"Ah! By the way, do you close the gates at night?"

"No, sir. Mr. Hubbard sometimes comes back late; and he likes to have the gates open always." "H'm! Well, I don't think he'll worry about that in future. The police will probably want to interview you before long about his comings and goings. Nothing more you can remember?"

But the lodge-keeper had nothing further to add to the Colonel's stock of information.

As Colonel Sanderstead turned away to follow Flitterwick, he admitted to himself a considerable satisfaction with the progress of his investigation. A motor had been there on the previous night—the tracks proved it. Now, by his inquiry at the lodge, he had established that its visit must have occurred not earlier than, say, 10.45 p.m. That was a factor in the case which he alone knew. Cyril, for all his ironical superiority, had missed this point—the presence of an extra man on the scene.

At the gate of the Bungalow, Colonel Sanderstead left the Vicar in order to pay his call on Jimmy Leigh.

"Good morning, Mrs. Pickering. Is Mr. Leigh in?"

The housekeeper's reply took him aback.

"No, sir. Mr. Leigh went off first thing this morning quite unexpectedly. It took me by surprise, sir, when he waked me up and said that he had to catch the first train. I got up and got him some breakfast; but he did not take much. He seemed very worried, sir, as if he'd had bad news."

The housekeeper knew that the Colonel was an old friend of the family and was more communicative with him than she would have been to a casual caller.

"Did he say when he was coming back, Mrs. Pickering?"

"No, sir. He just went off without a word."

"Not even his address?"

"No, sir, nothing."

"Well, I suppose that means he'll be back very shortly, perhaps this evening."

"He took his suit-case with him, sir."

"Indeed. Possibly he is spending the night in London; going to the theatre, perhaps."

But in his own mind the Colonel had very different ideas. The blackmail case, Jimmy Leigh's abnormal mood, Cyril's evidence with regard to Jimmy's nerves, the meeting with Hubbard, and now this sudden departure: there seemed to be a sinister thread running through the whole thing, a thread which, try as he would, the Colonel could not ignore. One might call it a 'departure'; but the real word that suggested itself to the Colonel was 'flight.'

"He's bolted. That looks bad. That looks very bad," he said to himself. Then aloud he continued:

"I'll just step into the laboratory and leave a note for him, Mrs. Pickering. Please see that he gets it as soon as he comes in."

At any cost, thought the Colonel, this sudden decamping must not be bruited abroad at that precise moment. Until he knew more of the mystery, he did not propose to let a connection be drawn between the murder and this apparently unforeseen departure. If the village supposed that Jimmy was returning almost immediately, no one would think of linking up his flight with the tragedy.

He went into the laboratory, scribbled a note asking Jimmy to play golf with him two days later, sealed it in an envelope and left it on the desk. Then, for some reason which he himself could hardly have explained, he began to look round the room.

Some changes in the arrangement had been made since his previous visit. The big iron tube of the 'shooting gallery' had been dismantled; and the sections stood piled beside the French window. The apparatus generating the Lethal Ray had been dragged into the centre of the room, where it now stood with its power-cables stretching across the floor to plugs in the wall. Beside it was a small table on which a sheet of paper was spread; and Colonel Sanderstead, half incuriously, stepped over to inspect this.

"Queer thing for Jimmy to be using," he murmured to himself as he examined it. "A six-inch-to-the-mile local section of the Ordnance map."

Two pencil lines ruled on the map caught his attention.

"H'm! The map's oriented as it stands. North and south line through the Bungalow. Second line ruled from the Bungalow to— Hullo! To Swaythling Court! That's funny. And here's a protractor. He's been reading off the bearing of the Court on the map. Now what interest could that have for him?"

The Colonel's eye wandered to the adjacent stand of the Lethal Ray machine and his glance caught something which made him start. A compass was lying on the top of the fine brass pointer of the machine. Colonel Sanderstead stepped round the table and read the bearing of the pointer. Then, with the protractor, he measured the angle made by the two lines on the map.

"Whew! He's got that pointer bracketed on Swaythling Court. And he told us that the Court was well within the range of the machine! There's more here than meets the eye, it seems to me. That's a nasty state of affairs."

He pondered over this new evidence for a time without being able to bring it into relation with the data already in his possession.

"Well, no matter what one thinks of this," he concluded, "no Lethal Ray was ever able to put a knife into a man's back. That's clear enough. Jimmy may have had murderous intentions; but that's not quite the same thing as being a murderer. I expect he rigged this infernal thing up during a hot fit; then thought the better of it; and did nothing further. But then, why has he bolted? For it is a bolt—undoubtedly. It looks fishy."

Then a possible interpretation struck him.

"Suppose Hubbard threatened immediate exposure; and Jimmy's bolt was on that account? He may have fitted this beastly contrivance up; then had a cold fit; felt unable to see the thing through; and simply decamped before Hubbard could publish the business, whatever it was. That would fit the facts all right. And then it would be a mere coincidence that Hubbard was murdered that very night. Just a mere coincidence."

But though the Colonel, in his anxiety to keep Jimmy Leigh's name out of the affair, repeated to himself again and again that 'it was just a coincidence,' he did not feel altogether reassured. Some coincidences are too pat to be purely accidental. And there, before him, was the damning evidence of the Lethal Ray machine, which proved beyond a doubt that at one moment Jimmy Leigh had at least begun to consider the elimination of Hubbard.

For a while longer the Colonel remained plunged in thought. Then, coming at last to a resolution, he picked up the map and compass and transferred them to his own pocket. After that, he slightly shifted the position of the Lethal Ray generator so that the brass needle no longer pointed towards Swaythling Court.

"I suppose this makes me an accessory after the fact," he reflected, rather ruefully. "But I can't help it. It wouldn't be justice to hang Jimmy Leigh on account of a blackmailing beast like Hubbard."

7
THE OPENING OF THE INQUEST

THE CORONER SEATED HIMSELF in a chair at the end of the long table in the dining-room of Swaythling Court and, after opening his book, glanced over the faces of the jury. His expression seemed to indicate that he had a poor opinion of their intelligence.

Formal evidence of Hubbard's identity was given and then the coroner, before calling further witnesses, addressed a few words to the jury.

"It will perhaps make matters easier for you, gentlemen, if I explain to you the purpose for which we are here this morning. You have inspected the body of a dead man in the room upstairs; and you have also been shown the apartment in which he was first discovered after his death. Formal evidence of his identity has been submitted to you—not that there is any dispute on that point, for I believe he was well known to some of you by sight. The question before us, which you have to settle for yourselves in your own minds, after hearing the evidence which we shall bring before you, is: 'In what way did this man come to die?'"

The coroner paused for a few moments, evidently to let his words sink into the minds of his hearers. Colonel Sanderstead took the opportunity to inspect the group of people before him. The jurymen, all looking slightly self-conscious, were familiar to him: the village butcher, Corley; old Swaffham, the Fernhurst grocer; Simon, the motor-man; and some farmers of the neighbourhood. Much to his disgust, the Colonel discovered that Simon had been chosen foreman of the jury.

The reporter of the *Micheldean Gazette* was sharpening his pencil at the foot of the table; and one or two spectators seemed to have been admitted.

Scattered about the room were the witnesses; and the grouping into which they had fallen seemed significant to the Colonel. He and Cyril Norton sat on adjacent chairs; slightly removed from them was Mrs. Pickering, Jimmy Leigh's housekeeper; at a respectful distance, Bolam had taken his seat. Then, near the coroner's chair, looking even more pompous than usual, was young Mickleby, fingering some notes of the evidence he meant to give. Isolated from them all, at the end of the room behind the reporter's chair, Leake the butler sat impassively in his place, his face composed into a mask out of which his eyes appeared to peep furtively from time to time as he raised his lids.

"In order that you may have sufficient information before you to enable you to form a correct judgment in this case," the coroner continued, "it is necessary to explain that this man, William Blayre Hubbard, carried on a business in artificial perfumes, in which products he was a wholesale dealer in a small way. His income from this business would not have enabled him to keep up a house like Swaythling Court; and evidence will be given to show that he practised blackmailing—extorting money by means of threats. That fact may or may not have a bearing on the manner of his death; but in any case you must take it into consideration. I wish to make clear, however, that we are here for one purpose only: to determine what caused the death of this individual. We are in no way concerned with the details of his blackmailing operations. That is an entirely different question, which cannot be opened up at this inquest, except in so far as it touches the matter of his death."

Colonel Sanderstead breathed a slight sigh of relief at this ruling. The coroner proceeded with his explanation.

"In order to make the matter as clear as possible, I have arranged to call the witnesses in an order which will lay before you, in proper sequence, all the events which can be connected with his decease; so that, as the evidence is unfolded, you will get an almost connected story of the last day of his life."

At this moment, the door opened; and the Colonel, glancing towards it, saw Hilton on the threshold. Cyril Norton, looking in his turn, allowed a frown to pass across his face as he recognized the new-comer. Hilton paused for a second or two, as though afraid to interrupt the coroner; then, after searching for a vacant seat, he walked across the room and took his place beside one of the windows. His appearance roused the Colonel's interest considerably. Here was a witness who would be able to fill in some gaps in the story, if he chose to speak the truth.

Hilton had barely seated himself, before the coroner called upon the butler to give his evidence. Leake came forward and took his place opposite the jury, on the other side of the long table. Seen thus, in the Swaythling Court dining-room which was part of his normal environment, he suggested nothing to the Colonel, who was watching him keenly. He took the oath without betraying any particular emotion; and, when prompted by the coroner, he delivered his evidence almost as though he had previously learned it by heart.

"My name is Thomas Leake. I have been butler here ever since Mr. Hubbard came to Swaythling Court. On the day of his death, Mr. Hubbard went up to town as usual in the morning. He returned in time for lunch. About three o'clock, Mr. Hilton called . . ."

The eyes of the jury swung round from the butler to Hilton; but as he was sitting between them and the window, they evidently could see nothing of interest; and they re-concentrated their attention on the witness.

"Mr. Hubbard at that time was rearranging his collection of butterflies in the study. I showed Mr. Hilton in. In about half an hour he came out again and left the house. Except for a few minutes when he went upstairs, Mr. Hubbard remained in his study until I served dinner in this room at seven o'clock. Mr. Hubbard had given all the domestic staff permission to go to a dance in Micheldean Abbas that night; and the maids and chauffeur had left the house at half-past six. After dinner, about half-past seven, I took whisky and a syphon of soda into his study and left it beside him on the desk; and I looked to see that a breakfast-tray had been left in the pantry, according to his orders."

Simon got up from his seat, a bulky figure in a light-grey dusty suit, very shiny on the back and at the elbows. He had the air of a man who means to get to the bottom of a puzzling affair, even though it costs him trouble. Colonel Sanderstead, noting the motor-man's side-glance at his fellow-jurors, let his dislike bubble up. Posing brute! Trying to show off before the yokels, no doubt.

"Witness, will you be so good as to tell us what orders the deceased gave to you about this breakfast-tray?"

Having delivered himself of this, Simon glanced again at his neighbours and sat down with great deliberation.

"Mr. Hubbard had given orders that we were not to return before half-past ten or eleven on the following morning; and I was to leave a breakfast-tray ready for him. He may have meant to take it up to his room with him and breakfast in bed."

"I must ask the witness to confine himself to facts," interrupted the coroner. "The jury must draw their own conclusions from the evidence."

"When I placed the whisky on Mr. Hubbard's desk, I noticed lying there a steel paper-knife which he frequently used. I left the house shortly afterwards, having carried out Mr. Hubbard's orders to see that all the doors and windows were fast and having dropped the catch of the Yale lock on the front door. I did not return to the house until the following morning, when I found the police in possession."

Leake seemed inclined to resume his seat; but the coroner checked him with a gesture.

"You identify this decanter and this tumbler as the ones which you took into the study?"

"I do."

"And this implement is the steel paper-knife of which you spoke?"

"Yes."

"On your inspection of the house after you returned, did you find anything abnormal?"

"One of Mr. Hubbard's exhibition cases of butterflies had been broken open and there was one butterfly missing, one which Mr. Hubbard had told me was his best specimen, very valuable."

"Anything further?"

"After the police had gone, I found the pantry window broken and the breakfast-tray contents scattered about the floor."

One of the jurymen nudged his neighbour, and both stared at Bolam with apparent interest, much to the constable's vexation. The coroner took no notice. Seeing that Leake was about to be dismissed, Simon lifted himself once more from his seat; and, holding tight to the table in front of him with both hands, he leaned forward and put a question:

"Witness, are we to understand from your evidence that you were alone in the house with the deceased between 6.30 and the time you departed for this dance?"

If Leake appreciated the bearing of this question, he gave no sign of the fact. He fixed his gaze on the exhibits which lay on the table before him; and in a perfectly clear voice he admitted the correctness of Simon's suggestion.

"I was certainly in the house alone with Mr. Hubbard for about an hour, I think."

Simon thought he had extracted something of value; and he sat down once more with the air of a man who knows more than he cares to tell.

At this moment, the Colonel became aware of someone in the room whom he had overlooked in his original survey. Sitting almost behind the coroner, he discovered a middle-aged man with a close-clipped moustache, whose face seemed faintly familiar to him.

"Who's that?" he inquired from Cyril, in a whisper.

"Angermere. Chap who writes books," Cyril retorted brusquely.

The Colonel inspected Angermere's face again, as closely as politeness allowed: and across his memory flitted the recollection of a shelf on a railway bookstall filled with volumes bearing titles like: *The Secret of the Green Oak* and *The Ravenshaw Mystery*. Each jacket displayed the author's portrait; and the Colonel now understood why Angermere's face had seemed familiar to him at first sight.

"What's he doing here?" speculated Colonel Sanderstead. "Probably a friend of the coroner; and came up here to see if he could pick up an idea or two for a book."

The next witness called by the coroner was Cyril Norton. Like the butler, he contributed nothing to the case which the Colonel had not heard before. And to the Colonel's relief, he succeeded in keeping Jimmy Leigh's name entirely out of the affair. "My friend communicated this to me." "I will read a copy of a letter purporting to come from the deceased and demanding money from my friend under menaces." "It was agreed that I should look after my friend's interests in this matter."

The dusty figure of Simon rose again from its seat at the end of the evidence.

"Witness, the jury wish to know who is this person whom you refer to continually as your 'friend.'"

Cyril Norton turned upon him with a scowl.

"I have no intention of answering that question, Mr. Foreman. If I were to give you the name, it would not throw the faintest light upon this matter; and I have no desire to wash dirty linen in public."

Simon was obviously very ill-pleased at the snub.

"I think that the jury have a right to know the full facts of the case before them. If you cannot tell us the name of the party, perhaps you can give us the person's sex; whether it was a man or a woman that the deceased was said to be blackmailing."

Cyril Norton's frown deepened.

"I do not propose to answer that question. I am quite satisfied that the person to whom you refer did not commit the murder, if that is what you are intending to suggest."

The coroner intervened sharply.

"The witness must not prejudice this case by referring to a 'murder.' We are here to discover how the deceased died."

Simon reseated himself with a sulky scowl; and the coroner proceeded to call Hilton as the next witness. As the name was announced, Colonel Sanderstead glanced at his nephew and was struck by a change to alertness in Cyril's attitude. When Hilton came forward to give his evidence, Cyril's face became an almost expressionless mask; his whole intentness seemed to be concentrated in his eyes. He seemed to be expecting something; and the

Colonel, remembering Cyril's air of knowing more than he cared to tell, turned with a growing interest to the new witness.

But when it came, Hilton's evidence apparently threw no fresh light upon the problem.

"I called at Swaythling Court on 30th September—about three o'clock in the afternoon, I think. I wished to see the deceased on a matter of business. I had no previous appointment. The butler admitted me; and I found the deceased in his study. He appeared to be busy with his butterfly collection at the time. We had some discussion of the business which took me to see him."

"Can you give us any indication of the nature of your business with the deceased?" inquired the coroner.

"It was purely private business—nothing to do with the present case."

"You had a disagreement with the deceased?"

"I had."

"And after that, you left the house?"

"Yes."

"Can you give us no idea what the business was?"

"It had nothing whatever to do with the death of the deceased. I am quite positive of that."

"Did you go to the deceased of your own free will?"

"Yes, I wanted him to do me a favour, which he refused."

The Colonel, almost subconsciously, noted a slight relaxation in Cyril's attitude as this answer came out.

"You speak of a 'favour'; but you also called it a 'matter of business.' Which was it?"

"It was a favour for which I was prepared to pay him."

"After you left Swaythling Court, what did you do?"

Hilton evidently saw the underlying meaning of the question.

"I went back to my hotel at Micheldean Abbas and stayed in the smoke-room until dinner-time, talking to some people. After dinner, I came back to Fernhurst Parva to see a friend. I was in that friend's company until about a quarter to ten o'clock. After that, I returned to my hotel and played billiards with the marker for an hour or so. Then I went to bed."

Mrs. Pickering was the next witness; and Colonel Sanderstead in his turn grew alert. Here was a chance of discovering what had happened during that mysterious interview between Jimmy Leigh and Hubbard at the Bungalow. He felt a certain apprehension as Mrs. Pickering took her place before the jury. She was obviously nervous; but she gave her evidence quite frankly.

"My name is Susan Pickering. Since the end of the war, I have been housekeeper to Mr. James Leigh at the Bungalow. On the evening of 30th September, I was in the kitchen there. Mr. Leigh had been out to dinner, and I heard him come in again shortly after half-past eight, I think."

Simon rose ponderously from his seat.

"Can the witness not tell us exactly when the man Leigh came in?"

Mrs. Pickering disliked Simon and evidently resented his interruption. She looked him over witheringly, fixing her gaze particularly on a grease-stain which disfigured his grey sleeve.

"No. And if I'm badgered with stupid questions, I'm sure to get muddled up. I'm telling you what happened as well as I can remember it."

"The times when things happened are most important," Simon commented pompously.

The coroner evidently sympathized with the witness.

"I think it will probably facilitate matters if witnesses are allowed to tell their stories with as little interruption as possible."

Several of the jurymen smiled broadly at Simon's discomfiture, which made the foreman still more angry. Mrs. Pickering continued:

"At a quarter to nine, Mr. Leigh went to the front door and opened it."

Simon could not resist this opening.

"How do you know it was exactly a quarter to nine?"

"Because I heard the church clock chime the quarter just at that time," Mrs. Pickering retorted, rather acidly. "When I say a thing happened, you can take it that I did know it happened, and when it happened, Mr. Simon."

The coroner frowned at Simon, who sank back into his chair. Quite obviously he was not making such a good impression as he

had expected. Mrs. Pickering, with a triumphant smile at the foreman, went on with her evidence:

"I heard Mr. Leigh open the front door and say: 'Good evening,
Hubbard. Come in.' I heard their footsteps come down the hall and
go into Mr. Leigh's workshop."

Corley, the butcher, had been following the evidence with interest; and he now put a question:

"If Mrs. Pickering doesn't mind, I'd just like to get that clear.
She heard footsteps. Was it quite clear that there were two people
in the hall?"

Corley was a favourite of Mrs. Pickering. She beamed on him
as though he had been giving her help.

"I heard the two sets of footsteps quite distinctly; and I heard
Mr. Hubbard drop his walking-stick into the umbrella-stand as he
passed. In about a minute or so"—she turned to gaze witheringly
at Simon as she gave this information—"Mr. Leigh came out of the
workshop and tapped at my door. He had a letter in his hand; and
he asked me to go out with it to the post, as he wanted it to go that
night, and he couldn't leave Mr. Hubbard. I hurried to put on my
things and went out with the letter immediately."

"Did you notice the address on the letter?" demanded Simon,
the tone of his voice showing that he believed he had hit on something of importance.

"I did not. I'm not so inquisitive as some of my neighbours."

The coroner again interrupted. Evidently he believed that Mrs.
Pickering would tell her story best if she were left alone.

"I think we shall get on faster if the witness is allowed to give
her evidence without unnecessary interruption."

Simon shrugged his shoulders sulkily under the reproof.

"At nine o'clock—I heard the church clock strike again as I came
in at the gate—I got back to the house and went into the kitchen.
The kitchen is next the workshop and the walls are very badly dead-
ened, so I could hear voices talking next door. I recognized Mr.
Hubbard's voice quite distinctly, though I couldn't make out what
they were talking about. I wasn't listening specially. They went on

talking, with occasional stops in the talk, until I went to bed. That was at half-past ten, because I always go to bed then. Just after I got into bed, I heard Mr. Leigh opening the front door and letting Mr. Hubbard out. I heard him say: 'Good night, Hubbard,' quite distinctly. After that, I fell asleep. Next morning, when I was dusting the hall I found Mr. Hubbard's stick in the umbrella-stand. I looked at it and found a silver plate with his name and address on it. I have seen that stick in his hand several times."

"You identify this stick on the table as the stick you found in the umbrella-stand?" inquired the coroner.

"That is the stick," Mrs. Pickering replied, picking it up from the table. "I happened to notice that one of the corners of the silver plate was rough. It caught my hand when I took it out of the stand; and you can see the rough bit here if you look at it."

Corley the butcher had evidently been thinking over the evidence. Again he ventured to put a question:

"Did you hear Mr. Leigh in the house after the deceased had gone away that night?"

"Yes, indeed," Mrs. Pickering hastened to add. "I forgot to say that immediately after leaving Mr. Hubbard at the door he went back to the workshop and began pulling heavy things about. He kept me awake for quite a while with the noise he made."

The Colonel pricked up his ears at this information. What the housekeeper had heard, evidently, was Jimmy Leigh shifting the Lethal Ray apparatus to bring it to bear on Swaythling Court.

The next witness was a stranger to the Colonel.

"My name is Timothy Simpson. I'm a clerk; and was employed by the deceased at 'is office. 'E visited 'is office as usual on the morning of 30th September. When 'e left for lunch, I gathered that 'e intended to return on the following morning. I 'ave a telephone in my 'ouse, put in at the expense of the deceased. At about five past eleven on the night of 30th September, the deceased rang me up and told me that 'e would not be at the office on the following morning. 'E then rang off."

"Was this a common practice of his?" inquired the coroner.

"'E did things like that from time to time, when 'e thought it advisable. There might be appointments that 'e couldn't keep at the office."

The coroner had been scrutinizing the faces of the jury while the witnesses were giving their evidence; and it was plain that he felt they stood in need of some assistance. When Simpson had concluded his statement, the coroner turned to the jurymen.

"I think you will see the bearing of the evidence which has been submitted to you. We are fortunately able to follow the doings of the deceased from the morning of 30th September right up to 11.5 p.m. on that day, with only two gaps in the period. The first gap is between 7.30 p.m. and 8.45 p.m.; but part of this is accounted for, since we know that the deceased must have walked from here to the Bungalow during that period, a distance which would take him perhaps a quarter of an hour to cover. The second gap is between 10.45 p.m., when he left the Bungalow again, and 11.5 p.m., when he rang up his clerk; but this gap obviously represents the time occupied by him in walking from the Bungalow back to Swaythling Court. Since he was last heard of at 11.5 p.m., it follows that his death must have occurred after that hour. We have no further evidence to bring forward until about nine o'clock on the next morning."

Constable Bolam was the next witness. His evidence was an old story to the Colonel, dealing as it did with the matter of the warrant, the visit to the Court, the finding of the body, the state of the room, and the broken window in the pantry. It was obvious that Bolam had digested his short-hand notes well; and he delivered his evidence in a way which made a very favourable impression on the coroner.

Colonel Sanderstead himself was then called. As Bolam had already covered most of the ground, the Colonel contented himself with identifying the paper-knife as the one which he had found in the ashes. He mentioned also the candle and the belt-fastener which he had discovered on the floor. When he had finished his story, Simon heaved himself out of his seat and proceeded to put a question.

"Witness, do you collect butterflies?"

For a moment, the Colonel was dumfounded. Then the insinuation behind the question grew clear to him; and he lost his temper.

"Do you mean to suggest that *I* stole the missing butterfly?" he demanded angrily.

Simon thought he had detected something.

"Witness, I asked a plain question; and instead of answering it, you shuffle and ask another question. That will produce a very serious impression on the minds of the jury. Will you be so good as to tell us —'yes' or 'no'—Do you collect butterflies?"

The Colonel glared at his *bête noire*; then mastered himself sufficiently to snap out:

"No, I do not collect butterflies; nor have I ever taken the faintest interest in butterflies. And to be quite definite about it, I did not remove the missing butterfly from its case."

Simon seemed in no way crestfallen. If he had not gained any information, at least he had managed to ruffle the Colonel.

The coroner intervened: and suggested to Simon that only questions connected with the case should be asked. They were engaged in an inquest and not a roving inquiry.

Mickleby was the next witness. It was apparent that he considered this an occasion demanding the greatest impressiveness at his command.

"I was called in to this case at half-past nine on 1st October. On my arrival, I found the body of the deceased in a chair at his desk; the head and arms of the body resting on the table as though the deceased had fallen asleep. The temperature of the body was about 80° Fahrenheit; and assuming that the body had lost four or five degrees of temperature in each of the first two hours, and approximately one degree per hour after that, then death must have occurred about eleven hours previously—say about midnight. Rigor mortis had set in, which points to the same conclusion."

"The jury will take note of that point," interjected the coroner.

"On examining the body more minutely, I was struck by a strong effluvium of almonds which emanated from it."

"Excuse me, Dr. Mickleby," the coroner interrupted, "would it be too much trouble if we asked you, for the sake of clearness, to use the simplest language? I wish the jury to understand that the body smelt strongly of oil of almonds. Could that smell be accounted for by the fact that the deceased was a dealer in synthetic perfumes?"

Mickleby considered for a few moments.

"My recollection is that not only the clothes but also the body of the deceased had a strong smell of almond oil. How it was produced is hardly in my province. I am not a perfumery agent."

The coroner took no notice of Mickleby's insolence; but nodded to him to continue his evidence.

"Further examination of the deceased showed that his eyes were markedly dilated; the pupils were widely expanded, I mean."

"Do you draw any inference from that?"

"It is a symptom in the case of poisoning with belladonna and some other drugs. I am giving you my observation."

Something in Mickleby's manner at this point suggested to the Colonel that the doctor had in reserve some striking fact with which he expected to surprise the jury.

"I now come to the wound in the body of the deceased. This is a punctured wound."

"Excuse me, Dr. Mickleby," interrupted the coroner. "Gentlemen, I think I had better explain that by the technical term 'punctured wound' we mean a wound of which the depth is much greater than the length of its free opening on the skin."

Mickleby distributed his contempt between the coroner and the jury; and then continued his evidence:

"Very little trace of bleeding was to be observed around the orifice of this wound. In fact, the quantity of blood exuded was hardly sufficient to stain the outer clothes of the deceased in the neighbourhood of the wound itself. The wound was less than an inch in its longer diameter and considerably narrower in the cross-diameter. It appeared to have been inflicted by some weapon like this paper-knife on the table."

Mickleby indicated the Colonel's find.

"On examining the edges of the wound, I could find very little sign of retraction of the skin, such as normally occurs in any wound such as a knife-cut. Usually, the edges of the wound tend to draw back from each other owing to the tension of the skin. I examined the whole surface of the body for bruises; but I discovered nothing of the kind. There was no sign of any struggle having taken place."

From Mickleby's expression, the Colonel judged that he was about to spring his surprise soon.

"I carried out a post-mortem examination of the body in order to determine the internal track of the weapon. The wound was between the sixth and seventh ribs at the posterior part of the body; and the weapon had penetrated to a point in line with the lower margin of the seventh rib in front. Any instrument taking this course would penetrate the heart in passing; and my examination showed that the weapon had passed through that organ."

Simon was on his feet again.

"Witness, from your knowledge, could you say whether this blow was struck by a powerful person?"

Mickleby examined Simon curiously, as though he were some strange animal in a menagerie:

"A wound of this kind might have been inflicted by anyone. An average man, or even a woman, would have had strength enough to inflict it, if they had the luck to strike just at that particular place."

Simon apparently attempted to think of a supplementary question, but failed to hit upon one on the spur of the moment. Mickleby continued:

"As the jurymen are laymen who cannot appreciate the full bearing of these facts, possibly the coroner will not object to my indicating the clear meaning which they present to the trained medical eye. They establish, beyond any doubt, the fact that *this wound was not the cause of death*."

If Mickleby had hoped to surprise his audience, he certainly achieved his object. Everybody except the coroner showed their astonishment at the turn which the case was taking.

"Any wound penetrating the heart during life is certain to bleed copiously: this wound did not bleed. A wound inflicted during life will show marked retraction of the skin at its edge: this wound shows no retraction. Finally, if this wound had been inflicted during life, I should have expected to find some trace of movement, or spasm, in the body before life became extinct: but the position in which I found the body seemed to negative anything of the sort. All the evidence, then, points to the fact that whoever inflicted that wound was only stabbing a body which was already dead."

For a few moments Mickleby sunned himself in the admiration of the jury and witnesses. He had produced his sensation; and he enjoyed it.

"Since the deceased obviously did not die from the effects of this wound," he continued, "I sought elsewhere for the cause of death. The skin of the body, I found on examination, was tinged slightly violet—quite different from the normal tint. There was a slight foam or froth at the corners of the mouth. The jaws were firmly closed, as though in a spasm. The hands and toes of the deceased were contracted; and, as I have said already, the pupils of the eyes were widely dilated. In view of these symptoms, I removed some of the internal organs of the deceased, under the directions of the coroner."

Mickleby stepped back; and the coroner took the proceedings into his own hands again.

"Gentlemen, the evidence of the last witness has established conclusively, I think, that the deceased did not die in consequence of the wound which you have inspected. That wound, therefore, falls out of our consideration; and the cause of his death must be sought elsewhere. Under my directions, the contents of the deceased's stomach and other organs have been submitted to a chemical expert, as well as the liquids contained in the whisky decanter, the soda-water syphon, and the tumbler which were found on the desk beside the body. The contents of a bottle also found on the desk have likewise been submitted for expert examination. I adjourn this inquiry until we have before us the evidence of the chemical expert to whom the matter has been referred. As soon as he has completed his investigation, you will receive due notice that your attendance is again required."

He rose, closed his book, and walked out of the room.

8
THE VERDICT

As Colonel Sanderstead came down the steps from the door of Swaythling Court, he found himself beside Angermere, who had left the house a little before him. The Colonel had a natural leaning towards hospitality to everyone who thought it worth while to stay for a time in his village; their visits were in some way flattering to the affection he felt for Fernhurst Parva; and he liked, if possible, to make things pleasant even for such birds of passage.

"Mr. Angermere? I see you've no car with you. I'd be very glad to give you a lift down to the village in mine, if you care for it."

Quite unconsciously, the Colonel assumed that anyone who stayed in Fernhurst Parva would recognize him without any introduction. In Angermere's case, he was not mistaken.

"That's very kind of you, Colonel. This affair lasted a bit longer than I expected, and I'm rather late for lunch as it is."

They got into the car. Cyril Norton, coming out of the house, nodded to the Colonel and went off in search of his motor-cycle. The coroner had already gone; and only a few of the witnesses and members of the jury were scattered about in groups, discussing the evidence,

Short as was the run down to the 'Three Bees,' it was long enough for the Colonel to form a favourable impression of Angermere's personality. Much to his host's relief the author put on none of the airs of superiority which the Colonel had feared; in fact, he seemed to be rather a likeable personality.

"How long are you staying here?" the Colonel inquired, as the car drew up at the hotel door.

"Since I've seen the beginning of this case, I suppose I may as well stay on for a few days more and hear the end of it. I don't suppose the adjournment will be a long one. The coroner—he's a friend of mine, by the way—told me that there would not be much delay."

"I'd rather like to hear what you think of it," Colonel Sanderstead suggested. "You must be rather an expert in this sort of thing."

"Because I scribble mystery yarns? That's a different thing altogether, you know. It's easy enough to solve a mystery when you've constructed it yourself. But this business strikes me as complex in some ways. I've really no settled ideas about it at all, just now. Wait till we've heard the whole story; and then I might have some notion or other. But, honestly, I'm no more of an expert in the matter than the first man you meet in the street. What do you think about it yourself?"

"It seems complicated enough for me," admitted the Colonel. "But I'd like to hear what you make of it after you've heard all the evidence. Suppose you dine with me on the evening after the inquest closes and give me your impressions while they're fresh in your mind? I'll send the car down for you. But of course I'll see you at the next meeting before then. We can fix it up there."

As the Colonel drove home to Fernhurst Manor after leaving the novelist at the 'Three Bees,' he turned over in his mind the evidence which had been given at the inquest, in the hope of finding some fresh light upon the death of the blackmailer; and the more he reflected upon the matter, the more uneasy he grew. Cyril Norton's evident perturbation about the part which Jimmy Leigh might have played in the drama returned to his mind. He recalled that Cyril's clinching argument had been that Jimmy Leigh would never have stabbed a man in the back: but now it appeared that Hubbard had been dead before that wound was inflicted. If so, then the manner of his death did not necessarily exclude the chance that Jimmy had had a hand in it. There was the Lethal Ray machine, that factor in the problem which was known to the Colonel alone, since he had destroyed the evidence by shifting the position of the generator. And there was this sudden departure of Jimmy which had to be accounted for. Much to his discomfort, the Colonel began to feel suspicious.

"Well, if he did do it," he summed up to himself as he stepped out of his car, "I can't bring myself to blame him over much. Black-mailers are vermin; and any man who takes the risk of putting them out of the way is a public benefactor of sorts."

But for the next day or two, Colonel Sanderstead was worried. Try as he might, he could see no solution of the mystery. Its complications defeated him at every turn. As Cyril Norton had said, one could find a theory to fit parts of the affair; but the Colonel could imagine nothing which would account for the whole of the facts. Even if Jimmy Leigh had done the actual killing, there must have been at least one other person on the scene. There was the man in the motor to fit somehow into the puzzle; there was the candle-wax to be explained; there was the broken window and the Yale key on the doorstep. Try as he might, Colonel Sanderstead was unable to put together any hypothesis which would bring all these points into a clear relationship.

When the inquest was resumed he went across to Swaythling Court with very mingled expectations. At least he would learn the true cause of Hubbard's death; and that would be so much to the good: but he feared that instead of clearing things up, the new information might complicate the problem still further.

The first witness called was the expert to whom the examination of the contents of some of the organs had been entrusted.

"My name is Laurence Shuttleboard. I am an analytical chemist. I have examined the various organs which were submitted to me in sealed jars, with the following results. The stomach contents on first inspection had a strong odour of hydrocyanic acid—prussic acid, as it is commonly called. I submitted the material to chemical examination and found that a very large quantity of cyanide was present."

"Did you succeed in estimating the total quantity in the stomach contents?" inquired the coroner.

"I should put it roughly at a quarter of an ounce at least."

"Can you give the jury any idea of the fatal dose of a cyanide?"

"What I found in the stomach contents was apparently potassium cyanide, which would generate prussic acid when taken into the stomach. The lethal dose of the cyanide is not known with accuracy; but it is one of the most formidable poisons known to chemists. I should say that even as little as five grains of the solid salt might cause death. A case is known in which a dose of that size killed a person in a quarter of an hour."

"So that you found in the stomach contents a quantity of cyanide equal to between twenty and twenty-five times the fatal dose?"

"Yes."

"Death would supervene with great rapidity in the case of a person swallowing a dose of this amount?"

"Almost instantaneously, I should imagine; but the time varies from case to case when cyanide is concerned."

"Could the deceased have lived for, say, a couple of hours after swallowing the quantity you found in the stomach?"

"I should have difficulty in believing that."

"Did you examine the food contained in the stomach and could you draw any inference from its condition as to the time which elapsed between the deceased's last meal and the time of his death?"

"My examination showed that the deceased suffered from chronic indigestion. His digestive machinery was evidently very sluggish and he probably suffered from dilated stomach. I noticed various partially digested foods in the stomach contents which had obviously been derived from different meals, so that the progress of digestion in his case throws no clear light upon the time which elapsed between his last meal and his death. Death might have followed almost immediately after the meal, or it might have been hours after his dinner, when he died."

The coroner made a note and then continued his interrogation:

"In addition to the stomach contents, some other materials were submitted to you for examination?"

"A decanter containing whisky, a small quantity of liquid obtained from a tumbler, a bottle with a wide mouth, stoppered, which was said to have been found on the desk beside the body, and a bottle stated to have been discovered among the deceased's effects."

"Can you tell us what you found in each case?"

"I examined the contents of the decanter first. So far as my analysis goes, it contained nothing but ordinary whisky."

"There was no trace of cyanide in it?"

"None whatever. The liquid was quite innocuous."

"Then obviously the deceased could not have met his death by drinking from that decanter?"

"No. That is quite impossible."

"Now with regard to the contents of the tumbler, Mr. Shuttleboard, what did your examination bring to light?"

"The contents of the tumbler submitted to me amounted to about a dessert-spoonful of liquid. On examination it proved to be mainly whisky similar to that found in the decanter. But in addition to the whisky, I found a certain quantity of the drug paraldehyde."

"How much paraldehyde would you estimate to have been present, assuming the tumbler had originally been half-full of whisky and soda?"

"I should say that some eight drachms may have been present in the ordinary quantity of whisky and soda that a man would pour out."

"Can you tell the jury the usual dose of this drug?"

"I believe that anything between half a drachm and two drachms is used."

"Can you inform the jury of the effects of this drug?"

"It is usually employed as a narcotic."

"Has it any marked taste—I mean could a man swallow it without knowing it was present in a liquid?"

"When pure, it has a very biting taste, irritating the mucous membrane of the mouth and tongue; but taken in whisky I think its presence might easily escape notice. A man taking a long drink of whisky and soda might quite well fail to perceive it until he had drunk a large quantity."

"You say it is a narcotic. Is it rapid in its action?"

"Very rapid indeed when taken in large doses."

"Have you ever heard of it being used for criminal purposes?"

"I have heard it connected with the so-called K.O.—'knock-out drops'—used by some criminals to drug their victims for the purpose of robbery."

"Is it ever used by persons suffering from insomnia apart from a physician's prescription?"

"I believe it is. I have used it myself at times."

"Would you attribute the deceased's death to the presence of this drug in his drinking tumbler?"

"No. I doubt if it was present in sufficient quantity."

"Did you find any traces of it in the stomach contents?"

"I found some of it, enough to show that he had certainly swallowed some of the contents of the tumbler."

"You do not attribute any share in his death to this drug?"

"Certainly not. I believe that the symptoms noted in the post-mortem examination pointed to cyanide poisoning."

"Now, Mr. Shuttleboard, would you tell us what you found in the wide-mouthed bottle submitted to you?"

"It contained 427 grains of cyanide of potassium."

"Was the bottle large enough to have contained much more of this substance?"

"The bottle was a four-ounce bottle, so that it might, if full, have held another three ounces of the cyanide. I should doubt, however, if it contained as much as that."

"Can you give us your reasons for that statement?"

"The bottle submitted to me was of a well-known pattern used by entomologists for killing butterflies and moths. When used for this purpose, it is never filled with cyanide, as space has to be left for putting the moth into the bottle to kill it. I believe the deceased was a butterfly collector; and I suspect that this was his killing-bottle. In that case, it would only be partially full of cyanide."

"Then the cyanide found by you in the stomach contents might have come from this bottle?"

"Yes."

"And the quantity found by you in the stomach would approximate to the quantity missing from this bottle, assuming the bottle originally to have contained a usual amount of cyanide?"

"That is so."

"I am sorry to repeat questions, Mr. Shuttleboard, but I wish the jury to be absolutely clear upon this point. Death, you believe, was produced by a dose of cyanide?"

"Yes."

"The other drug—the paraldehyde in the tumbler—had nothing to do with the death, though it must have been swallowed at an earlier period than the cyanide?"

"That is my belief."

"The quantity of cyanide found by you, if replaced in the so-called killing-bottle, would bring the total quantity of cyanide there up to the normal quantity of cyanide usually found in a killing-bottle?"

"That is my estimate."

The Colonel had been watching the witness carefully; but his attention was now diverted by a shadow passing across the window. He glanced up and saw the great vacant moon-face of Sappy Morton peering through the glass, as though fascinated by the spectacle of the proceedings.

"Poor devil," thought the Colonel. "I wonder what he makes of it all. The ways of ordinary humanity must be puzzling to Sappy at times. Here are a lot of people sitting down at a dinner-table, with nothing on it except some odd scraps of stuff, obviously quite uneatable. He must think we're a rum lot—quite mad."

But Bolam had evidently noticed Sappy's presence at the window; and, at a gesture from the constable, the idiot recoiled sharply and disappeared.

"Now," continued the coroner, "perhaps you would be good enough to tell us the nature of the contents of this last bottle which was submitted to you."

He held up a four-ounce medicine-bottle as he spoke.

"That is the bottle which was submitted to me. I analyzed the contents and found that they corresponded with the name written on the label: 'Paraldehyde.' I applied the usual tests and I found nothing there except that drug."

The coroner indicated that he had no further questions to put; and the witness withdrew. Constable Bolam was recalled.

"On information received, I instituted a search for a bottle of paraldehyde among the effects of the deceased man. No bottle of this kind was found in the room in which his body was found; but on the wash-hand stand in his bedroom I found a number of bottles, among which was this one, labelled 'Paraldehyde,' which I now identify. I passed this bottle to the coroner in accordance with his instructions."

Bolam clicked his heels together and returned to his seat. The coroner indicated that he had forwarded the bottle to the analytical expert; and then proceeded to recall Leake.

"Do you remember seeing this bottle on the wash-hand stand in the deceased's bedroom at any time before his death?"

The butler took up the bottle, examined it carefully for a few moments, and then shook his head:

"No, I can't say that I recall it particularly. But it might easily have escaped my notice. I had nothing to do with the deceased's bedroom, except that occasionally he asked me to valet him. I remember that he had a large number of bottles on his wash-hand stand—hair washes, mouth washes and things of that sort. He seemed to have a fad for things of that sort; and there were a good many bottles on the stand."

"Was there any other place where this bottle might have been kept usually?"

"The deceased had a medicine cupboard fitted up in the bathroom. He kept a good many drugs there. His digestion was very poor; and he was always tinkering with drugs."

"Did the deceased, to your knowledge, ever suffer from sleeplessness?"

"I could not say. He sat up late at times, but I could not take it upon myself to say that he was a victim to insomnia."

"Had you any reason to suppose that the deceased was a drug-taker—I mean a man addicted to the immoderate use of narcotics?"

"No, I have no knowledge on the point."

"That will do."

Leake retired to his seat. The coroner turned to Bolam.

"Call Eleanor Shore."

This was a new name to Colonel Sanderstead; and he turned with interest to see who the witness was. He recognized her, after a glance, as one of the Swaythling Court maids. The girl was obviously very nervous; and the coroner proceeded to help her in her evidence by putting questions.

"You were employed by the deceased for some time before his death?"

"I was."

"Part of your duties was to look after his bedroom?"

"Yes."

"When you set his wash-hand stand in order daily you must have handled the bottles which he seems to have kept standing on it?"

"Yes."

"Do you recognize this particular bottle?"

"It's just a bottle."

"Did you ever see it on the wash-hand stand?"

"I can't remember it. One bottle's very like another."

"Did you ever read the labels on the bottles?"

"No."

"You had no curiosity in the matter?"

"No."

"Then this bottle may have been there without your noticing it?"

"Yes."

"You know that the deceased had a medicine cabinet fitted up in the bath-room?"

"Yes."

"Did you ever see this bottle in that cabinet?"

"No, he always kept that cabinet locked."

"Then this bottle might have been there without your knowledge?"

"Yes."

"That will do."

Eleanor Shore escaped with evident relief.

"Call Henry Wood Bottesford."

This was another new name to the Colonel.

"My name is Henry Wood Bottesford. I am employed by the Syndicated Drug Shops, Ltd. This bottle bears the label of that firm, with the word 'Paraldehyde' also printed in addition to the firm's name."

"From your knowledge of that firm's methods, can you say if it would be possible to trace the purchaser of that bottle?"

"It would be quite impossible. Paraldehyde requires no prescription in order to get a supply. This bottle might have been sold over the counter of any of our branches."

"How many branches has your firm?"

"Sixty-seven, scattered up and down the country."

"And this might have been bought at any of them?"

"Yes.

"Have you the name of the deceased on the books of your firm in this connection?"

"No. But if this drug had been bought over the counter for cash there would be no entry in our books. It is not on the poison schedule which requires the customer's signature."

The coroner took up another line of inquiry. "Potassium cyanide is a scheduled poison?"

"Yes."

"'Have you any knowledge that the deceased purchased that substance?"

"Yes. His signature is written in this book. Here is the page."

"What book is that?"

"It comes from the Micheldean Abbas branch of my firm."

"That proves, then, that the deceased purchased a quantity of this poison last month?"

"Yes."

"Can you suggest why he required a fresh supply? He had been using the substance in killing-bottles before that."

"Potassium cyanide is gradually attacked by exposure to air, and loses its potency; so that sooner or later he would need to re-new his supply."

The coroner dismissed the witness and turned to address the jury:

"Gentlemen, I think that the fresh evidence which we have had before us to-day has cleared up the matter very considerably. It may, perhaps, be of some utility to you if I summarize the main points which have been brought out in the course of the examina-tion of these various witnesses.

"In the first place, the cause of death is now perfectly clear. You have heard the evidence of the analytical expert which estab-lishes beyond question that the body of the deceased contained a super-dose of one of the most formidable poisons known to sci-ence. No man could possibly have lived for even a short time with such a quantity of this poison in his system. The only other drug which has come under our notice is this narcotic, paraldehyde; and, as you have heard, it is not a compound which is legally restricted in its sale, since it is not dangerous in ordinary doses. You may leave it out of consideration, so far as its poisonous character is concerned in this case. As you heard, we are not able to determine whether or not the deceased was addicted to the use of this narcotic; but in any case, paraldehyde had nothing to do with the actual death of the deceased man.

"As to potassium cyanide, you have heard evidence which proves that quite recently the deceased purchased a quantity of this poison. He had it in his possession; and we know that some of this substance was found in a bottle on his desk beside his body.

"It is therefore established that the deceased had the poison and that, further, he had it beside him when he died. The question which you have to put to yourselves and to answer in your verdict is: 'Did he administer the poison to himself, or was it admin-istered to him by someone else?' And if you decide that it was administered by someone else, you must make up your mind whether that person is known to you or is some person unknown.

"In considering that question, you may have to take into consideration the fact that the deceased was threatened with exposure of his blackmailing practices. He knew that his criminal career was about to become public property; and that if he were convicted, he might have to undergo a long term of imprisonment. It is for you to consider whether that fact has any bearing on the manner of his death. You will weigh the possibility that these circumstances may indicate a motive for the taking of the poison, if it were self-administered—it may have been a last act of desperation on his part. That is a matter for you to settle according to your own satisfaction.

"You will not fail to bear in mind that the deceased, as a butterfly hunter, kept one or more of these so-called killing-bottles at hand. One of them was found beside the body. And you have heard the evidence of the chemical expert which goes to prove that the quantity of cyanide swallowed by the deceased is approximately the amount which is missing from this particular bottle, assuming it to have contained the amount of cyanide usually present in bottles of that sort.

"You must dismiss from your minds anything connected with the wound of which we heard so much on the previous day of this inquiry. That wound, you will remember, was shown to have been inflicted after death; and it therefore should play no part in your deliberations, which are to be devoted exclusively to the question of the manner of this death.

"As to your verdict, you should state in it what you find to be the cause of death and also, if necessary, add a clause stating whether the deceased voluntarily caused his own death. If there is any point upon which you desire information, this is the time to bring it forward."

Simon had sat silent during the whole of the proceedings up to this point; but he availed himself of the coroner's offer at once. Heaving himself ponderously out of his chair he put a question:

"There is one matter on which I think the jury are dissatisfied—at least, one member is. How does it come that although James

Leigh was one of the last people—if not actually the last person—to see the deceased alive, we have had no evidence from him at all? Why has he not been called before us like everybody else?"

The coroner, ignoring Simon pointedly, turned to the rest of the jury:

"Gentlemen, I should inform you that we had the intention of calling James Leigh as a witness in this inquiry. It was found, however, that he has left Fernhurst Parva; and on inquiry we learned that he furnished no address, nor did he give any indication by means of which he could be put in communication with us. We have done our best to secure his attendance here; but we have been unable to find him. The matter is of little real importance; for the evidence of the housekeeper at the Bungalow covers the period about which James Leigh could have testified. Should you desire a further adjournment of this inquiry until James Leigh can be found, I have no objection; but unless there is any real demand on the part of the jury for this course, I think that we have sufficient evidence before us to enable you to arrive at your verdict. The medical evidence, as you will remember, indicated midnight or thereabouts as the time of death. But long before midnight the deceased had left the Bungalow, had returned home to this house, and had rung up his clerk. I fail to see how James Leigh's evidence could throw any particular light on the stage of the affair—the crucial stage—which mainly concerns us here, since that stage was reached at least an hour after James Leigh saw the deceased for the last time."

At the suggestion of a further adjournment, most of the jury showed by their expressions that this was the last thing they desired. One or two of them even summoned up enough courage to murmur protests in undertones; and their glances in Simon's direction were anything but friendly. The coroner had no difficulty in interpreting the general feeling:

"Very good, gentlemen. I take it that you wish to consider your verdict now. If you will withdraw to another room and discuss the matter, we shall be ready for you on your return."

While the members of the jury were filing out of the room, Cyril. Norton came across to Colonel Sanderstead.

"Suppose we go out and smoke a cigarette while they're talking it over? Or several cigarettes—they may take a while to argue it out among them."

The Colonel agreed; and together they went out to the front of the house.

"Well, what do you make of it?" demanded Cyril, when they had passed out of earshot of the waiting chauffeurs.

Past experience had made the Colonel rather chary of taking his nephew into his confidence in the matter of his theories. Before answering, he flicked the ash from his cigarette with meticulous care, as though its removal were of the greatest importance. However, in the end he made up his mind that he could hardly fall into a trap on this occasion: and he put his views into words:

"Suicide, it seems to me. Your letter threatening him with exposure seems to have done the trick; and he lost his nerve. There was the cyanide, ready to his hand; and he hadn't enough grit to wait and take his gruel. But, even assuming that, there's one thing that puzzles me badly. What did he want with other stuff, that drug—what's its name, paraldehyde or something?"

Cyril Norton knitted his brows for a moment as if considering the point:

"The paraldehyde's a snag, sure enough, in a plain, straightforward suicide case. But was it a case like that? You seem to take it that he was never in doubt about his choice between the two alternatives: arrest or suicide. But suppose Hubbard was in two minds about the best course. One minute, say, he thinks suicide's the only way out; next minute be believes he sees a chance of brazening out the business and getting off scot-free—by putting on the screw harder than ever. He sits down at his typewriter and begins his last letter to Jimmy Leigh, in the hope that one final bluff will scare Jimmy stiff and pull the business out of the fire. Then, in the middle, he changes his mind; goes into the cold fit again; and sees suicide as the only way out. Suppose he gets hold of his killing-bottle, to be ready. Then suppose he thinks matters over again. Perhaps he changes his mind once more; decides he'll see the thing through and hope for an acquittal. But in that case, he'll need to be fresh in the morning: no good facing the final racket when he's jaded from lack of sleep. So off he goes to his bedroom, with his tumbler in his hand; gets the bottle of paraldehyde off his wash-hand stand; pours his last dose into his whisky and swallows it down. Then, before it has time to act—perhaps while he's muzzy with the stuff—he changes his mind for the last time; gets the wind up completely; and swallows the cyanide. It seems to me that that fits the whole case all right. You seem to think that suicide's a straightforward business; but I'll bet every prospective suicide wobbles a bit when he gets to the edge; and a good few of them draw back at the last moment."

The Colonel was forced to admit that Cyril's suggestion had a good deal in its favour. It fitted the unfinished letter on the typewriter neatly into the scheme of things; and it seemed to be based on a very reasonable reading of psychology.

"He must have been in a rather frantic condition at the tail-end of things, if your interpretation's correct," he commented. "But I suppose he was really in a pretty awkward fix either way. Gaol would be a change from Swaythling Court."

As they made their way into the entrance hall, Colonel Sanderstead noticed Bolam on guard at the door of the room into which the jury had retired. The constable's face betrayed a feeling of extreme annoyance.

"Well, Bolam," inquired the Colonel, "you seem to be worried over something? What is it, eh? Anything I can help to put right, by any chance?"

"Sir, I was fair taken aback by that woman's evidence."

"What woman?"

"The chambermaid, sir. I questioned her most carefully, sir, at the time I found the drug-bottle in his bedroom; and when I spoke to her about it, she gave me definitely to believe that the bottle was quite familiar to her. By her way of it, she'd seen it often. I reported that to the coroner, sir. And when he puts her on her oath, she goes right back on what she said to me. She swears she never saw the bottle before. I feel fair affronted, sir. Making me look a fool before the coroner."

"I shouldn't worry too much over it, Bolam," advised the Colonel, tolerantly. "I expect she was flurried, or something, when you showed her the bottle first of all, and just agreed with anything you suggested to her by your questions. Then when she was on oath, she'd had time to think over things; perhaps she thought over them so much that she got completely muddled up—one does confuse one's memory if one thinks too hard about a thing; and so quite probably she was honest enough both times. Anyway, it's no fault of yours. I'll mention it to the coroner, though, if you still feel sore about it."

Before Bolam could reply, the door opened and the jury began to file into the dining-room where the coroner was waiting. Cyril Norton and his uncle followed them in.

"Well, gentlemen, have you considered your verdict?"

Simon rose to his feet, inflated to an even greater bulk than usual by the dignity of his position:

"We find that William Blayre Hubbard died from the effects of cyanide poisoning; and that the poison was self-administered."

"You have nothing to add to that verdict? Nothing to suggest as to his state of mind at the time he took his life?"

Simon looked puzzled. The coroner thought it well to explain:

"The verdict you have brought in amounts to *felo-de-se*. If that verdict is given, the body of the deceased can be buried in a churchyard, but not in consecrated ground; and the question of holding a religious service at the interment is left to the clergyman responsible for that burial-ground. He may object, if he chooses, to take part in a religious service over the corpse of a suicide. If you add a rider to the effect that the deceased was of unsound mind at the time when he took his life, then the body can be buried in consecrated ground. But unless you are quite satisfied as to the state of mind of the deceased at the time when he took his life, you should not offer an opinion on the point."

The jury hastily consulted among themselves in whispers for a few moments; and finally Simon intimated that they had nothing to add to their verdict.

"Then these proceedings are now closed, gentlemen."

9
THE THEORY OF THE NOVELIST

DURING DINNER, Colonel Sanderstead avoided the subject of the inquest; but when he and Angermere settled down in the study after their coffee, Hubbard's death crept into the conversation almost immediately. Angermere was free from all prepossessions in the matter; he was a casual visitor who had chanced to be on the spot in time to see the unfolding of the Hubbard affair: and the Colonel felt a keen curiosity to know how the problem presented itself to a detached observer. Nor was he without hope that Angermere, with his long practice in mystery-concocting, might throw fresh light on the problem.

"It's a pretty puzzle," Angermere admitted, "a very pretty puzzle. I've been turning it over in my mind since I heard the evidence; and I think that from my point of view at least it has the makings of something."

The Colonel made no attempt to conceal his interest:

"And you've hit on the solution, perhaps?"

Angermere's faint gesture deprecated anything so definite.

"No, I'd hardly like to go so far as that, hardly so far as that. You see, Colonel, I approach this affair from a very definite direction. I'm professionally interested in it, if I may put it so. What I want to get out of it, if possible, is simply the germ of a yarn, nothing more. I'm not really interested in getting at the true solution; all I need for my-purpose is a solution which can be used as the basis of a 'shocker.' I'm a seeker after sensation, you know, and not necessarily an inquirer into truth."

The Colonel nodded, though he felt a certain disappointment with Angermere's outlook.

"I expect that we part company at the very start," the novelist continued. "For instance, are you yourself satisfied with the suicide hypothesis? Do you think the jury hit the nail on the head when they brought in that verdict?"

Colonel Sanderstead shifted uneasily in his chair. He had meant to question, not to be interrogated:

"Well, frankly, I don't see what other verdict they could have brought in. Of course, it doesn't clear up the case; it leaves the whole affair very much of a puzzle: but so far as it goes, it seems to me a very satisfactory verdict."

Angermere smiled faintly at this reply, but the Colonel could see that there was no disagreeable superiority in the expression. The novelist was merely pleased to find that his opinion was verified.

"That just illustrates what I said. You're quite satisfied with the verdict; and from your own point of view I think you're perfectly right. It's a mysterious affair in many ways; but all the evidence points towards that verdict. For my particular purpose, however, that verdict would be totally useless. It makes things too simple. What I want to get out of the thing, you understand, is a good tale, a downright mystery-tangle that will keep the reader wondering about the real story which underlies the surface-presentation, if you see what I mean.

"Now from that standpoint, there's nix in a suicide case. There's no conflict, so to speak. To make the thing readable, somebody's got to be suspected of something; he's got to be cleared or convicted in the end. That's how it presented itself to me as I sat there at the inquest; and naturally, from that standpoint, the verdict was the least interesting part of the affair—rather an anti-climax, in fact. Or even worse than that, for it left no loop-hole for a possible criminal."

"Then you don't think it was suicide after all?" demanded the Colonel, rather perturbed to find that Angermere's line of thought was approaching so closely to his own.

"For my particular purpose, suicide would be no good at all. And, remember, I'm not trying to get at the truth of the thing. All I care about is to rearrange the affair so that I can make a murder yarn out of it. The facts are all right, except that there are too many of them. I shall probably have to drop out a few of them—a good many, in fact—before I can get the thing to fit together and make anything out of it."

The Colonel's good manners saved him from showing that this view of the case was a disappointment. He had hoped to get a clear analysis of the situation as it appeared to an unbiased mind; and now it seemed that the most he could hope for was a 'rearrangement' of the facts, with most of the puzzle omitted during the re-distribution process. However, he fought down his feelings and decided to let Angermere have his say without interruption:

"Would you mind giving me some idea of how you go to work in a case of this kind? It's all fresh ground to me, you know, and I've often wondered how that kind of thing is done."

Angermere had apparently failed to notice the Colonel's slight discomfiture. He bent forward in his chair and began to study the pictures in the fire.

"Well, of course, with my pre-conceived object, I went to that inquest in search of what we may call the First Murderer. It was of no importance whether there ever was a murder or not; all I needed was a suggestion. I wanted to look over the witnesses and find somebody I could cast for the part. By the way, you'll remember that this was a mere academic exercise, I hope, and you won't be offended if I give you the thing just as it happened?"

"Of course not," the Colonel hastened to reassure him, "I quite see your point. You can suspect me, if you like."

Angermere laughed softly.

"Well, it's not quite so bad as that. I began by ruling out the obviously impossibles from the fiction point of view; and of course you were the first to go. Your part in the yarn is evidently the part which you actually played in the real affair: the discoverer of the crime."

"And who else did you rule out?"

"The constable, for one; he wouldn't fill the bill as a murderer at all—at least not that kind of murderer. From what I saw of him, he has no great imagination; and this murder is stamped with imagination from start to finish. Perhaps I ought to say 'theoretical murder'; but I take it that you'll read the adjective in without my repeating it."

"And your next suspect, who was he?"

"Let's eliminate the witnesses in order. I think one can throw out the housekeeper at the Bungalow. She could hardly be dragged in on any reasonable grounds. Nor do I see any way in which Mickleby could be connected with the affair. He's only a temporary inhabitant, a *locum*; and the chances of making him a probable criminal seemed to me slight. That leaves young Leigh, your nephew, Hilton, and the servants on the list of possibles, doesn't it?"

"That's so," Colonel Sanderstead agreed, cautiously. He was beginning to feel uncomfortable. Angermere's analysis was narrowing the circle; but three of the remaining suspects were connected, more or less closely, with the dominant caste in Fernhurst Parva.

"I forgot one other possible," Angermere went on, "that mysterious woman who appeared for a moment in the village and disappeared by the first train on the morning you discovered the body. Her meteoric visit seems to have stirred up Fernhurst Parva considerably, to judge by the amount of gossip I've heard about her. I noticed that she didn't appear in the evidence, though."

"No, there was nothing to connect her definitely with the case," the Colonel commented, wondering how much Angermere knew about the matter.

"Village gossip is pretty unreliable," Angermere went on, "but down in Fernhurst Parva they seem to have connected her with one of the local magnates. From all I gathered, she was rather a flamboyant person, not exactly the type that one finds in the family circle. However, we may neglect her, I think, so far as the actual murder goes; there isn't a scrap of evidence to connect her directly with it, though she may have played a subsidiary part somewhere.

"Now let's continue the elimination process; and again, remember, I'm trying to make a yarn out of it and not retrace the real story. You mustn't imagine that I'm throwing out real suspicions, you know.

"First, there's Mr. Cyril Norton. I must confess he played a peculiar part in the business. He struck me—you won't mind my saying so—as a particularly tenacious person: the last sort of man that one would care to have as an enemy. But then, that very tenacity and blunt down-rightness of his happen to be the characteristics that were needed for the part he played in the affair. He was just the sort of man to whom people would go for help if they got into deep water. He knew a good deal about the inside of the case; but nobody got much change out of him in his evidence. In fact, going back to the real case and not the sham one that I'm putting up, it struck me that quite probably Hubbard must have felt that he had come up against it once for all when his affairs passed into Norton's hands. I know that if I'd been in Hubbard's shoes and Norton had threatened to expose me, I'd have skipped on the spot; for I'd have felt sure he'd carry out his threat without the faintest hesitation.

"I don't mind saying that on the face of it Cyril Norton would have made a good First Murderer in some respects. But when I tried to fit the thing together on that basis it obviously fell to the ground at once. Norton had his grip on Hubbard and he had no need to go any farther. He had got him into such a corner that either flight or suicide was the only chance of escape. In that state of affairs, there was nothing to gain by murdering the creature. So I think we can drop your nephew out of consideration. Besides, his part in the drama is quite well defined—like your own and the constable's: he pulled the trigger that set the machine in motion."

Angermere threw the stub of his cigarette into the fire; and the Colonel passed him the box to take another. After he had lit it, Angermere continued.

"Hilton was the next person I looked at. He played rather a mysterious part in the business. You know the usual detective yarn—some character makes episodic appearances from start to finish and the reader's attention is carefully diverted from him until at the last moment he turns out to be the master-crook or murderer or whatever it is. Now Hilton might quite well have filled that bill for me. Suppose that he were the mysterious person whom Hubbard was blackmailing—the man that your nephew was trying to shield. Hilton, so far as my judgment of physiognomy goes, is a person with a certain violence of temper mixed with a considerable amount of—shall we say—craft, or subtlety. He's just the kind of man who might get into difficulties and use either violence or manoeuvre to get himself out of the scrape. I must confess that he tempted me—speaking purely professionally, of course. He would have made an excellent character, with a little rearrangement. One could imagine him putting his affairs into the hands of your nephew and then, at the last moment, in a fit of temper, taking the control of the business back into his own hands with fatal results. But that won't fit in with the rest of the facts. A violent man doesn't use poison as a weapon. He might have stabbed Hubbard; but I doubt if he'd have turned to the cyanide. Certainly if he changed his mind at the last moment, I don't think he'd have done the thing that way. No, whatever part he played in the business, it wasn't that of a poisoner."

The Colonel was now on tenterhooks. Jimmy Leigh's name was the next for treatment; and he wondered what Angermere had made of him. But much to his relief, the novelist did not linger over that character in the drama.

"As to young Leigh of the Bungalow, I left him out of the rearrangement almost at once. In the first place, there was nothing whatever to connect him with Hubbard, beyond a casual acquaintanceship. Then, I hadn't seen young Leigh in the flesh, but I gather that he doesn't look anything like a criminal but quite the reverse, rather a harum-scarum personality apart from his scientific work. And to my mind, he had a perfect alibi even if one did go the length of suspecting him."

The Colonel interrupted for a moment to confirm this:

"He dined with me here that night and went straight off to the Bungalow. Hubbard was there till nearly eleven; and the housekeeper heard the two of them talking most of the time. She heard

Hubbard go out; and after that Jimmy Leigh kept her awake for a long time. Hubbard died about midnight, when Jimmy Leigh was still fumbling about in his workshop."

Angermere sat up suddenly.

"Just wait a moment! Suppose that it wasn't young Leigh in the workshop at all. Suppose someone else came in and took his place! One man's fumbling about makes the same noise as another man's; and all that's in the evidence is this racket. I must make a note of that idea; one could use it in another yarn."

He pulled out a notebook and made a jotting.

"And so, you see," he continued, putting his book back into his pocket, "we've eliminated everyone except the servants. But before I got that length, I had paid some attention to the late Hubbard himself.

"I've studied the case of the blackmailer pretty thoroughly—merely theoretically, of course, for literary purposes; and the more I think over it, the more precarious a trade it seems. You see, Colonel, if a blackmailer makes a single mistake, he's got to pay for it, and steeply, too. If he misgauges the character of a single victim, he may find himself in Queer Street before he knows where he is. It isn't merely at the start of any particular episode, either. He may have been blackmailing a man for years and getting paid his hush-money regularly; and then, suddenly, the man may find his resources overtaxed and may take the short way out, even at the cost of a scandal. Of course, that's bound to be a pretty rare affair; once you start paying blackmail, you generally go on. But still, there's always the off-chance that a victim may cut up rough.

"And it isn't a certainty that the police are the worst that a blackmailer has to fear. A victim may get crazed and decide on more direct methods of righting his wrongs—take the law into his own hands and save scandal in that way. It certainly looks to me a very risky business. I've often wondered if some of these apparently aimless murders cases where there seemed to be no traceable motive—hadn't that at the back of them if the truth were only known."

Colonel Sanderstead had no need to feign interest at this point. Angermere, whether intentionally or not, was coming very near to the possible inner history of the Hubbard case; and the Colonel was on tenterhooks to see what turn would come next in the exposition. Here, in spite of all the talk about 'theoretical' and 'professional rearrangements,' was a detached observer approaching the case with an unbiased mind; and his host was disturbed to find how close he seemed to be getting to the solution of the mystery.

"The only one of the male servants whom I saw," continued the novelist, "was the butler, Leake. How did he strike you?"

"Hang-dog fellow," blurted out the Colonel, voicing his original impression of the man.

"Quite so; that's how he appeared to me. I had the feeling that all his frankness wasn't quite the right stuff, somehow. As soon as I set eyes on him while he was giving his evidence, I made up my mind that he was the sort of person one might cast for the villain of the piece. He was so infernally suave, you know; and yet somehow one got the impression that he wasn't naturally a suave person at all. He'd put on a kind of mask; but underneath that there was a pretty tough character."

"I agree with you there," the Colonel concurred. "When he turned up at the Court that morning he showed a good deal less surprise than one might have expected under the circumstances."

"Ah," the novelist commented. "That's a useful point if I ever use this affair in print. I like to have things right, even in a shocker."

He jotted something down in his ever-ready notebook.

"Now we've been a long time getting down to dots," he continued, replacing the book in his pocket, "but you asked me to explain how I went about things; and I've taken you at your word. I think we can go straight ahead after this.

"Suppose that our hang-dog butler has gone astray from the path of rectitude at some earlier period. From the look of the man, I'd say it was a highly probable assumption. And suppose, further, that he fell into the grip of the late Hubbard as a consequence. Quite obviously Hubbard would not be able to make much out of him pecuniarily; butlers aren't big game financially. But one may have other uses for a man beyond merely bleeding him white. A blackmailer might quite well require help in one form or other:

say a cat's-paw to do the preliminary go-between work in a ticklish case, or a spy who could do some of his dirty business for him in
certain eventualities. I can quite see the possibility that Leake may
have been a blackmailer's tool. He doesn't strike me as a man who
would revolt against that sort of thing merely for moral reasons."

"That's a pretty sound suggestion," the Colonel put in. "Now
that you've stated it, I wonder I didn't see the possibility myself.
But I certainly didn't."

"Well, suppose we assume that as a starting-point. If you think
over it for a moment you may see more light still. As I told you,
blackmailers are in a ticklish position if their victims cut up rough.
But suppose that the victim who cuts up rough chances to be every
bit as big a scoundrel as his persecutor, what then? Assume that
he rids himself of his tyrant once for all, what about the tyrant's
assets? Hasn't every blackmailer a mass of compromising documents in his safe? Certainly, if he's a big man in his line, papers
are the thing he must have gone after—compromising letters, and
so forth. Wouldn't that be the very swag to attract his late victim?
Wouldn't it be a fine double stroke of business to rid yourself of a
blackmailer and then set up in his place with his documents and
carry on where he left off? I should think it would."

Angermere paused for a moment or two, as if to let the Colonel
assimilate this fresh idea; then he continued:

"That was how I looked on the case after I had seen all the witnesses. And that's why I paid very little attention to the verdict. I
can't quite see a blackmailer suiciding until he's absolutely in the
grip of the police. Why should he, since he has always the chance
of escape? And any man with the cunning to carry on the blackmail business is sure to have enough liquid assets stored away
somewhere, a nice nest-egg which he can get at on short notice if
he has to make a bolt for it."

The novelist seemed to have dropped the pretence that he was
merely 'rearranging' the case for literary purposes. From the tone
of his voice, Colonel Sanderstead got the impression that this was
Angermere's real opinion on the business; and it came as a considerable relief. Besides, Angermere's theory had a good deal to

recommend it. It fitted the 'hang-dogness' of the butler into the sequence of events; and in so doing, it chimed in with the Colonel's own prepossessions with regard to Leake. He had always had an uncomfortable feeling about the fellow, although he could not assign any specific reason for his dislike.

"Now suppose we look over the evidence from this new point of view," Angermere continued. Let's assume that it really was a case of murder and not of simple suicide. The man was undoubtedly poisoned. Who could have done it? Obviously someone in the house. I think one may take that for granted as a start."

The Colonel fastened on this point. He felt a certain desire to show Angermere that he was not the sort of person who would accept the easiest solution simply because it was easy.

"But Hubbard died about midnight, according to the medical evidence; and at that time he was alone in the house. How are you going to get round that? Cyanide kills almost instantaneously."

Angermere evidently had his reply ready.

"You've raised two points there, two points of very different bearing. Let's take 'em seriatim, if you don't mind. You say he was alone in the house at midnight; but how do you know that? What you really know is that nobody came forward to testify that they were there then; but you don't expect the murderer to put that into his evidence, do you? If the murderer were on the premises during the night, it's the last thing he'd want to advertise in the newspapers or anywhere else. Therefore, there's no evidence that Hubbard was alone."

The Colonel acquiesced, though with certain mental reservations on the validity of Angermere's assumption.

"Then your second point," continued the novelist. "It was that cyanide killed instantaneously; and therefore, since by your way of it, Hubbard was alone at midnight, no one could have administered the poison to him. But . . . I think I'd better give you my reconstruction of the business. You'll see an easy way round these difficulties."

Angermere took a fresh cigarette, lit it, and leaned back in his chair.

"Here's my idea of the train of events that night. We can begin at the point when the chauffeur and the maids went off to the dance. The butler serves dinner, as per evidence. Hubbard goes into his study, ditto. Then Leake goes to his pantry, and *he doctors the decanter of whisky with cyanide before bringing it in.* He takes it and the soda in on his tray and leaves it on Hubbard's desk, ready to his hand. Then Leake goes off to the dance on his motor-cycle. The next stage of the evening passes as per evidence: Hubbard doesn't touch the whisky; he goes out to call on young Leigh; he returns and rings up his clerk. Now comes the critical point. He pours out some whisky and squirts in his soda. Then he feels wakeful; and he thinks of a dose of a sleeping-draught—that paraldehyde which he kept in his bedroom, as per evidence, though the evidence was more than foggy on the point. He has filled his tumbler on the tray, so he goes off and digs out a second tumbler in Leake's pantry on the way upstairs. He pours out his dose, leaves the bottle up there, and comes down with the tumbler in his hand. When he gets to the study again, he puts a dash of whisky into the paraldehyde to disguise the taste, which is a chronic one, I can tell you. He swallows down the dose; and then he sees his whisky and soda on the table, so he gulps that off—including the cyanide. Result, almost instantaneous death."

"But there was only a single tumbler on the tray when we found him; and this theory of yours needs two glasses," objected Colonel Sanderstead.

Angermere's gesture restrained him from further comment.

"We've now come to midnight or thereby. But what happened at midnight? That Cinderella dance broke up. And so Leake passed out of ordinary observation. He went straight to bed at the inn, by his way of it. But I've been over to the 'Cat and Fiddle' in Micheldean Abbas; and I've made a few cautious inquiries—very cautious inquiries—on my own hook. And the result was that I found Mr. Leake's bedroom on the ground floor of the place, a little room away from the main run of traffic in the hotel. And after midnight, there's not much traffic at the best in a tiny pub of that sort."

"You mean he might have got out of the window in the night?"

"Exactly. And he had his motor-cycle with him. Ten minutes would bring him back here; and there's no one on the roads at that hour to identify him."

"I can tell you one thing, though," Colonel Sanderstead interjected, "he didn't come up the avenue on his motor-cycle, for I went over all his tracks and there wasn't the extra pair needed by your theory."

"Of course not," the novelist countered, "he'd never bring his machine inside the lodge-gate. The noise of the motor might have wakened the lodge-keeper. My notion is, for what it's worth, that he left his motor-cycle parked in a field beside the road and then cut across country straight to the Court, so as to leave no tracks whatever on the avenue.

"Then came the problem of getting into the house itself. If he's as smart a man as I take him to be, he wouldn't go to the front door, although he had a key of it. He might have left tracks there on the soft ground of the approach. No, he cut along by the paved path that runs under his own pantry window; and he got into the house by that window, which he'd left open."

"Why assume he left it open when the glass was smashed to smithereens?" demanded the Colonel.

"Let's take things as they come," returned Angermere. "I'm giving you a chronological yarn; and I don't think the window was broken at that stage of the proceedings. Now let's see what Leake came back to the house for. The only thing that connected him with the murder was that doctored decanter of whisky. Even that wasn't a fatal bit of evidence, for he could always have argued that Hubbard—with cyanide in his killing-bottle—had shoved the stuff into the decanter himself when he intended to commit suicide. Leake's procedure was based on making it look like suicide. So he had to wash out that poison and refill the decanter with plain whisky.

"But when he crawled through the window, I suspect that he saw something that set him thinking on a new line. The constable told me about the upset tray and the dog you found outside. Leake probably saw the dog—it would be all over him as soon as he appeared—but the tray was the thing that gave him his sudden idea. Why not make it appear that the house had been burgled and Hubbard murdered? He himself had his alibi all right already; he was supposed to be snoring at the 'Cat and Fiddle,' you know.

"These last moment improvements are the death of most murderers; but Leake seems to have pulled it off, more by luck than anything. He'd have been far safer to leave the business in its initial simplicity. However, in he crawls, gets a candle and drips a liberal trail of grease through the house to the study. That represents the arrival of the murderer. In the study he finds, as he expected, the body of Hubbard. He sticks his candle down on the desk—a good bit of evidence for investigators and with the merit, also, of leaving no finger-marks on the wax, which is bound to melt away altogether as the candle burns out. Then he picks up the paper-knife and sticks it into Hubbard's back. The finger-mark question presents itself again, so he draws it out and pitches it into the fire. Being steel, it will be there all right in the morning—he can find it himself if no one else spots it—and his finger-marks won't survive the flames.

"Then he sets about his main business. Much to his astonishment, no doubt, he finds a couple of tumblers there instead of the single one he left. Both contain whisky; but one smells of something else—paraldehyde, of course. He doesn't quite know what to make of it, so decides to leave it alone. One never can tell what may turn up, you know. He washes out the decanter and replaces it, refilled to the same level, on the tray; and he cleans up the poison-tumbler and puts it back in the pantry. That clears him, personally, of any future trouble.

"Next he begins to make hay while the sun shines—or at least by starlight. He gets the keys of the safe out of Hubbard's pocket— I expect he wore gloves while he was in the house; and he collars all the blackmailing material in the safe. To account for it, I dare say he shoved a lot of old unimportant letters into the fire, so as to make enough ash for investigators."

The Colonel winced slightly at this description; but Angermere failed to notice it.

"Finally, the job's done. But here again he falls into the usual murderer's error of trying to make things too complete. He wanted to make it absolutely certain that people would look elsewhere for the criminal. So he smashes the butterfly case and takes out the star-piece of the collection—shoves it into the fire, I've no doubt. Then he remembers he has a small automatic in his possession. He gets it from his room, say, and cleans off all finger-marks on it—I suspect he was obsessed with the finger-mark notion. Then he drops it on the mat. That was taking a risk; for it might have been traced back to him; but I suspect he got it in some under-hand way and was pretty sure it couldn't be identified as his."

"It certainly had no finger-marks on it," the Colonel confirmed. "It was pretty carefully examined; and the last person who handled it had gloves on."

"So I heard from the constable," Angermere went on. "Now we come to a pretty point. You must remember that Leake came into the house with all his plans cut and dried to make the thing look like suicide; and he must have been repeating to himself the directions he had laid down to carry out that idea. Just before he left, I suspect that he went over these directions in his head; and the principal one must have been: 'Leave the lights burning.' Nobody would turn out lights before committing suicide, you know. So at the last moment he forgets about the candle left burning on the table; and he switches on (or leaves switched on, rather) the study lights and the hall lights.

"Then he goes into the pantry to get away. And when he is getting up to the window, it occurs to him that a final stroke would be to underline things a bit—smash the window in such a way that no one could help seeing the damage, and so call attention to the supposed burglarious entry. So once he's outside, he picks up a stone and does the job thoroughly, as you found next morning. Then he cuts across to his bike and gets over to the 'Cat and Fiddle' without attracting any notice. And I think that covers everything."

"Everything except one thing," admitted the Colonel aloud. "Everything but two things," he would have said, if he had uttered his full thought.

"And that is?" inquired the novelist.

"Hubbard's latchkey. I found it on the doorstep in the morning. How did it happen to come there?"

"Oh, that!" Angermere airily waved the difficulty aside. "One has to admit ordinary possibilities, you know, even in a murder case. I've often left a latchkey in a lock myself out of absent-mindedness. I expect Hubbard did the same when he came back from the Bungalow; and if he slammed the front door when he came in, the key would drop out on the doorstep all right."

"Yes," conceded the Colonel, half-heartedly, "I suppose one has to allow for a thing like that. And apart from it, you seem to have fitted things together very neatly indeed. Your assumption about the post-mortem stabbing clears the business up. Without the medical evidence, I'd never have looked beyond the stab for a cause of the death; and I expect Leake took it for granted that nobody would go any further either. The P.M. evidence must have been a staggerer for him when it came out. But, by the way, you've left out one point. If he didn't burn the papers, what did he do with them?"

Angermere dismissed that question with a wave of his hand.

"Obviously the man is no fool; so he wouldn't conceal them in the house. I expect he had a biscuit-tin ready for them and buried them somewhere on his way back to his motor-bike. He could dig them up again safely when the hue and cry was over."

"Well," the Colonel summed up, "it's been most instructive to an old fogy like myself. You've thrown quite a fresh light on the business, for me; and I'll look forward to seeing the book you make out of it. I can't tell you how much you've interested me."

But later in the evening, after Angermere had gone, Colonel Sanderstead poked up the fire with an expression on his face that might almost have been a sardonic smile.

"A clever devil, that man. That's the first connected yarn I've heard that might fit the affair. He's smarter than the rest of us. But there's just one thing that he didn't account for; because he didn't know about it. I wonder if he could have fitted in the man who drove the motor up to the Court that night. Whoever that was,

I'm dead certain he must have played some part in the business; and Angermere's story is complete without him. That makes rather an inky blot on the Angermere theory, I think.

"And yet, perhaps Angermere's stuff is right in the main outlines. It hinges together so very neatly. Possibly the man with the motor was only a super in the play. Possibly he came up to the door, rang, got no answer, and went off again without being inside the house at all. But in that case, why didn't he come forward to give evidence?"

He put down the poker and sat down in his easy-chair. The case still puzzled him; and the Colonel hated to be puzzled.

"I still believe that motor had something to do with the business. But a motor may have come from anywhere within a radius of a hundred miles; the chance of it turning up again is pretty small. Still, I'd like to know who the fellow was. I'm not going out of my way to find out; but if by any chance I come across the track of that non-skid tyre, I'll go quietly into the affair on my own. Vulgar curiosity, I suppose, or morbid curiosity; but I can't get rid of it."

He would not admit even to himself that his real motive was to clear up the part which Jimmy Leigh had played in the affair. In spite of all Angermere's lucid reasoning, the Colonel had uneasy feelings on that point.

10
THE INVISIBLE MAN

CURIOUSLY ENOUGH, the effect of Angermere's conversation upon the Colonel was stimulative rather than sedative; far from allaying his uneasiness over the Hubbard case, it increased his discomfort. Some imp of contradiction insisted on gaining a hearing in his mind and prevented him from accepting the novelist's hypothesis, as he would gladly have done if he could.

Angermere's reconstruction had been eminently satisfactory from the Colonel's stand-point, for it excluded from the drama all the members of the ruling caste in Fernhurst Parva; and this was precisely what the Colonel, in his heart, desired to see. Not only so, but the novelist's view accounted for practically everything— except the mysterious individual in the motor-car. But that piece of evidence, having been acquired by himself, had assumed great importance in the Colonel's mind; and with the best will in the world, he felt himself unable to accept any theory, no matter how complete, which left no gap into which that character could be fitted.

Smoking his pipe on the terrace after breakfast, he found that he could not shake himself free from the affair. Some subconscious influence kept insisting that he should go forward and satisfy himself about the business.

"At any rate," he concluded, "we'll have no washing of dirty linen in public, whatever's at the bottom of it. I'm uneasy; but that's my own private affair. The police have had the thing in hand; and it's not for an amateur like me to set them right if they've made a slip."

Though he would hardly admit it, even to himself, the thing that lay behind his troubles was simple enough. He remembered Jimmy Leigh's statement that every animal killed by the Lethal Ray had cyanide in its stomach after death. For some reason, this information insisted on emerging from the Colonel's memory, in spite of all his efforts to shelve it. For now it was linked with two other points of crucial importance: the cyanide found in Hubbard's body; and the fact that Jimmy Leigh had left the Lethal Ray generator aimed at Swaythling Court. Try as he might, Colonel Sanderstead could not dissociate these three facts from each other; and when they were allowed to associate, they pointed straight in one direction—to the guilt of Jimmy Leigh.

That was why Angermere's reconstruction had failed to convince the Colonel, though he was only too eager to accept any explanation which would clear Jimmy Leigh. And there was the further fact that the novelist's theory left the motorist out of account. But then, as the Colonel reflected, the motor-car was equally out of joint with the view that Jimmy Leigh had murdered Hubbard by means of the Ray. Whichever way one turned, that unidentified nocturnal visitor blocked the road. He, if anyone, ought to be able to fit the keystone into the mystery. He must have been on the premises just about the time when Hubbard returned from the Bungalow; possibly he met the blackmailer in the avenue or at the door of the Court.

"If one could only run across the track of that tyre somehow," he said to himself. "But I'm afraid it's only a chance in a million."

Putting his hand in his pocket, he found he was running short of tobacco; and he decided to walk down to the village and get some more. The Fernhurst Parva tobacconist kept a stock of his brand, for the Colonel encouraged local trade.

"Anyway," he reflected as he moved away from the house, "if I run across that car, I'll have it out with the owner. I promise myself that."

At the foot of the avenue, just as he turned into the main road, the Colonel was overtaken by Constable Bolam.

"Good morning, Bolam. Fine day."

"Very fine, sir."

The constable pondered for a moment or two, as though doubtful if he should broach a fresh subject. At last he made up his mind.

"Sir, after the verdict of the coroner's jury, I suppose there will be no further investigations of the Hubbard case?"

"I should imagine not, Bolam. Has anyone given you instructions on the point?"

"No, sir."

"The county authorities are quite satisfied, then?"

"It would seem so, sir. I've heard nothing from them on the matter."

"What's going to happen to Swaythling Court, now? Do you know?"

"Sir, Hubbard's lawyer was over here this morning—or so I heard—and it seems they're going to sell the Court as soon as they can get things fixed up. The lawyer said—so I heard—that Hubbard's clerk, the man who gave evidence, is coming here soon to go through Hubbard's papers."

"I thought most of his papers were burned, that night."

"It seems not, sir. A number of documents referring to his perfume business were stored elsewhere in the house. The lawyer found them; and the clerk is to go over them."

The Colonel was relieved to learn the nature of the surviving papers; for the first mention of them had suggested the possible existence of another store of blackmailing material.

"Who inherits all this stuff, Bolam? Have you heard?"

"Sir, it seems to be a second-cousin or somebody like that. Hubbard had no near relations. At least, so it was reported to me."

"Well, it's satisfactory that we'll have no more of that breed at the Court."

"Very satisfactory, sir."

For a few moments Bolam relapsed into silence; but it was evident to the Colonel that the constable had something more on his mind.

"Out with it, Bolam, whatever it is that's troubling you," he said, at last, to encourage Bolam to begin.

The constable seemed to hesitate; but finally he screwed himself up to the pitch of speaking.

"Sir, there's been a good deal of talk in the village about Swaffham's shop; and I'd like you to know the rights of it, so that you won't think I've had anything to do with it."

The Colonel became suddenly alert. Anything that touched Fernhurst Parva was of importance to him.

"What's wrong with Swaffham?" he demanded. "Who's been complaining about him? He's a thoroughly honest man."

"Sir, it isn't that kind of talk. You've taken me up wrong. Nobody's got a word to say against Swaffham. It's something quite different. I hardly like to repeat it, sir, seeing it's so silly; but it's bound to come round to you sooner or later; and seeing I was mixed up in it, I don't want you to be getting the idea that I was in any way responsible for putting about such nonsense."

"Well, what is it?"

"Sir, the talk in the village is that Swaffham's shop's haunted."

"Rubbish!" interjected the Colonel, rather nettled by the suggestion.

"That's what I say, sir. But I'd better tell you how all the talk arose."

"Go on," said the Colonel encouragingly. A haunted shop in his village! Absurd! Who ever heard of such a thing? The sooner this silly idea could be scotched, the better.

Bolam put on his best orderly-room manner.

"Sir, on the night of the affair at the Court, I was in the street at 11 p.m. The church clock had just struck when I met Ellen Farrar, the maid at the Vicarage, sir. I stopped to pass the time of day with her; and, seeing it was so late, I walked along with her towards the Vicarage. She told me she had been to see her mother over at St. Nicolas village; and she'd stayed later than she intended, owing to her watch having stopped. When we came to Swaffham's shop, it was shut up and dark; no one lives on the premises, as you know, sir. Just as we were passing the front door, we heard the telephone bell ring inside the shop. I stopped, and we looked into the shop. There was no one there. I inspected the fastenings; and they were all secure. In about a minute, while I was still examining the windows, I heard the telephone bell ring again."

Bolam suddenly dropped his orderly-room manner and became an ordinary man under irritation:

"And then, sir, if you'll believe me, that girl had a fit of hysterics! Indeed, sir, she had. And there was I, at that time of night in the main street, with a young female on my hands, crying and laughing fit to split—excuse me, sir. As it so happened, no one came by; and after a time I got her quietened down, sir."

"A most unpleasant situation for you, Bolam," commented the Colonel, sympathetically. Inwardly he was considerably amused by the picture which Bolam had drawn.

"Very unpleasant indeed, sir, I can assure you." With an effort, Bolam recovered his orderly-room manner:

"I asked her what had excited her, sir; and she replied that she believed the shop was haunted and that a ghost was ringing up on the phone. I told her not to be a little fool; and I saw her to the Vicarage gate."

"An imaginative girl, evidently," the Colonel commented.

"A proper young ijjit!" said Bolam, wrathfully. "And by the next morning, she'd spread it all over the village that the shop was haunted. And, to tell you the truth, sir, the story's grown and grown since then, until I hardly recognize it myself. Everybody seems to add a bit to it every time it's repeated. The last I heard was that the Green Devil had come back again; and had rung up Hubbard on the phone; and that was what made him suicide!"

Bolam's expression betrayed a mixture of injury and contempt.

"Sir, I knew you were bound to hear about it; and I didn't want you to think that I had anything to do with spreading such a nonsensical tale. I'm fair exasperated with the whole thing; for they're all saying: 'And Constable Bolam saw it himself.' As if I would ever dream of seeing such a thing! And half the children in the place after me, trying to get me to make their flesh creep for them. I've made some of their ears ring, anyhow."

Colonel Sanderstead fastened upon the important point.

"Have you any idea why the telephone rang at all, Bolam?"

"No, sir."

"A ring means an inward call, of course. Now who would think of ringing up a shop that was bound to be empty at that hour? Everybody who deals with Swaffham knows that he doesn't live in the shop, so he couldn't hear the bell. It seems a pointless affair."

"Yes, sir."

"No explanation forthcoming yet?"

"None, sir."

"It's strange. Why should anyone ring up a number which couldn't answer? But perhaps it was a mistake—crossed wires, or a wrong number, or something like that. Probably that would account for it."

"Very probably, sir."

"Well, Bolam, don't worry over the matter. No one who knows you would ever accuse you of putting a ghost-story abroad—especially a story like that."

The constable seemed satisfied with this and parted from the Colonel with a punctilious salute, acknowledged with equal punctiliousness by the Colonel.

Moved by a faint curiosity of which he was rather ashamed, Colonel Sanderstead turned into the St. Nicolas road in order to look at Swaffham's shop as he passed. A small child was standing on the pavement near the shop, examining with awe the telephone wire over which "the ghost" had spoken; and the Colonel's eye turned in the same direction. Swaffham's telephone was the only one in the village itself; so if the mysterious ringing had been due to accidental contact, it must have originated farther out. Colonel Sanderstead moved on a little until the line of posts carrying the wire came into view; and he followed that with his eye across the fields. So far as he could see, Swaffham's cable had supports to itself until it ran across the Bungalow garden; but at that point it was joined to two other wires: one coming from the Bungalow itself and another from the police station on the outskirts of the village.

After that point, all three wires ran on the same posts. Farther up the slope, he could see the poles of the line from Swaythling

Court which converged upon the trio and joined them somewhere farther along the Micheldean Abbas highway.

"It must have been somebody ringing up the wrong number," the Colonel concluded, as he continued his walk in the direction of St. Nicolas.

He was well outside the village when he recognized a figure approaching him. Lonsdale, his gamekeeper, lived in a cottage a little way off the road to the left; and apparently he had noticed the Colonel and had come down to meet him.

For the second time that morning, the Colonel found himself in the presence of someone with news to communicate and hampered by a fear of being laughed at. Lonsdale, most evidently, had something on his mind which he wished to tell his employer; but Colonel Sanderstead had practically to drag it out of him. When it did come, the Colonel was not surprised that Lonsdale had had some difficulty in putting it clearly.

"I just wanted to consult you, sir, about a matter that came up lately. It's really about the inquest on that man Hubbard. I'm not sure whether I shouldn't have volunteered my evidence at the inquest; but at the time I didn't feel inclined to do it. Some people would have thought I was just making it up, sir; telling a silly story for the sake of being called as a witness. I thought it out; and I made up my mind to say nothing about it to anybody then. But after the inquest, I thought it over again; and it seemed to me, just in case the thing went any further, that I'd better mention it to someone; so that if anything further turned up, it wouldn't look as if I had anything to conceal."

The Colonel nodded encouragingly but said nothing.

"So I thought I'd better mention it to you, sir; you being a J.P. and knowing me and not being likely to let it go any further unless there was need for that."

"Quite right, Lonsdale. Go ahead."

Lonsdale fidgeted slightly, as though trying to find the proper opening:

"It's this way, sir. You know the Sproxtons of Upper Greenstead village?"

The Colonel nodded again. The Sproxtons were a family that had been rooted in the Fernhurst soil for generations; and they now kept the tiny solitary shop of Upper Greenstead. A very sound family, by the Colonel's standards. He began to wonder how they came to be mixed up in the affair of the inquest.

"Well, sir, for some months back, Kitty Sproxton and I have been looking each other up and down, so to speak, and trying to see if we wouldn't suit each other."

"Sensible man, Lonsdale," commented the Colonel. "She's a pretty girl, and a good girl, too."

"She's that, sir. So you see it was only to be expected that I'd be often at Upper Greenstead. I used to go up there in the evenings and come back through the High Spinney. I've been a bit doubtful about the birds there lately; there's a poaching fellow I've had my eye on lately—not from the village, sir—and I thought it would do no harm to be going through the Spinney at odd times in the night."

The Colonel smiled covertly at Lonsdale's combining business with pleasure; but he said nothing, and Lonsdale continued his story.

"On the night of this Hubbard man's death, I was over in Upper Greenstead; and Kitty and I went for a walk in one of the lanes up there. I could see she was a bit upset over something; and gradually I got it out of her. It made me fair furious, sir."

Even the recollection seemed to make Lonsdale angry. His face flushed and his brows contracted as he went on with his narrative.

"She told me, sir, that the day before that she had been down in Fernhurst Parva, doing some shopping; and as she was walking home along the road, this beggar Hubbard overtook her in his car. He was alone; and there was no one else in sight. He stopped the car and offered her a lift into Upper Greenstead. Kitty isn't that kind of girl, sir."

"I know that," said the Colonel. "Go on."

"Hubbard, it seems, wouldn't take a civil no for an answer. He got down from the car and began to talk to her. She walked on; and he followed her along the road. Then he began to get familiar, sir. I didn't ask her to tell me all about it; but I could see from the way she spoke that he must have got beyond bounds altogether. Anyway, there was a bit of a struggle and she got away from him. He followed her up in his car, keeping beside her and talking to her until they got in sight of the village; and from what she said, his talk was worse than what he did."

Outwardly unconcerned, the Colonel was raging in his mind. Here was another story of Hubbard pestering the village girls. Another black mark against the hound! Quite obviously a man of that sort was better dead.

"Go on, Lonsdale."

"I'm not an easy-tempered man, sir; and that story fairly made me rage. Kitty had some trouble in calming me down after it. In fact, sir, we made up our minds about things that evening and we're going to get married next month."

"Ah! That's good news, Lonsdale. She's a very nice girl in every way; and you're a very lucky man. I must drop in at Upper Greenstead and congratulate her, too. I'm very pleased to hear about it."

Inwardly the Colonel was estimating what increase in pay he ought to offer Lonsdale when the marriage took place. He liked both the keeper and the girl; and young folk ought to be made easy in their minds at the start.

"Thank you very much, Colonel. I'm sure Kitty will be very pleased if you take notice of her. If I may say so, sir, she thinks a lot of your opinion."

The Colonel was not too dense to see the implied hint.

"That's all right, Lonsdale." He smiled. "I'll tell her just what I think of you; I'm sure that will please her. But go on with your story."

"Of course, sir, when we got things fixed up definitely, it put the Hubbard affair out of my mind for the moment. I'd no thoughts for that then. But after we'd got back to Upper Greenstead and I'd said good-night to her, I turned off into the High Spinney on my road home; and somehow the whole business came back to my mind and made me madder than ever. I left her at the shop about ten o'clock; and I walked slowly through the Spinney, looking about to see if there was anyone about; and it was some time before I came out of the wood at the end nearest Swaythling Court. I was that mad over the affair that I made up my mind I'd go right off and have it out with Hubbard then and there. I'd have half-killed him if I'd got my hands on him just then.

"I cut across the slope and got into the Swaythling grounds at the west end and then I tramped up to the house. The church clock in Fernhurst Parva happened to chime half-past ten as I got over the fence. When I got near the house itself, I saw there was no light burning in it except in the hall, so I'd had my pains for nothing. The beggar was out, that evening. However, to make sure, I trudged up to the front door and rang the bell. Nobody answered. I rang again—kept my finger on it for the best part of a minute, enough to wake the dead, but still no one came. So I left it at that and went away again."

"Do you remember it raining that night?" inquired the Colonel.

"Yes, sir. It began to rain a bit just after Kitty went into the shop. I think it cleared up again just about the time I reached the Swaythling Court grounds."

"So that you were actually on the premises about half-past ten; and Hubbard was not in the house?"

"No one answered my ringing, at any rate."

"That fits in perfectly with the evidence at the inquest."

"Yes, sir. That's one reason why I didn't feel there was any need for me to come forward. So far as that went, they had the information from other people. But it wasn't altogether that that made me keep quiet. You see, sir, I'd have had to explain how I came to be there; and that meant dragging Kitty's name into it; and perhaps having her put into the box to confirm my story. I wasn't going to have my girl made a show of if I could help it."

"I quite see your point, Lonsdale. I think you were quite right to keep quiet. Your evidence carried the matter no further anyway."

Lonsdale fidgeted again at this comment.

"But you see, sir, that wasn't quite the only thing. The rest of the story was so downright impossible that if I'd told it to the coroner he'd have said straight out that I was either drunk or making up a yarn. I can hardly believe it myself, now I come to look back on it. Sometimes I think I must have been dreaming and got mixed up."

The Colonel brushed aside Lonsdale's commentary.

"Let's have the facts first, Lonsdale. You can give me your impressions about it afterwards. What happened after you stopped ringing the bell at the Court? That was about half-past ten, wasn't it?"

"Yes, there or thereabouts, I should think. I didn't go down the avenue; I just cut straight across into our own grounds and went down past the sixth green to the road at the Bungalow."

Colonel Sanderstead's face betrayed very little; but there was a certain eagerness in his voice which puzzled the keeper:

"Ah! By the way, Lonsdale, did you by any chance notice a motor in the avenue or near it, about that time?"

But the keeper's reply dashed the hopes of the Colonel.

"No, sir. Certainly there was no car near the house while I was about the place."

The Colonel made no comment. Inwardly he was making a note that the mysterious motor must have reached the house after, say, 10.45 p.m.; for the avenue of Swaythling Court. was commanded by the links, and if the car had arrived while Lonsdale was crossing the golf-course he would certainly have seen its lights.

"All right. Go on, Lonsdale."

"Well, sir, I crossed the Micheldean Abbas road at the Bungalow and went through the Bungalow gate. Mr. Leigh allows me to go through his garden instead of walking round by the road. It cuts off the best part of a mile for me. So I pushed open the gate and walked up the drive towards the Bungalow door. I usually turn off into the shrubbery just before reaching the front entrance. I don't like tramping past his front door-steps. It looks like presuming on a favour."

The Colonel nodded his approval of this tact.

"I'd just reached the place where I usually turn off and I'd taken perhaps a couple of steps into the shrubbery, when I heard the Bungalow door open. Quite without thinking, I looked across. You know the Bungalow door, sir? You'll remember there's a porch outside it, a fairly roomy thing, so that people can stand at the door and not be seen from outside. I could see the light from the open door and that was all. Then I heard Mr. Leigh's voice; and that made me pull up in my tracks. He said: 'Good-night, Hubbard. See you again soon.' And with that he closed the door."

Colonel Sanderstead had some difficulty in maintaining an outward appearance of unconcern. Here was a piece of evidence worth having; an account by a completely unbiased witness of the parting between Jimmy Leigh and Hubbard after that final momentous interview which hitherto had been wrapped in obscurity.

"By the way, Lonsdale, excuse my interrupting your story, but can you remember anything more about that incident. For instance, could you recall the tone of voice Mr. Leigh used?"

Colonel Sanderstead was rather proud of that inquiry. To the keeper, it would merely appear that his recollection was being tested; whilst actually the Colonel would extract the crucial information as to whether the two men had parted on bad terms or not.

Lonsdale paused and reflected for a moment or two before he answered. Quite evidently he thought that the Colonel was applying a memory test. .

"I don't seem to remember anything particular, Colonel. My recollection is that Mr. Leigh spoke just as you or I might speak in a casual way; just the way I'd say, 'See you to-morrow,' to anybody I met in the ordinary way."

He paused again and tried to gather something further from his memory:

"No, sir, I can't remember anything out of the way. It was the ordinary good-night business. Nothing more was said, if that's what you mean. I'm quite certain about *that*."

But the Colonel had learned enough already to make him think furiously. Here, on absolutely credible evidence, was the proof that Jimmy Leigh had parted from Hubbard, after that crucial interview, on terms which were not in any way removed from the normal. But if that were so, then Jimmy Leigh could hardly have had a hand in Hubbard's death at all. They hadn't parted in a passion; therefore they must have come to some arrangement which did not hit Jimmy Leigh too hard. Perhaps Hubbard had climbed down completely and agreed to stop the blackmail. A great wave of relief passed over Colonel Sanderstead's mind.

"And what happened after that?" he inquired.

Lonsdale fidgeted more markedly than before.

"Well, sir, I hardly expect you to believe the rest; but it's gospel truth. I stood there under cover of the bushes and all at once it flashed across me that I'd got my chance after all. I'd missed Hubbard at his house; and now he'd dropped clean into my hands—a regular gift o' Providence, so to speak. I could have it out with him after all. And with that all my rage came back again; and I promised myself he'd get the biggest drubbing any man ever got. So I waited for him to come out. I meant to follow him back into his own avenue, where it would be quiet and there'd be nobody to interfere; and then I was going to take it out of his hide."

The keeper paused again, with an artless dramatic effect.

"I kept my eye on the porch, waiting for him to come out; for I had to let him get ahead of me before I crept out of the shrubbery. I waited for five minutes, I'm sure. Nobody passed me. I was near enough the avenue to have touched a man with a stick if he'd passed down. I don't think I'd have heard him, perhaps, for there was a wind rustling among the dead leaves. But I'll take my oath that I saw nobody. So I took it that Hubbard was still sheltering in the porch after Mr. Leigh went in and shut the door. Seeing that he wasn't coming out, I changed my plans and I tiptoed up to the porch myself. If it came to a noisy scrap, I thought I could trust Mr. Leigh to stand aside once I'd told him the rights of the case."

"I expect you were right in that," the Colonel agreed.

"So I crept quietly up the avenue, sir, until I came in full view of the porch. I could see every corner of it. And you may believe me or not, Colonel, but it's the cold truth that there wasn't a soul there. He'd slipped past me somehow. You could have knocked me down with the tip of your finger, I was so taken aback. I didn't know what to make of it."

Even the mere recollection of his surprise seemed to affect Lonsdale. He looked at the Colonel with eyes in which amazement struggled with something almost akin to fear.

"I didn't know what to make of it," he went on. "Did you ever hear tell of an Invisible Man, Colonel? That's what Hubbard was that night. I've been wondering if it was one of Mr. Leigh's scientific dodges—he's a great hand at doing weird things with these instruments of his. Do you think that could have been it, sir? He might have made Hubbard invisible for a bit."

"I'd rather try for some simpler explanation first," the Colonel commented. "Suppose Hubbard had simply opened the front door and gone inside after Mr. Leigh?"

"It won't do, sir. Mr. Leigh has a Yale lock on the Bungalow door; and when I got into the porch I tried the door, and it was locked."

"Aren't there any cupboards or lockers in the porch? Hubbard might have spotted you, you know, and concealed himself."

"There wasn't cover enough for a cat in the porch, sir. I had my flash-lamp with me; and I went over every corner."

"Well, I'd want very sound evidence that Hubbard did go out of the house then before I swallowed this Invisible Man notion of yours, Lonsdale. The thing's ridiculous."

A certain obstinacy appeared in the keeper's face.

"That's what I thought you would say, sir. And that's just what kept me from offering my evidence at the inquest. What sort of a figure would I have cut if I'd brought out that story on oath? Nobody'd have believed me, any more than you do yourself. But it happened, right enough. And what's more, I've got proof that Hubbard did leave the Bungalow then."

Again the Colonel became alert. Here was something else of importance coming out.

"How can you prove that?"

Lonsdale answered the question by asking another: "How long would it take you to walk from the Bungalow door over to Swaythling Court, sir, taking it just at an ordinary pace?"

"It's roughly three-quarters of a mile from door to door, I should think. That's near enough anyway. Taking it at three miles per hour, that would work out somewhere round about fifteen minutes."

"That's what I make it," confirmed Lonsdale. "I've walked it with a watch in my hand since then; and it came out at thirteen minutes. But that Hubbard was a slug of a man; and he might have taken a couple of minutes longer."

His expression became tinged with a certain triumph.

"Well, sir, just before Hubbard came out of the Bungalow door, the Fernhurst Parva church clock chimed a quarter to eleven. As soon as I'd satisfied myself that Hubbard wasn't concealed about the premises, I cut off sharp to my own cottage. From the higher ground there you can see right over the Bungalow to Swaythling Court. When I got to my cottage door, the windows of Swaythling Court were all dark; only the hall lights were burning—just as I'd left it. I took out my watch and waited; and I kept my eye on the Court. I might have saved myself the bother with my watch; for almost immediately after the Fernhurst Parva clock chimed again, eleven o'clock, the light flashed up in the study windows of Swaythling Court. And that meant that Hubbard had got home to the house again. He'd taken just the quarter of an hour that you allowed for it. And there in that study you found him dead next morning. Can you get round that, sir?"

The Colonel idly traced some lines on the road with his stick. Certainly Lonsdale's evidence seemed neatly hinged together, and what especially struck the Colonel was the fact that only a man with his wits about him would have thought of applying the last check to the business. Most people would have had quite enough when they discovered that Hubbard had vanished. One could not rule Lonsdale out as an incompetent witness. And yet . . . an Invisible Man was a bit of a mouthful for anyone to swallow. That sort of thing simply didn't happen; and that was all about it. But perhaps it was some dodge of Jimmy Leigh's: a conjuring trick with mirrors or something like that. But Jimmy Leigh had more to think about than aimless conjuring just then.

Lonsdale was anxiously awaiting the Colonel's verdict; but Colonel Sanderstead wanted time to think the matter out. At last he took refuge in a non-committal phrase:

"I must say, Lonsdale, I think you were quite right in not volunteering that evidence of yours. I'm not throwing any doubts on your veracity; but other people might have been less broad-minded. An invisible man takes a lot of swallowing, you know."

The keeper was obviously disappointed.

"It's gospel truth, sir, whether anybody believes it or not. Do you think I'd be fool enough to make up a cock-and-bull story like that? If it hadn't been the plain truth, no more and no less, I'd never have spoken to you about it, never."

The Colonel suddenly stopped tracing lines with his stick. Hallucination! That would cover the case. And, of course, a man suffering from a hallucination would be absolutely convinced that he was speaking the truth. Most probably the whole yarn originated in some vivid nightmare that the keeper had had after he went to beds His mind would be full of Hubbard; and no doubt the blackmailer bobbed up in his dreams. He turned to Lonsdale again.

"If I were you, Lonsdale, I think I'd keep this affair to myself. You've got it off your mind by telling me about it; and I shan't let it go any farther. And if anything turns up, I'll be able to say that you didn't attempt to keep it quiet. But you know what people are; they'd scoff at the whole affair if you told them about it. Much better to keep it between ourselves, I think. And now I must be moving on. I'll be over at Upper Greenstead soon to look up Kitty. We must see about getting you a better cottage, if we can, or else build something on to your present one; and Kitty may be able to give me some notion of the kind of thing she would like. That'll do. No thanks. I'm only too glad to do something for a young couple."

And with a certain relief, the Colonel escaped under cover of the keeper's gratitude.

He was frankly puzzled by this latest addition to the evidence in the Hubbard case. He repeated to himself the word 'Hallucination'; and he tried to convince himself by these repetitions. But he had known Lonsdale long enough and well enough to doubt whether the keeper was a likely subject for delusions. That possible explanation hardly rang true when one judged it fairly. But then the alternative, the Invisible Man, was even more improbable. Unless . . . unless one accepted the idea that Jimmy Leigh had been up to some new scientific stunt, something even more wonderful than the Lethal Ray itself.

"Damnation!" complained the Colonel, who seldom swore, "I seem to come up against Jimmy Leigh wherever I turn in this infernal affair. And even if there is an Invisible Man mixed up in it, that doesn't exclude the possibility that the Lethal Ray was at the bottom of the whole business. I've simply got to get at the truth of this thing, or I'll never feel satisfied."

He walked back toward the village, switching his stick in irritation.

"I used to wonder how a plain man would feel if he were set down to solve a mystery. Well, I know now. What's wrong with this case is that there seem to be far too many clues; and hardly a pair of them point in the same direction. One would think they had all been carefully contrived to lead nowhere in particular. I wonder what Angermere would have made of Lonsdale That's another bit of evidence that his theory couldn't account for anyway. He's just as far astray as I am myself. Upon my soul, I believe Cyril took the safest course of us all when he admitted straight off that it was beyond him. He's saved himself a lot of unnecessary worry by keeping clear of the affair. I wish I'd never heard about it. It's getting on my nerves."

But before his walk was finished, Colonel Sanderstead was destined to have yet another complication of the case thrust upon his notice. As he turned into the main street, the Vicar almost ran into him; and it was evident that Flitterwick was suffering from a bad attack of suppressed news.

"Oh, good morning, Colonel. Delighted to meet you. The weather is exceptionally fine for this period of the year, is it not? Just the very morning for a pleasant walk, *aequo ammo*, if I may put it so, with a mind at ease."

"Very pleasant, very pleasant," said the Colonel, shortly.

"A terrible business, this Hubbard case. *Animus meminisse horret*, as Virgil has it; my soul shakes with horror when I recall it."

"Unpleasant business. I shouldn't dwell on it," advised the Colonel, unsympathetically.

"That reminds me," Flitterwick went on, coming to his real news, "there is a most surprising rumour in the village."

"Indeed?" Colonel Sanderstead's voice was very dry; and anyone with a thinner skin than Flitterwick would have left his news untold. The Vicar, however, was by no means dashed.

"It appears, Colonel, that young Leigh's sudden departure has been explained at last."

If Flitterwick hoped to produce a sensation in his audience, he certainly succeeded. The Colonel stared at him with an expression in which astonishment and a certain apprehension seemed to be blended. Much encouraged, the Vicar proceeded.

"A very strange affair, very strange; not at all what one would have suspected. I never imagined for a moment that young Leigh was that sort of person."

Apprehension was now the Colonel's chief emotion. What had come to light about Jimmy Leigh? But he kept his feelings in hand; it would never do to let Flitterwick think the matter was being taken seriously. Impatiently he waited for the Vicar to divulge his news.

"*Horresco referens*," the Vicar went on, "I'm sorry to have to repeat such a thing."

Completely sceptical on this point, Colonel Sanderstead fumed with impatience and, to hasten Flitterwick's procedure, looked at his watch pointedly. The Vicar noticed the glance and, afraid lest the Colonel might hurry on to some appointment, he came straight to the point at last.

"It appears, Colonel, that young Leigh has . . . what shall I say? . . . eloped with that . . . well, with that . . . I should say with that rather flamboyantly attired woman who paid a flying visit to the 'Three Bees' on the night before he disappeared."

Colonel Sanderstead had difficulty in suppressing any outward signs of his internal relief. So they weren't connecting Jimmy Leigh with Hubbard's death after all! That was something to the good, anyway. And from the relief he felt, the Colonel was suddenly aware of how far he himself might go if it became a question of shielding

Jimmy Leigh. Somehow, the further he penetrated into the case, the more inclined he felt to side with the culprit—if, indeed, there was a murder at the bottom of the business at all. Even Lonsdale's evidence had helped to tip the scale farther; for the more one heard about Hubbard, the more one hated the beast.

Flitterwick was evidently disconcerted to find that the explosion of his gossip bomb had produced so trifling a result.

"I can assure you, Colonel, there is no doubt in the matter. I have questioned the station porter myself. One owed it to young Leigh to have the facts clearly before one, if I may say so, before one sat in judgment in any way. But it's all quite clear. This abandoned woman left Fernhurst Parva by the first train. She was early at the station; and as she walked up and down the platform she seemed to be expecting someone. She walked two or three times down the platform to the entrance and looked about. At last she gave it up and took her seat in a carriage. Just as the train was moving, young Leigh dashed up the platform, glanced along the train, and flung himself into her compartment. To my mind, the whole thing must have been prearranged between them. And that would account, of course, for his having left no address behind him. I must confess, Colonel, that I am gravely disappointed in young Leigh."

"Jimmy Leigh's a friend of mine," said the Colonel abruptly.

And with that he crossed the road, leaving Flitterwick puzzled and aghast upon the pavement.

11
THE NON-SKID TYRE

CYRIL NORTON AND COLONEL SANDERSTEAD had finished a round of the links when a heavy thunder-shower broke upon them; and they decided to retire to the Manor smoking-room until the weather became settled, one way or the other. Neither of them was of the golfing type which finds it necessary to replay verbally every stroke of the preceding round; and when they had settled themselves comfortably by the fire, it occurred to the Colonel that Lonsdale's story might help to set Cyril's mind at rest with regard to the relations between Jimmy Leigh and the blackmailer. Cyril was a person to whom one could safely mention a thing of that sort; Colonel Sanderstead felt that it would not be a breach of his understanding with the keeper if he repeated the gist of the affair.

"I've come across something fresh on the Hubbard case, Cyril," he began.

Cyril Norton looked up with an expression into which the Colonel read a faint tinge of irony. "At it again?" his nephew seemed to inquire, without uttering any verbal comment. The Colonel disregarded the look.

"This is for your own information, of course," he continued. "It won't go any farther. The fact is, I've got some evidence to prove that Jimmy Leigh and Hubbard parted on perfectly good terms at the Bungalow, that night."

Rapidly he sketched in outline the story which Lonsdale had told him.

"Of course," he concluded, "Lonsdale's notion of an Invisible Man is nonsense. I expect that in some way or other he missed the scoundrel; though I don't understand how he managed to do it. But anyway, there's the story for what it's worth. And it appears to me to clear Jimmy completely, so far as Hubbard's death is concerned. It seems to me that Jimmy and Hubbard must have come to some agreement; and if they had done that, then there was no need for Jimmy to eliminate Hubbard at all."

Cyril Norton listened to the story with concentrated attention. For some moments he remained silent, his pipe clenched in his teeth, gazing into the fire. At last he broke silence.

"I've told you before, uncle, that I don't understand the ins and outs of this business. It looks as if a dozen kittens had been rolling amongst the clues and tangling them up. Even this Lonsdale affair doesn't seem to me to make them much easier—quite the reverse, in fact. By the way, you don't propose to publish this evidence abroad?"

"No."

"Suppose you came across something that told on the other side—against Jimmy—would you show the same masterly restraint."

The Colonel was nettled by Cyril's tone. He had uneasy memories of the map and compass episode. Off his guard, he blurted out his real views:

"Certainly! I'm not a detective paid to catch Jimmy out. Besides, to tell you the truth, Cyril, I'm beginning to discover a certain sneaking sympathy with the man who finished Hubbard—if it turns out in the end to be murder and not suicide."

Cyril looked at his uncle curiously.

"So you're coming round to a sensible point of view? What's a dead blackmailer, after all, eh? 'A rat, a rat' and all that sort of thing? That's the line I took at the start, myself. I never was the kind that raises a hullabaloo about the extermination of vermin."

Colonel Sanderstead was experiencing a certain relief at the turn of the conversation. For some days he had been suffering from too much concentration, uncomfortable concentration, upon the

Hubbard case; and now he felt that with Cyril he might safely ven-
ture to discuss the matter. Cyril would not betray any confidences.
And, in the very earliest stages of the case, Cyril had shown a hard,
critical spirit, which was just the thing his uncle wished now to see
applied to the affair.

"Haven't you got any ideas about the business?" he asked. "Does
it suggest nothing to you at all?"

Cyril Norton smiled a little grimly; then the grimness faded out,
as though something amusing had come into his mind.

"Have you come across Flitterwick lately, uncle? He's got a fine
explanation of Jimmy's departure. Bolted with the damsel who
came to see Hilton, you remember. Well, well, boys will be boys!"

He laughed with obviously genuine amusement.

"So you don't believe that either?" demanded the Colonel.
"Flitterwick's an idiot, of course; and he annoyed me by his muck-
raking and sniffing for scandal: but although one doesn't swallow
his story, there's no denying that Jimmy's bolting does require
some sort of explanation. Have you any notion why he went off?"

Cyril's amusement came to a sudden end.

"I suppose it was the usual reason: he didn't want to stay where
he was."

Colonel Sanderstead recognized the tone; whatever Cyril
knew—and it looked as though he knew something—it was evident
that he did not feel justified in giving information. He decided to
be frank with his nephew.

"The fact is, Cyril, this Hubbard affair has given me a great deal of
worry lately. It's no affair of mine; but there's something about it that
makes me uneasy. I hate to be puzzled by a thing; and that creature's
death does puzzle me. If Jimmy Leigh's out of it, then why did Hubbard
commit suicide? There's no reason that I can see. If they parted on
friendly terms, then Hubbard could count on Jimmy stopping your
mouth; so he needn't have suicided at all. Angermere thought that
the butler was at the bottom of it. What do you think of that?"

Cyril's face lighted up for a moment as though he had seen a
beacon on a dark road.

"The butler? Now *that's* an idea! That would help to clear up some of the tangle, perhaps. I can't say I was impressed by Leake. Let's hear Angermere's notion."

The Colonel rapidly outlined the theory of the novelist.

"H'm! He seems to have got it down to dots. That might account for some parts of the thing. The belt-fastener we found on the carpet, you remember; that might have been Leake's. Yes, I'll admit that Leake might have played a part in the affair."

He thought for a moment.

"Did you take Lonsdale's story as being correct all the way through? Did he give you the impression of a man remembering or did he look like a fellow reciting a prepared story?"

"I've known Lonsdale—and you've known him too—for years, Cyril. You don't suggest that he murdered Hubbard, do you?"

"Everybody's a potential murderer, uncle, given the proper circumstances. I bet that with your ideas, you'd be on the side of Judge Lynch if you lived in the Southern States. It's just because you live over here that you're clear of that."

"I'm down on any man who mishandles a girl, admitted."

"And Lonsdale, maybe, thinks the same when it's *his* girl."

"I don't believe Lonsdale killed Hubbard, if that's what you mean," declared the Colonel, emphatically.

"Not quite that; but he may have seen more of the affair than he told you. Are you sure he didn't go inside the house?"

"I believed the story he told me, up to the Invisible Man episode. It sounded perfectly straightforward. Besides, how could Lonsdale have poisoned Hubbard?"

"It was the stabbing I was thinking about."

"But that was aimless, apparently."

"Of course it was," Cyril assented. "Quite futile. That's what puzzles me about it. Hubbard was dead some time before the stabbing was done. Now a sane man doesn't stick a knife into anyone unless he has a sound motive for it. And where's the motive here?"

"There's Angermere's theory," the Colonel pointed out. "Suppose the stabbing was done to hide the poisoning."

"I doubt it. Everybody knows that there's a P.M. examination in murder cases and that was certain to bring the cyanide to light. Besides, the room stank of the stuff, you remember. The weak point in Angermere's theory is that it assumes first of all that Leake is a bit of a super-criminal; and then it makes him fake evidence of a murder by stabbing, which is an obvious mistake under the circumstances. It's trying to prove too much in the evidence you leave behind."

"But don't all murderers make mistakes?" objected the Colonel. "Isn't that the usual hall-mark of that crime. They always get caught by being too clever."

Cyril took his pipe out of his mouth as if to lend force to his reply.

"Yes, the ones who are too clever get caught. But when they're not too clever they don't get caught, because nobody thinks it's a murder at all. Do you really suppose, uncle, that every murder is detected or even suspected of being a murder? Not a bit of it."

The Colonel went back to his original trouble.

"Are you sure that Jimmy Leigh's not mixed up in the affair? I don't mind telling you I've been very worried over it, Cyril. I've come across some things that made me uneasy—not suspicious exactly, but troubled. Have you any notion why Jimmy cut his stick just at that moment?"

Cyril Norton pondered over his reply for a few moments before speaking.

"Between ourselves, uncle, I do know why Jimmy cleared out. You can set your mind at rest on that point, if it's troubling you. I've gone into this business very fully; and you may take it from me as absolutely straight that Jimmy did not kill Hubbard. I could establish that to-morrow without the faintest difficulty if I were put to it. I've got all the evidence I need."

"Then why did he bolt?" demanded the Colonel. "It looks queer."

"You needn't ask me why Jimmy went off," Cyril said, with an air of finality. "I'm not going to tell you. And you needn't apply to me for a solution of the mystery either; for a good many parts of it leave me just as much in the dark as you are yourself. I've got my own views about some sides of it; but the rest beats me entirely. And for that reason if you've noticed, I've confined myself to knocking down other people's theories. I've set up none of my own. I'm not going to start throwing suspicion on anybody, because I simply don't know the whole story of what happened on that night at Swaythling Court. A silly owl like Flitterwick bubbles with theories—half of them libellous, like this latest effort about an elopement—and possibly some of his dirt may stick in some people's minds. I'm not going to fall into that mistake, anyway."

Cyril Norton got up and walked across to the window, where the rain was drumming a diminuendo upon the panes.

"Not worth playing another round," he commented, gloomily, as he looked out over the wet surface of the sweep. "The greens will be sodden after that waterspout, and we'd only cut them up by walking on them. I think I'll clear off home once this rain stops."

He came back and re-seated himself by the fire.

"Give Hubbard's affair a rest, uncle, and take up a fresh line. The village seems to be buzzing with a new sensation. All this nonsense about a haunted telephone has revived the old Green Devil. You'd better look into that yarn for a change. Local folklore and all that."

The Colonel made a sound suspiciously like an angry snort.

"Where do they pick up stuff of that kind nowadays?" he demanded with some vexation.

"General chatter, with the assistance of Flitterwick, I suppose. Rot, anyway. The only eyewitness seems to be Sappy Morton—just the sort of person one might expect to see a thing of that kind. I understand he swears he met the Green Devil one night; describes it in detail, too. All green, with great gnarled claws—quite in the old tradition. I suppose he had a nightmare of some sort."

"I'll have a little chat with poor Sappy one of these days," the Colonel decided. "A little kindly talk will probably get these notions out of his head."

"You'd better hurry up, then; or we'll have some penny-a-liner down from London to write it up: 'THE GREEN DEVIL OF FERNHURST. REAPPEARANCE OF WELL-KNOWN SPECTRE.

ALL TEETH AND CLAWS. WHAT DOES IT MEAN?' That sort of thing."

The Colonel ground his teeth at the prospect of seeing his village held up to ridicule in the cheaper Press.

"I'll see Sappy as soon as I can."

The rain had ceased and a watery sunlight came through the windows. Cyril got up.

"I think I'll clear off now while there's a dry blink. I hate splashing through a downpour on a motor-bike."

The Colonel let him go; and soon he heard the purring of Cyril's motor-cycle receding down the avenue. He refilled his pipe and sat down again beside the fire.

The blunt statement of his nephew had taken a load off his mind; for Cyril was a trustworthy person. If he said that he could produce certain evidence, the Colonel knew that the evidence would be forthcoming if necessary. Cyril was the last person whom one could accuse of empty bragging in matters of that kind. That meant that Jimmy Leigh's conduct, curious as it seemed on the surface, did not connect him with Hubbard's death. And that, again, fitted in quite coherently with the evidence of Lonsdale, showing that Jimmy and the blackmailer had parted on friendly terms. That, in itself, was a sound corroboration of Cyril's assertion.

But how had Cyril got hold of this evidence which he had not disclosed? He was, quite frankly, holding back something. The Colonel admitted to himself, as he thought over the matter, that he, too, had done the very same thing; he had kept his thumb on his discovery of the track of the defective nonskid tyre and had said nothing about it to Cyril. Possibly Cyril had seen something else that day, something more important, which had escaped the Colonel; and thus he had got ahead in the race.

"Smart man, Cyril," his uncle reflected. "But I wonder what he noticed that I didn't see. From the way he talked, one got the feeling that he had a fair idea of the whole case—more than I have, anyway—but that he wouldn't be hustled into saying anything until he'd got it completely straightened out. Probably he'll tell me what he thinks by and by."

His attention was caught by the faint sound of a car passing under the windows of the study; and in a few moments a maid opened the door.

"Mrs. Hilton, sir."

The Colonel rose to his feet as the maid stood aside to admit a grey-eyed girl in tweeds. Colonel Sanderstead's face lit up. He liked Stella Hilton. "She looks you straight in the eye, and she doesn't stare when she does it," was his form of praise. He had known her since her childhood right up to the outbreak of the war; and when he came back after that interlude he had found her grown almost out of recognition, more responsible from the effect of her war-work and—married. It had come as something of a shock to the Colonel; a chit of fifteen reappearing as the mistress of a household; it made him suddenly feel older. But his affection for Stella had not been lessened; there was no difference in the side she showed to him.

"Gardner wanted to immure me in the drawing-room; but I insisted on being shown in here. You don't mind?"

The Colonel reassured her with a gesture.

"The fact is, I want a quiet talk with you about my affairs; and I don't want to run the risk of some other visitor dropping in on the top of us. I want your advice."

The Colonel needed no further enlightenment. Stella's 'affairs' could mean one thing only: her relations with her husband. Colonel Sanderstead had long been in the secret of all her troubles; she had turned to him from time to time. And he had admired her more than ever for the way in which she had taken them. It was what he had expected of her: she wasn't the whining type with a wet pocket-handkerchief. Without ceasing to be feminine, she had faced ill-fortune as bravely as a man could have done. When her whole happiness had gone down in disaster, she had wept, if she wept at all, in private; and to the world she had turned an inscrutable face. Only Cyril Norton and the Colonel had had glimpses of what went on behind that mask.

"Well, sit down, Stella; make yourself comfortable; and then tell me all about it. By the way, did you leave that chauffeur of yours out in the rain? I'd better get him brought under cover."

"The rain's quite off. He's all right; and he probably wants to smoke a cigarette. 'Sit down; make yourself comfortable,' as you say; and I'll tell you all about it. It's more of the same, of course."

The Colonel nodded.

"Surely he hasn't been giving you any more trouble? You got your decree *nisi* all right; and it'll be made absolute in another month or so, won't it? What more do you want?"

Stella stretched a pair of neatly shod feet towards the fire.

"The trouble's this. Has he any right to come to Carisbrooke House; force his way in there; interview my servants; and make himself generally a nuisance?"

The Colonel found no difficulty in making up his mind on that point.

"The house doesn't belong to him. For that matter, it doesn't belong to you, either: it's Jimmy's really, isn't it?"

"Yes, that's the trouble. If Jimmy were at hand, I'd turn him on to deal with that man; but Jimmy's away just now and he hasn't left any address, even with me. The only person I can get at is his lawyer; and he seems to be a regular old stick-in-the-mud. He 'can't take the responsibility' of doing anything; and he 'has no instructions providing for the case'; and so on and so forth. So I came to you to see what could be done. I simply won't have that man approaching the premises."

"He's got a certain amount of nerve to put in an appearance at all, it seems to me," the Colonel commented. "But I don't think you need fear any further trouble. Of course, if Jimmy were at home, you could have got him to work—he's the natural person to tackle the business. But since he's away, I must see what I can do myself. If you like to complain to me formally that Hilton is molesting you, then I'll see to it that Bolam keeps an eye on the matter; and all you need do then will be to ring up the police station and they'll send up someone to fling Hilton off your doorstep. I never heard of such a thing!" the Colonel continued, with rising indignation. "What's he after, anyway?"

"He seems to be trying to get hold of something; I'm not sure what it is. He even had the nerve to tackle my maid and cross-question her about my affairs; but she seems to have sent him off with a flea in his ear: and the result is that she didn't discover exactly what he was after. And there have been other funny things happening that I don't like."

"What, for instance?"

"Well, not long ago, a packet of letters disappeared out of a drawer. I hadn't much difficulty in tracking down the person who took them—Jeal, a housemaid I had then. I taxed her with it; but she denied taking them, flatly. Of course, I couldn't prove that she did it—supposition was all I had to go on. But I got rid of her."

"What sort of letters were they?" inquired the Colonel, rather anxiously.

"Oh, some of Cyril's. Nothing in them that could interest anyone except our two selves."

"You're sure?"

The grey eyes met the Colonel's blue ones with obvious sincerity.

"Quite sure. As a matter of fact, anybody might read our letters— much good it would do them! Why, I didn't even keep this packet under lock and key. It was lying in one of the drawers of my writing-desk. There was nothing in the letters but appointments, bulbs I'd asked him to get for me in London when he was up in town, books, and so forth. We see each other almost every day and there's no need to put anything on paper. I'd have destroyed the things long ago if it weren't that they were Cyril's letters. Sentiment, you know."

"I understand."

The Colonel knew that he could believe Stella implicitly. She would have had no hesitation in telling him, if the letters had really been important.

"Do you think Hilton bribed the girl to steal them in the hope that he might make something out of them?"

A shadow passed across Stella's face.

"Possibly he did. Or possibly it may have been something else. I don't know. But anyway, I don't like that sort of thing happening. And I'm not going to stand that man prowling around any longer."

"We'll see that he doesn't. Leave it to me and Bolam," the Colonel reassured her. Then, to change the subject, he bethought himself of another matter. Stella went about a good deal. Why not, without giving her any hint, enlist her in the search for the imperfect non-skid tyre?

"Oh, by the way, Stella, I'm on the look-out for a motor with a defective tyre—a non-skid with one stud missing. You might keep your eyes about you; and if you come across anything of the kind, you might let me know."

"Why! . . ."

Then, with a change of tone, she demanded: "What do you want to find it for? Has there been an accident and a car going off without showing its number?"

The Colonel's mask of impassivity failed to stand him in good stead under the scrutiny of a keen pair of eyes.

"It's nothing very important; but I'd like to know who owns that particular car."

"Not an accident?"

"No, nothing worth mentioning."

Stella looked at him with a puzzled expression.

"I wonder what it is. Can't you tell me? You don't usually play the mystery-monger with me. What is it all about?"

But the Colonel refused to be drawn.

"All I want to know is who owns that particular car."

Stella made no reply for a moment. Something which the Colonel could not identify clouded the grey eyes. When she spoke again, it was evident that she felt hurt at his reticence; and she seemed to be trying to cover up her feelings by a rapid change of subject.

"I'm very nearly starving. Do you mind if I hint that it's just about tea-time, even if it isn't really? I had a miserable lunch; and I think I could surprise you with a display of appetite."

The Colonel rang the bell and ordered tea. Stella rose and walked over to the window, where she stood for a time looking out.

"The rain's over for the day, I think," she commented, as she turned back towards the room again. "By the way," she added, as though by an afterthought, "could you lend me a pencil and a sheet of paper? I want to send Hales with a message into the village. He can go down while we're having tea; and that will save me some time."

The Colonel got writing-materials out of his escritoire; and she scribbled a note.

"If you'll ring for the maid, she can take it to Hales."

When the maid appeared, Stella handed her the note.

"Please ask Hales—the chauffeur at the door—to do what is in this note and come back again for me as soon as he is finished."

In a few moments they heard the engine of the car starting.

"And now, tea," said Stella. "I'm dying for it."

But in spite of her eagerness, she seemed to have the very poorest appetite. She toyed with her bread and butter, making it last as long as possible.

"I think I'd rather have a cigarette," she admitted, when the Colonel hospitably attempted to force cakes on her attention. "I suppose I must have got to the over-hungry condition when one really doesn't want to eat much after all."

She selected a cigarette from the Colonel's box and allowed him to light it for her.

"Do you know, I must be losing my nerve. I know it's silly and all that; but somehow I wish that decree *nisi* were made absolute and that I were done with that man completely. I've a sort of haunting feeling that things may not come right in the end; something may come in the way at the last moment. It's pure fancy; but it worries me all the same."

The Colonel, too wise to make an articulate comment, contented himself with a sympathetic murmur. Stella was obviously troubled; and he found it hard to blame her. It must be a very irksome business to have Hilton sneaking about the place, interviewing her servants behind her back, possibly even attempting to arrange thefts of her letters. There could be nothing in it, really; for Stella was not the sort of girl who would go off the rails, no matter how strong the temptation might be; but merely to be suspected of such a thing would be enough to irritate her in her most sensitive spot. And all these doings of Hilton's pointed to something of the kind. One doesn't gossip with maids or attempt to steal letters unless one thinks that there is something to be gained by it all. Hilton must imagine that he was on the track of something. And the Colonel, with a mixture of wonder and indignation, reflected how little this man must have known of his wife when he could suppose such a thing. If Cyril Norton was sure of Jimmy Leigh's innocence in one field, the Colonel was equally certain of Stella's innocence in another. There must have been a good deal more of this privy persecution than she had described; for she was not the sort of girl who would take a thing of that kind meekly. She was very well able to look after herself, the Colonel remembered.

"Hilton's an idiot!" was his final conclusion; and he was surprised to find that he had uttered it aloud.

Stella seemed taken aback by the remark. Evidently she had not been following that train of thought.

"An idiot?"

She appeared to get her bearings.

"Oh, yes, an idiot of course. I wasn't thinking of it in that way. You know, somehow I look on him from the outside, now; he doesn't seem to be in my life at all. Funny, isn't it? And that's what makes all this peering and poking about so annoying. It's just as if a stranger were doing it. The whole of that affair seems to have been wiped out. I can't persuade myself nowadays that I was ever in love with him. Perhaps I never was."

The Colonel attempted to get away from an unpleasant subject.

"Have you seen Cyril lately? He was here this afternoon. You just missed him."

"What a pity. When did he go?"

"Just before you drove up. I wonder you didn't meet him in the avenue."

"I came round by the back road, through Upper Greenstead, otherwise I'd have met him in the village, I suppose. It doesn't matter. We see each other almost every day. And we haven't long to wait now, anyway."

Her quick ear caught the sound of her car in the avenue.

"There's Hales back again with my parcel. I must fly now. Thanks so much for the tea; I was dying for it. And thanks for getting Bolam to work, too. I'll be able to sleep in peace now without having nightmares of that man crawling down the chimney."

"Was it as bad as all that?" inquired the Colonel, smiling.

"Quite bad enough," she retorted soberly. "It's not so much his actually coming, you know; it's just the feeling that he may be coming: prying about, suspecting one of all sorts of things—a beastly feeling! It gets on my nerves."

The Colonel opened the study door for her and together they went out to the front of the house where her car was waiting. Colonel Sanderstead shut the tonneau door behind her, waved a farewell as the car moved off, and stood watching as it disappeared down the avenue.

When it had vanished round the bend, he cast his eyes mechanically on the ground before him and as he did so, he saw something which made him stoop in order to see more clearly. The surface of the drive was wet and the soil had taken a sharp impression of the car's tracks. There, before him, he saw, clean-cut and vivid beyond a doubt, the impress of the imperfect non-skid tyre which in his mind had become associated with the key to the mystery. It was Stella's car that had driven up to the door of Swaythling Court on the night that Hubbard died.

For some moments the Colonel stood looking blankly at the damning tracks. Stella mixed up in the business! It seemed unthinkable. What possible part could she have played in the affair? How could an absolutely straight girl like Stella come to associate with a blackmailer? Incredible! And would any girl go voluntarily to the house of a man like Hubbard at that time of night? The Colonel refused to let himself believe it. There must be some other explanation.

Then a flood of relief poured into his mind as an alternative explanation occurred to him. Stella's car had undoubtedly been at Swaythling Court on the fatal night; but that did not necessarily imply that she herself had been there. The car might have been driven by someone else. Why, her chauffeur might easily have taken it out for purposes of his own. He might be the 'supernumerary man' of whom the Colonel was in search. And as the Colonel reflected again, this idea gained ground. All this spying, stealing of letters, and so forth. Suppose that Hubbard had taken a hand in the game as well as Hilton. If there had been something to rouse Hilton's suspicions it might just as easily have caught Hubbard's attention, whatever it was. And Hubbard might have suborned the chauffeur to do his spying for him; and the chauffeur might have gone to the Court to report progress that night. That would account for the whole of the facts—and leave Stella out of it.

But just as the Colonel had reached this satisfying conclusion, he saw something further on the ground before him which demolished his line of reasoning. The only tracks before him were those of Stella's car—and they were not identical. Two of them showed the imprint of the tyre with a missing stud; the other two displayed instead the track of a fresh tyre.

"So *that* was what she wanted when she sent the car into the village. She ordered Hales to change the tyre before coming back. And that was why she wrote down her instructions—because she didn't want me to hear them, as I would have done if she'd given them verbally. The first two tracks, with the non-skid tyre, were made when she came here first and when the chauffeur went off to the village; the second two tracks, with the plain tread, are the ones made by the chauffeur coming back and going off again afterwards with her. That clinches the business. Whether she was in the car herself that night or not, she knew the car had been out on some fishy affair; and when I asked about the tyre she remembered the missing stud and got it changed right away, so as to leave no more of these infernal tracks behind her. O Lord! Little Stella mixed up in this affair! This is a bad business!"

12
ONE PART OF THE STORY

THE HUBBARD CASE had already given Colonel Sanderstead some uncomfortable half-hours; but the discovery of the non-skid tyre increased his troubles ten-fold. He had been perturbed when he thought that Jimmy Leigh was connected with the affair at Swaythling Court; but in that instance his anxiety had been partly on account of the fact that the ruling caste of Fernhurst Parva was implicated. After all, Jimmy Leigh was a man; and a man could be expected to look after himself in a thing of that sort. Benevolent neutrality was all that could be demanded from Jimmy's friends; and that neutrality the Colonel had already adopted as his policy in the affair.

But when the net extended its folds to enclose Stella Hilton, the Colonel found that he could not force himself to maintain a passive attitude. Girls were incalculable creatures. One never could tell what they might do in given circumstances. Jimmy Leigh, for all his erraticness, could be depended on to take a clear line and follow it out consistently; but Stella's probable course of action was by no means a certainty in the Colonel's mind.

Quite obviously she had got mixed up in the business in some way or other. Equally obviously, she must have known the importance of the non-skid tyre. And, learning the facts suddenly, she had acted immediately—correctly enough in the circumstances, so far as the Colonel could see. She had avoided leaving any more dangerous tracks behind her car.

It was that very rapidity of action that perturbed Colonel Sanderstead.

"As it so happens, she did the right thing in this case; but she might quite well have done the wrong thing. And she acted on the spur of the moment without having time to think out the affair in detail and follow the possible results. That changing of the tyre might have been a damning affair if it happened to come out. And for all one knows, there may be other things she left behind."

He lay back in his chair and thought for a long time.

"That's it!" he said to himself at last. "Probably she did leave something else behind, something that I didn't see. And Cyril spotted it. I knew he must have seen something that I missed, and of course that accounts for his attitude in the business. He's keeping his mouth shut on her account, just as I kept quiet about the Lethal Ray machine to prevent Jimmy Leigh being dragged into the business. That's *that*, anyway. Things are growing a shade clearer."

But on further meditation, the Colonel did not find them any more satisfactory on that account.

"One thing's certain. This isn't the kind of affair to be handled in a slap-dash way. Stella's too much inclined to take the shortest cut in a difficulty; and in a case of this sort that impulsive way of doing things may land her in terrible difficulties. She wants a steadier mind behind her to keep her from rushing at things. Cyril's the man for the job."

Before he had got half-way through his next pipe, however, the Colonel had discovered the difficulties of that solution.

"I can't go to Cyril and say to him: 'Look here, the girl you're going to marry has been mixed up in some very fishy work.' After all, I don't know for certain that Cyril has any idea that she is mixed up in it at all. That's only a possibility. The less mud one stirs up the better. I've got to leave Cyril out of it. And she mustn't get any idea that Cyril does know anything—still assuming that he does know. That would make things just as bad, if not worse. And yet she ought to have a man behind her in this affair; and she ought to be warned against doing things in a hurry, like that tyre-changing. If only Jimmy Leigh were available, I'd talk it over with him; after all, she's his sister and he'd stand up for her and give her a hand.

But there's no getting at him. Cyril's out, Jimmy Leigh's out: there's nobody but myself left to tackle the business. I'll have to take it on. But it's a most damnably awkward thing to do."

He passed to another line of thought.

"I wonder what Cyril can have spotted."

Colonel Sanderstead went over the case again in his mind, trying to see where a missing piece of evidence could have come in. The paper-knife, the broken show-case, the open window and the latchkey he dismissed as outside the question.

"That leaves . . . the automatic pistol. H'm. *That* was never traced. I wonder, now. Suppose it was hers and Cyril recognized it. He had a good look at it, I remember. He may have noted the number of it and said nothing about that. Perhaps he gave it to her himself when Hilton began to be a nuisance. It's the sort of toy one might give to a girl to make her feel she had something to fall back on in case of need; and at the same time it's too much of a toy to do any great harm except by a sheer accident. That fits in neatly enough. It doesn't make things any clearer, certainly; but it would slip into its place without a wrench, anyway, if that idea's correct. It agrees with her being there in the car that night; and it would account for Cyril keeping his mouth shut so tight."

He refilled his pipe and continued his speculations.

"Question is: 'What am I going to do next?' She ought to be warned about that automatic—if it is hers; or else she may be doing something a little too smart, just as she did with the tyre."

It was some time before he could make up his mind as to the best line of action; but at last he came to a decision.

"That's what I'll do. It can't do any harm, anyway. I'll see about it to-morrow."

On the following afternoon the Colonel's car stopped at the police station and he went inside to interview the constable. In order to divert attention from his main object, he had devised an excuse for his call; and when that was disposed of, he touched on indifferent matters before coming to his real business. At last he ventured to touch on this.

"By the way, Bolam, what happened to that automatic pistol that we found at Swaythling Court? Have you still got it, or did the county police take charge of it?"

"I have it here, sir. They looked at it and made a note of the number; but they didn't take it away."

"Could I have a look at it, Bolam?"

The constable retired to another room and returned with the little weapon wrapped in paper and neatly labelled. The Colonel took the package from him and undid the string. As he unfolded the cover, he feigned to be a little in doubt.

"I wonder if I could borrow this for a day or so, Bolam? The Hubbard case is over and done with, now; so this thing is not needed any longer. I'm interested in automatics at present, and I'd like to see whether these tiny ones are liable to jam. I don't suppose there would be any great harm in my taking charge of it for a short time, eh? I'll give you it back in a day or two. I may want to fire a shot or two from it; but that won't matter now, since the police have got all they want from it."

"No, sir. I see no reason why you shouldn't have it, so long as I get it back again."

"I'll give you a receipt for it now, if you'll let me have a piece of paper."

With considerable relief at having achieved his purpose so easily, the Colonel scribbled a receipt and passed it over to the constable. For a few minutes more he stayed, turning the talk to indifferent subjects, so as to divert the constable's attention from the pistol; then, putting the weapon into his pocket, he returned to his car and drove off.

"And now for the awkward part of the afternoon," he said to himself as he turned up the road leading to High Thorne and Carisbrooke House. He had telephoned earlier in the day to Stella and knew that she would be at home, waiting for him.

Colonel Sanderstead was by no means lacking in tact; but in this particular case he had already decided that bluntness would be the best policy. He intended to force himself as an ally on Stella, whether she wished for his help or not; and he did not propose to approach the thing cautiously. Far better to brusque matters, he thought, and bring things to a head at once, so that she should know almost immediately where he stood. He had no heart for sapping and mining in a case of this kind. Rush tactics would take her off her guard and disclose his own position without long explanations. No sooner had the maid closed the door behind him than he took the tiny pistol from his pocket and held it out to Stella in his open palm.

"I'm here as a friend, Stella. Understand that. Now this is your pistol, isn't it?"

Stella Hilton grew a shade paler and her eyes seemed to darken as the pupils dilated; but she looked the Colonel straight in the face as she replied:

"Yes, it's mine—at least I had one like it."

She put out her hand and took the automatic from Colonel Sanderstead's outstretched palm.

"It is mine. There's a scratch on the sliding part."

She lifted her eyes again to the Colonel's; but he could read nothing definite on her face. A slight arching of the eyebrows, a faint tension at the corners of the lips was all that betrayed emotion.

"Well?" she demanded, as he hesitated over his next phrase.

"Where did you get the thing originally?" Stella, the Colonel noticed, did not pause before she replied:

"Cyril gave it to me long ago—shortly after the outbreak of the war. He said he thought a girl ought to have something to protect herself with; one never knew what might happen. And he taught me how to shoot with it."

"And you've had it ever since? When did it go amissing?"

Again Stella answered without the faintest hesitation:

"I lost it on the night of the affair at Swaythling Court."

The Colonel heard the reply with very mingled emotions. On the one hand, he was relieved. Stella was obviously doing the thing he had expected from her, telling the plain truth without any subterfuge, although she must realize the seriousness of her admission. That he had been prepared for; it was all of a piece with her character: and yet it was reassuring to know that he had not misread her. This was a bigger thing than she had ever been up against before; and it delighted the Colonel to find that she stuck to the plain truth without any qualifications. She might easily have pretended that she couldn't recognize the pistol; one automatic is exactly like any other of the same calibre and make. But on the other hand he had heard her admission with something akin to fear. Before she spoke, he had been trying to persuade himself that he was off on a false trail and that Stella probably knew nothing about the inner history of that night at Swaythling Court. Somebody else might have taken her car there. But from her manner he could see that she was deeper in it than that. He resolved to get at the root of the thing as quickly as possible. It was kinder to do that than to keep her on the strain by rambling round the subject.

"So you were at the Court yourself that night?"

"Yes."

Colonel Sanderstead paused before putting any further questions. As he did so, it struck him that for the first time in the case he had got a witness who seemed prepared to answer frankly. This was a very different business from the butler's hang-dog look. He had bent his eyes to the automatic in Stella's hand; and now as he looked up again, he found her scrutinizing his face. She met his eye and that forced him into further speech.

"I'm not here as an inquisitor, Stella. I'm quite sure, before you tell me anything, that you've nothing to be ashamed of. But the fact is, I feel that you're in an awkward corner and two heads are better than one. As it happens, I seem to be the only person who has put two and two together and seen that they make four; but somebody else may be cleverer than I am, and one must be prepared for things. In a dirty business of this kind, one can't tell what may turn up; and I came to you because I want to help if it should become necessary. So far as I know, nobody else has any idea that it was your car that came to Swaythling Court that night; in fact, it's more than possible that no one else will ever know. But it might come out . . ."

The Colonel found that he was wandering into the very by-paths which he wanted to avoid. He broke off short and began again:

"I'll tell you exactly what I know. I know that your car was at the Court some time after half-past ten that night. And I know that this automatic of yours was found in the hall just outside the door of Hubbard's study on the morning after his death. Except for myself, no one, I think, has any idea that a car was there at all that night; and I don't believe that anyone else recognized this automatic as yours. I'm not a detective. It's no business of mine to investigate the affair. There will probably be no further investigation at all. But in case the matter goes any further, I feel that you ought to know that you can be quite frank with me if you want to. Nothing that you say will go any further without your explicit permission. And I'm very worried over the business. That changing of the tyre that you did at the Manor the other day wasn't altogether a good thing. If I'd been anybody but an old friend who knew you to the backbone, it would have made me more than suspicious about you. You acted in too much of a hurry there. And it's just that kind of thing that makes me want to help if I can. To tell you plainly, Stella, I'm afraid that you may do something else of the same sort that might lead to trouble; and I want to come in as an adviser, if you'll let me help. You don't need to tell me anything that you don't wish to, but I want you to let me give you advice in any moves you make in future. But it's just as you like. If you don't want me, you've only to say so; and we'll agree to forget all this."

Stella played with the pistol for a moment or two; then she made a gesture inviting the Colonel to sit down. She seated herself on the nearest chair so that they did not require to raise their voices much above a whisper.

"I've nothing to conceal in the matter—nothing, I mean, that would do any real harm if it came out. It would be unpleasant to have one's private affairs talked about; but beyond that, I've no reason for keeping silent. You believe that, don't you?"

The grey eyes looked straight into his; and the Colonel nodded assent. His experience was wide enough to tell him when a person was speaking the truth; and in this case it was clear that he was not being misled.

"I'm going to tell you the whole story. I quite see that you might easily jump to wrong conclusions; and I wish to be quite frank about it. I've nothing to conceal in the affair; and since you've got so much already, there's no reason why you shouldn't hear the rest. From what you've told me, I can see that you might easily have put a bad interpretation on things. It was just like you not to do that. And it was like you to offer to help me. I've had rather a rough time, you know, and one can appreciate a thing like that."

The Colonel looked uncomfortable.

"Anybody would do the same," he protested.

"No, some people would have done something very different. But I know you like your toast dry, so I won't say any more about that."

"Eh? What's that? Dry toast?" demanded the Colonel, who felt rather out of his depth.

"No butter, you know," Stella explained. "You don't care for flattery; though in this case it isn't flattery, only the plain truth. You're not the kind that sees a girl in a bad position and sets to work to make it worse, like some people. But I'd better go on with the story."

The Colonel nodded assent. His mind had been greatly relieved by that incident. If Stella could find it in her heart to talk nonsense at this stage in the affair, it was clear enough that things could not be very bad.

"You know, of course," Stella continued, "that this man Hubbard made his money by blackmailing. That came out at the inquest; and of course everybody hereabouts read it in the papers. But I knew it a good while before that. It may surprise you, but he tried to blackmail me. Me! You may well look surprised."

The Colonel was more than surprised. The idea that Stella Hilton could by any chain of circumstances have fallen into the hands of a blackmailer seemed incredible to him: and he showed that in his face.

"Nothing in it, of course," he hastened to interject.

"Nothing. At least no truth in what he said. But there was enough in his story to do harm, more harm than I care to think about."

"Let's hear about it," demanded the Colonel.

Stella's expression changed.

"I can't tell you about it just now. You'll simply have to take my word for it. Wait for a month or two, when it's all past and gone, and I'll tell you the whole thing. But just now I don't want to talk about it. All I can say is that he had got hold of something without a spark of harm in it; and he had twisted it into a form that made it the most serious thing in the world for me. You know me well enough to take my word for it; and I really can't say anything more about it for the present."

"It's no business of mine," the Colonel hastened to say. "Tell me when you like and as much as you like. I'm only trying to help you; not to poke my nose into affairs that don't concern me. And I may as well say bluntly that if Hubbard had published anything against you, I shouldn't have believed a word of it, no matter how nasty it looked. You're not the kind that does things you're ashamed of."

Stella nodded her thanks.

"He tackled me personally in the first place. Once I happened to meet him on a lonely by-road and he took his chance then. Of course, I was thunderstruck when I heard the interpretation he was putting on things—some of the things I didn't even know about myself at the time. I was absolutely taken aback. I didn't know what to think or what to do. He saw that; and I think he thought he had got away with it. I know that the surprise of the thing shook my nerves; I was quivering—I mean physically shaking—and he saw the state I was in. What would you have done?"

"Kicked him for the good of his soul," snarled the Colonel as he conjured up in his mind the picture of the girl and the blackmailer on that unfrequented road.

"I couldn't very well do that. I temporized, as best I could on the spur of the moment. Remember, I was in rather a state of nerves—it had all come so suddenly and he had managed to let me see what it meant. So I told him I would think over it and see him again."

Stella paused and looked down at the little automatic which she still held in her hand.

"I went home and thought it over. He seemed to have the whiphand of me. If I didn't knuckle down, so far as I could see, he had it in his power to hit me very hard. And the worst of it was that no one could touch him if he did hit me. I can't explain what it was; but he could have done all he threatened and legally he, was within his rights. I could see no way out of it. In the end, I decided to play for time as long as he would let me do that. I met him again and told him I didn't believe he could do anything. He got rather nasty; but finally he smoothed down a little and said he would produce enough evidence to convince me. We met a third time; and he brought with him a signed statement by some maidservant, witnessed by himself and that butler of his. And at that point I couldn't help seeing the game was up: he had me absolutely in a vice. There was no way out at all."

"Why didn't you consult me?"

"I was terrorized. You know how one broods over a thing until it seems to swell up and cover the whole horizon of one's mind? Well, that was what he managed to make me do. He had the knack of suggesting things that made me wake up in the night and think, until I couldn't get to sleep again. I've never had such a miserable time as I had then. And there were other things to worry me, too. It was about that time that these letters were stolen; and in addition to Hubbard I had that man prowling about here, cross-questioning my servants, and spying continually. Really, it's no great wonder that I wasn't able to look at things calmly just then."

The Colonel's face expressed the sympathy he felt.

"I can't understand," he said, "why you didn't come to me. I don't blab about my friends' affairs. I think you might have trusted me to look after that brute for you."

"I couldn't," she replied, definitely; but her glance thanked Colonel Sanderstead for his intentions.

"Now we come to the last stages of the affair," she continued. "He evidently began to see that I was trying to gain time; and he made up his mind to cut me short. He let me know that if I didn't come to terms—his terms—immediately, he meant to do something drastic. And he was going to be paid for his trouble in any case. If he didn't get his price from me, he'd get it from someone else; so either way he stood to gain. That put him on velvet, as he said himself. And if he got his price from this third party, the whole thing would come out—that was the bargain—and I would be done for. Can you imagine how I felt! I was desperate."

Again she fondled the little pistol in her lap.

"Now I'm coming near the day of the Swaythling Court affair. The next thing I got from him was this."

She walked across the room and took from a tiny safe an envelope which she handed to the Colonel.

Inside it was a single sheet of unheaded typewritten paper:

> I think that the matter can be arranged without any monetary payment if you will come to see me at 11 p.m. on 30th September. I shall be alone; and we shall not be disturbed. Use this latch-key, as there will be no servants in the house.
>
> A Well-Wisher.

The Colonel's brow darkened; and he read the letter a second time. One meaning was plain enough. And then, by some obscure mental conjunction, the word 'Paraldehyde' leapt up in his mind. 'Paraldehyde'—'knock-out drops'—that suggested something. Stella's story was convincing enough; and the Colonel knew he could take her word for it that Hubbard had been 'making a case' against her. But if the blackmailer had been able to induce her to go to Swaythling Court at night and had given her paraldehyde—in coffee, say—he could have let her sleep there until morning; and then he would have had a real hold over her. That would have been the crowning stroke from Hubbard's point of view. There would have been no question of a faked-up case after that. The trouble would be real enough.

While this idea was taking shape in his mind, the Colonel's eye mechanically scanned the typewritten sheet before him; and again his subconsciousness came into action. By some trick of memory he seemed to hear Cyril's voice: *"Look at the 'd' in 'don't' and the other 'd' in 'down.'"* These letters were defective in the blackmailer's letters to Jimmy Leigh; but in this new specimen of the Well-wisher's correspondence the 'd's' in 'arranged' and in 'and' were perfect.

"I suppose he changed his shuttle. And yet, this letter must fit in somewhere between the earlier ones to Jimmy Leigh and that last one we found on his typewriter that morning. It had the defective 'd' in it too."

The Colonel did not make this comment aloud; nor did he follow the line of thought further at the moment. Stella was obviously waiting for him to raise his eyes from the paper; and when he looked up, she continued her narrative.

"When I got that letter, I felt I had to consult someone. I consulted . . ." (she hesitated for an instant) ". . . I consulted Jimmy."

Colonel Sanderstead felt a momentary disappointment. Why hadn't she come to him? He had had far more experience of the world than Jimmy Leigh had. Then a fairer judgment forced him to admit that a sister would naturally go first to a brother in a case of this sort.

"And what did Jimmy say?"

"He advised me not to go."

The Colonel showed his astonishment.

"Was that all he had to say?"

"Oh, of course, he did his best to reassure me; said it would come out all right in the end, and so on. He was so certain about it that he convinced me, temporarily, that it *would* be all right. Jimmy can be very convincing when he sets about it, you know."

"And after that?"

"After I got home, the thing got hold of me again; but Jimmy had somehow managed to get me back into a more normal state of mind. I seemed to see things in truer perspective, somehow. Jimmy had managed to dislodge the terror or at any rate to shake it a bit; and the result was I could sit down and think more or less calmly— a thing I hadn't been able to do since Hubbard first sprang his mine. And suddenly I saw a way out and I wondered why I had been such a fool as not to see it before. Remember, I'd just been desperate—

absolutely up against it, so far as I could see. I don't suppose I'd have dreamed of such a thing in cold blood."

The Colonel was making an attempt to run two currents of thought through his mind at one time and was not succeeding very well. His surface attention was concentrated on Stella's narrative; for evidently the story was drawing near the crucial 30th September and he was going to hear her adventures on that night. But the second half of his mind was obsessed with the bearing of this fresh evidence on the doings of Jimmy Leigh. Here was a second score coming to light between Jimmy and the blackmailer. Hubbard had been trying to get the whole family into his grip at once. And Jimmy was fonder of his sister than of anybody else in the world. And yet, with all this knowledge in his possession, he could meet the black-mailer that very night and let him go off, throwing a friendly "Good night" after him as if he had been a mere casual caller. That would need a lot of explaining. Unless . . . unless the Lethal Ray were at the bottom of the whole thing after all. If Jimmy knew that he could snuff out Hubbard the moment he got home, there would be no need for a violent quarrel at all. In fact, it would be a fatal mistake to have one. Probably Jimmy had pretended to cave in completely to Hubbard, even to stand out of his way in the matter of Stella; and then . . . the Lethal Ray would square all accounts.

Stella's voice recalled the Colonel to the other strand in his thoughts.

"I thought over it and thought over it; and the more I thought, the simpler it seemed. He had terrorized me. Why shouldn't I ter-rorize him and force him to keep his mouth closed? So obvious, when one looks at it now. And, do you know, I began to take al-most a pleasure in the thing in anticipation. He had terrorized me. Well, I was going to get a little of my own back! And I positively gloated over the prospect. You've no conception what a lot of good it did me, to feel that I could put the fear of death on him—I mean it literally. That's what I meant to do. He had sent that insulting invitation to me. Very good; I would take him at his word; and I would go there at the time he fixed. But I'd take *this* with me."

She held up the 0.22 automatic.

"That's what I meant to do: go there and tell him that if he moved a finger against me, then or later, I'd shoot him with less compunction than I'd feel in killing a fly. I wasn't afraid of not convincing him. When I thought of what he'd made me feel, I hadn't the faintest doubt I could make him understand that if necessary I would put him through it. He wouldn't mistake what I had to say for bluff."

"And do you mean to tell me that Jimmy allowed you to go off on that insane errand?"

"Jimmy? I didn't say a word about it to Jimmy. I knew he'd have tried to stop me. Let me tell the thing in my own way. After dinner that night I got out the pistol and loaded it. Then I cleaned every finger-mark off it and put it back in its case. By that time it was getting on towards ten o'clock. I had given Hales leave to go to that dance in Micheldean Abbas, and I had told him not to bother about cleaning the car before he went. That meant I could use the car to go across to the Court and no one would know that it had been out.

"But just then I had a cold fit. Somehow I felt that I'd better have some reserves to call up in case things went wrong. So I rang up Cyril at High Thorne. But it seemed that he was out at a bridge-party at the Allinghams', on the Micheldean Abbas road. So I rang up the Allinghams' house, shortly before ten o'clock; and asked for Cyril. But by the time he came to the phone, I'd changed my mind again; and when he spoke to me I made some excuse or other. I asked him when he expected to be finished with his bridge; and he said they meant to play well on into the morning—two or three o'clock. So I said it didn't matter; and I rang off."

"Evidently you hadn't told Cyril your plans," commented the Colonel with a grim smile. "I can't imagine him letting you go to the Court, if he'd known anything about it."

"Of course, he knew nothing about it. Now I'm getting near the end. About ten o'clock I got fidgety; I simply couldn't sit in the house any longer. I wanted to be doing something—no matter what—so that I shouldn't have to sit about and think. So I went down to the garage, got out the car, and went for a spin up the

Bishop's Vernon road. I hadn't gone far before it started to rain. I came back; and just before eleven o'clock I turned into the Swaythling avenue. The lodge-keeper's windows were dark, I noticed; but the gates were open, fortunately.

"I forgot to tell you that before I went out I'd put on my driving-gloves; and then I'd gone up to my room and taken out the pistol. I'd thought out very carefully any chances of leaving finger-marks behind me—just in case I had to deny being at the Court at all. I made up my mind to keep my gloves on all the time I was at the Court. Oh, and another thing: I took with me the Yale key he'd enclosed in his letter."

Colonel Sanderstead made no audible comment; but he noted in his mind that one of the 'misfits' in the evidence was now accounted for satisfactorily. Clearly this was the Yale key which he had picked up on the doorstep of the Court.

"I was very pleased with myself as I drove up the avenue. I hadn't a quiver; and I stopped the car at the front door and walked up the steps as if I'd been going into my own house. When I took out his latchkey, I got it into the lock without the slightest fumbling. My nerves really are good, you know."

The Colonel nodded assent.

"I'm afraid I really shouldn't brag about it," Stella continued, "for, as you'll see, I hadn't so much to brag about after all. But I was quite proud of myself at the time. As I turned the key and pushed the door open, I even remembered to take the pistol out of my pocket. I thought I'd better have it handy as soon as I crossed the door-step."

"I suppose that was what made you leave the key in the door," commented the Colonel. "I expect you pulled it half-way out of the key-hole and then took your hand away to get the pistol. And so you forgot to pull the key out of the door."

"How do you know about that?" demanded Stella. "I hunted everywhere for that key after I got home again. I couldn't think what had become of it."

"I picked it up off the door-step next morning," explained Colonel Sanderstead.

"If I'd only known that! It would have saved me a lot of anxiety. I was in terror lest I'd left it lying about somewhere—dropped it out of my pocket into the car or something like that. And then somebody might have picked it up and connected me with the affair at the Court."

"It's all right," the Colonel reassured her. "Nobody made anything of it. Go on."

"When I got into the hall, I found the light burning. He had evidently left it on so that I could see my way about. I thought it funny that he had sent me the latchkey instead of letting me in himself when I rang the bell; but when I got into the hall I saw the reason. The whole place was in darkness except for the hall lights. Apparently he had been going out somewhere that evening and hadn't been able to get back in time to meet me. So I thought, at least; and that accounted quite satisfactorily for the latchkey. He was late for his appointment, that was all."

"What time was that?" the Colonel interjected.

"The Fernhurst church clock had struck eleven just before that. It must have been a little after eleven—perhaps two or three minutes after the hour."

The Colonel's interest was increasing; for now Stella was approaching a crucial time in the affairs of that night. From the next section of her narrative it would be possible to check the gamekeeper's evidence as to Hubbard's presence in his study at eleven o'clock.

"I saw a door ajar just a little way along the hall," Stella continued, "so I made my way to it. It used to be old Mr. Swaythling's study; so I thought that very likely it would be Hubbard's study also. As I came up to it, I saw that there was no light burning in it; so as I pushed the door a little I put my hand round to the switch— you know how one does that mechanically—and turned on the light before the door was really open.

"The light went up; and just as it did so, I heard Hubbard's voice calling: 'Get out! Shut that damned door. I don't care who you are. Get out!' And then he said a lot of other things that I needn't repeat. That beastly lisp of his made them sound rather dreadful—did you ever hear a man swear with a lisp?"

The Colonel shook his head. He was thinking of something else. Lonsdale had been right in his results, though he was wrong in supposing that Hubbard himself had switched on the study light. Anyway, the blackmailer had been at home at that particular moment; and part, at any rate, of Lonsdale's tale was accurate. The electricity had been switched on almost at the very moment he had mentioned.

"And now I've got to scramble down off my pedestal," Stella went on. "You've no idea what a shock that voice gave me. You know, I hadn't expected to find anyone in the room; and to be cursed like that out of the void, so to speak, simply knocked my nerves to fiddle-strings. You can't imagine the tone he spoke in. It sounded more like an angry animal than a human being—as if he'd lost all control of his temper. And of course I couldn't understand what it all meant. Altogether, it was a bit of a nerve test; and I didn't pass. I drew back from the door; and then I fell into a pure panic; and all I wanted was to get out of the place safely. I must have been in a pretty state; for I dropped the pistol and ran for the front door. Luckily I managed to get it open without any bother. I slammed it behind me; bolted down the steps and scrambled into the car almost without knowing what I was doing. Pretty inglorious, wasn't it? The only thing I can take credit for was that I didn't fall into hysterics. But there certainly wasn't much of the conquering heroine about that affair."

"Lucky you didn't faint, Stella. That would have complicated matters, wouldn't it? If you want my plain opinion, I think you had no right to go into a business of that kind at all; and you were extra lucky to get out of it safely. That's the main thing, after all."

"Nice of you not to rub it in; but I've rubbed it in myself often enough since then. I'm not over-proud of the way I behaved. I didn't know my own limitations—that's quite evident—but I've learned a good deal about myself. What a little fool I was to think that I could terrorize anybody! But I really thought I was up to the thing, quite fit for the job. I suppose I must have been a bit off-colour with all that worrying."

"Forget about it, Stella; that's my advice. Now if you'll get a duster and clean your finger-marks off that pistol, I'll take it away with me; and there'll be an end of the whole thing. Nobody else knows that you were there that night?"

"Nobody at all. I had to tell you, because you evidently had some information about it and I didn't want you to think I had anything to conceal. I could tell you the whole story and not feel particularly ashamed, except of having shown myself such a coward when it came to the pinch."

"I don't know if I'd have liked you any better if you had managed to carry the thing through. Tackling a blackmailer in that way is a man's business, Stella, not a girl's. I'm quite glad you didn't manage to carry it off. I mightn't have thought any the worse of you for it; but I'd have thought differently of you, if you understand me."

For a few moments the Colonel remained silent.

When he spoke again, it was evident that the non-skid tyre was still engaging his mind.

"By the way, Stella, did you drive straight home?"

"No. I kept my head enough to remember that I mustn't be identified as coming from Swaythling Court at that time of night; so instead of turning into the front gate and coming up the avenue here, I drove round through Micheldean Abbas and came in by the back approach. There was no one about, so far as I saw; but I thought it just as well to be on the safe side."

"Quite right," the Colonel commented. "And the main street of Micheldean Abbas is paved, so you'd leave no tracks there."

"So it is," Stella confirmed. "I never thought of that. All I wanted was to avoid the risk of someone seeing my car come out of Swaythling gate and then turn into my own avenue."

The Colonel did not extend his visit much longer. He had got what he wanted; in fact, he had got more than he expected. Although his interview with Stella had cleared up certain points in the Hubbard case, it had raised at least two fresh ones which puzzled him as much as anything that had gone before.

In the first place, there was the type of the 'Well-wisher' letter. How did it, with its perfect lettering, come to be interjected into the middle of a series of communications all containing defective 'd's'? That was a curious thing.

And the second puzzle was even more difficult. Why should a blackmailer arrange a meeting of that kind with a girl and then, when he had apparently got her into his power, order her off the premises in that fashion? And why should he commit suicide just when he seemed to have the ace of trumps in his hand? For quite obviously if Hubbard had played his cards properly, he had Jimmy Leigh at his mercy. Stella's wild-cat scheme ought to have been Hubbard's deliverance. All he had to do was to let Jimmy know that his sister had been at the Court that night and threaten to make the affair public. Jimmy would have done anything to save his sister's reputation; he would have agreed to any terms with *that* hanging over him; the projected prosecution would have vanished into thin air; and Hubbard could have continued his career without a qualm.

Colonel Sanderstead was driven to a fresh series of inferences. Admit that Hubbard at eleven o'clock had all the cards in the game. Still he needed time to play them. Jimmy Leigh knew nothing of his sister's visit. And suppose that meanwhile, before Hubbard could communicate with him, Jimmy Leigh had been getting his Ray into action and had wiped out the blackmailer shortly after Stella got away from the Court. That really seemed to be the only hypothesis that would fit the facts.

"Nobody will ever prove it now, that's one good thing," was the Colonel's mental comment as he turned his car into his own avenue.

13
THE VOICE FROM THE BEYOND

Colonel Sanderstead banked in Micheldean Abbas; and, a few days after his interview with Stella Hilton, he took his car over to the town in the afternoon in order to cash a cheque. As he came out of the bank, he noticed a man loaded with parcels standing on the pavement.

"I wonder who that is," he thought. "I can't place him; and yet he obviously recognizes me."

Not liking to appear forgetful, the Colonel nodded to the unknown and fell into casual conversation with him as they stood by the car; and as they talked, the tones of the stranger's voice recalled the scene at the inquest.

"You're Mr. Simpson, aren't you—Hubbard's clerk? I thought so. I remembered your face at once from seeing you that day at the inquest; but I couldn't place it for a moment."

Simpson seemed delighted to be recognized. Colonel Sanderstead, inspecting the laden figure beside him, was moved to one of his kindly actions:

"Been shopping? You seem fairly loaded. I'll give you a lift back in my car, if you like; that is, if you've finished your round of the shops."

Simpson accepted the offer eagerly; and they got into the car. Having encumbered himself with the man, Colonel Sanderstead sought for some common ground in conversation; and as the Swaythling Court case was never very far from the surface of his thoughts, he opened the talk with a question.

"I believe you're clearing up Hubbard's papers at the Court just now?"

Simpson seemed quite eager to follow this lead: "Yes, I've been busy over 'em. I expect to be done with 'em to-morrow, with luck."

"Have you come across anything that might throw some light on his death, by any chance?"

"Nothing whatever in the papers, so far's I can find—and I've done a fair bit o' looking, too, I can tell you. There's more in that case than ever came out at the inquest, Colonel; and you can take my word for that, you can."

"Indeed?"

Colonel Sanderstead took care to show only the most casual interest; but behind his mask he was on the alert. What had this clerk come across?

Simpson seemed in no way loath to discuss the subject.

"That was a rummy affair, if you ask me. Mysterious, I call it. There must ha' been a lot o' funny work, damn funny work. By the way, Colonel, you're not a spiritualist, are you?"

"Good Lord, no!" ejaculated the astonished Colonel.

"Well, I am," the clerk announced with the air of a martyr pre-pared to suffer for his faith. "Ignorant beggars laugh at us; but we know what we know. Now I believe in telepathy and materializa-tions and controls. 'Cause why? 'Cause I've got dead cert proof that it's all true. Gospel, I tell you."

"Indeed," said the Colonel, dryly. He felt little interest in the clerk's beliefs. Simpson interpreted the tone easily enough. It seemed to annoy him.

"You don't believe in these things, mebbe?"

"I'm afraid I've never taken much interest in spiritualism, so my opinion, one way or the other, isn't of much value."

The clerk seemed to imagine that this tepid statement marked the Colonel as a potential convert; and he made up his mind to try his hand.

"Would you believe in it if I was to give you absolute evidence that a disembodied spirit spoke to me? No hank about it either."

The Colonel fenced diplomatically with this. He had little liking for cranks; but the fellow was to a certain extent his guest; and the demands of courtesy had to be met. One can't laugh in a man's face after having invited him into one's car.

"Well, I can assure you, Colonel—and I'll take my oath on it any time you like—that no longer than a month ago an astral body spoke to me from a place where no man could 'ave got into in 'is material body. It was ole man 'Ubbard, if you want to know."

The Colonel was now all attention. Simpson noticed the change, but naturally ascribed it to personal interest in Hubbard. The clerk continued in a would-be convincing tone.

"You remember the evidence I gave at the inquest, eh? about 'Ubbard ringing me up on the 'phone the night 'e died?"

The Colonel nodded.

"Well, 'twasn't 'Ubbard at all. Or if it was 'Ubbard, then 'e must ha' been speaking from a place where 'e couldn't possibly 'ave been in at that time o' night. Now 'ow does that strike you?"

"Go on. I'd like to hear the whole story."

Simpson supposed that he was making an impression.

"After the inquest, I began to think over things, I did. There was something about that voice on the phone that I didn't quite like, as it were. It was 'Ubbard's voice all right. Nobody could mistake that lisp and 'is general way o' speaking. It was 'Ubbard sure enough. But it wasn't quite 'Ubbard, neither. There was something in the tone o' the voice that somehow 'aunted me; it came back and back; and I couldn't 'elp thinking about it. I can't quite explain what I mean, if you understand me."

"Do you mean he sounded as if he had a cold in the head or something like that?"

"No. You don't get what I mean, Colonel. There was a sort o' quality in the voice, if you understand me—something . . . I can't quite describe it. What I mean to say is that it was 'Ubbard's voice right enough and yet somehow it wasn't, so to speak."

The Colonel's face showed Simpson that he had failed to convey his meaning, whatever it might be. The clerk tried a fresh line.

"You don't understand what I mean? No? Well, anyway, that voice came back and back to me till I felt sure there was something behind it. A sort of command, like, to investigate into it. You know, Colonel, everything 'as a meaning if we can only guess what it is."

Politeness restrained the Colonel from comment.

"I made up my mind that p'raps, somehow, there was a warning in this affair," Simpson continued. "And so I began to look into it—careful. The more I worried my 'ead over it, the surer I got that the Powers was at work. They 'ave the strangest ways of manifesting themselves, y'know. It may be a knot in a bit of string or a tom-cat washing its ears or the way your ole lady puts your bloater on your plate in the morning; but no matter what it is, it ought to be followed up—and prompt. One never knows what it might lead to."

He paused, mysteriously, suggesting an unveiling of the wonders of an unseen universe.

"Now, as it 'appens," he went on after a moment or two, "I was able to trace that telephone call. You'd ha' called it a marvellous coincidence; but we know the Powers work that way always, smoothing away difficulties in the path of the honest inquirer. When one's able to trace out a thing easily, it's because the Powers are 'elping one on and making things easy."

The Colonel was engaged in drawing in to the side of the road, hugging the hedge to allow Simon's motor-bus to pass. He hated to meet Simon on the road.

"I knew that night-call must ha' come from the Micheldean Abbas exchange," Simpson went on. "Now the Powers—just see 'ow easily you can trace them at work!—the Powers 'ave arranged that a young lady friend o' mine is one o' the switchboard operators on that exchange, so I went to her about it. And it turned out that she 'erself 'ad put that call through to me. She remembered it, 'cause she knows my number, see? And see 'ow well the Powers 'ad fixed things up. At that time o' night there ain't but a few calls; and so she remembered where the call came from."

Simpson paused dramatically.

"It came from Swaffham's shop—the grocer's, y'know."

The Colonel's mind shot back in a moment to Bolam's story of the haunted telephone. Here was corroboration from an unimpeachable source. Wild as the clerk's tale was, it evidently had some substratum of fact.

"Indeed?" said the Colonel.

"Yes, Colonel, from Swaffham's shop. And Swaffham's shop was shut at that time o' night. Nobody could get into it, nohow. And what's more: everybody in the village knows that that night the telephone bell in Swaffham's shop rang, although there was no one on the premises. I 'ad that on the best authority myself. Now what d'you make o' that?"

"What do you make of it yourself?" retorted the Colonel.

"Oh, I know quite well what 'appened. It's all plain sailing to us initiates. What 'appened was this. 'Ubbard, somehow or other, 'ad got out of 'is body on to the Astral Plane. On the Astral Plane one does the same sort o' things as one does 'ere on earth—at least one does on the lower part o' the Plane, one does. So 'Ubbard, 'aving somehow or other got out of 'is body—'ow 'e did it I can't go so far as to say—but anyway 'e suddenly remembered 'e wanted to ring me up and give me a message. And so off 'e went to the nearest phone, of course. Being on the Astral Plane, 'e could walk through a stone wall as easy as you or me could go through an open door— it's all a matter o' the Fourth Dimension, same as you could step over a chalk-line on the floor. So 'e simply walked through the wall o' Swaffham's shop, rang up my 'ouse on Swaffham's phone, gave me 'is message—same as I told 'em at the inquest—and that was all about it. And, o' course, coming from the Astral Plane, 'is voice would sound a bit out o' the common, different from an ordinary voice. My medium, Miss Hesby Mulligan, she says there's always a slight inco-ordination of the dematerialized muscular system when one gets into the Astral Plane. Only a real expert can manage 'is astral body, she says."

"H'm!" The Colonel was considering the matter from a fresh angle. "And would an astral body be visible to the ordinary eye? Would the man-in-the-street notice it?"

"Oh, no! It requires the trained sight of an adept to see 'em. I c'n just see the astral figures faintly myself, after sitting a long time in the dark to polarize the retina. My medium, Miss Fleshy Mulligan, 'as been able to show them to me sometimes. But then I'm a very good sensitive, you understand. My retina polarizes quicker'n most people's, and the refraction of my choroid, Miss Mulligan says, is much above the average: so that gives me a pull. It requires a very active sclerotica to appreciate an astral body. I've no difficulty in seeing Miss Hesby Mulligan's control—Sandra's 'er name, a dark girl with short curly 'air. But for the ordinary person an astral body's very difficult to see, very 'ard indeed. I doubt if an untrained eye would see one at all. It's a question of the polarization of the retina, mainly."

The Colonel's mind was occupied with the bearing of all this stuff upon Lonsdale's story of an invisible Hubbard. It sounded like rubbish (in fact most of it was obviously rubbish): but so did the gamekeeper's tale of an invisible man.

"Suppose that an astral body were to pass within a couple of yards of an ordinary man with keen sight, would he notice it?"

"No, I don't think so. No, I'm sure 'e wouldn't. It takes a great deal o' practice and a lot o' knowledge to get to be an expert. It's taken me years to get to that stage myself. And one needs faith, too. No, I don't think an ordinary man would spot an astral body at all. Just as well expect a blind man to see a shadow on a wall. The Powers don't lend Their 'elp, you know, unless one 'as gone through a severe course o' discipline."

"And what would be happening to Hubbard's real body all the time that his astral body was careering about the country?"

"Very probably 'e would be lying in what you'd call a trance. 'E wouldn't really be there, if you understand what I mean. The mere body in the flesh is just a glove, so to speak. So Miss Hesby Mulligan says. And the astral body is the 'and that fits the glove, as one might say. When the astral body goes away, it leaves the empty glove be'ind it. And then Something Else may come in and take possession of the body, just as somebody might put on your glove if you left it about."

"Indeed?" The Colonel was more than a little bored, but he meant to get all the information he could extract. "And have you taken any further steps to clear up the Hubbard business?"

"I've done my best," Simpson declared angrily, "but one comes up against such a pack o' prejudiced blighters! 'Ere were the Powers 'elping me along no end; and I wanted to 'ave a séance at Swaythling Court and bring down my medium, Miss Hesby Mulligan, to try 'er 'and at the thing. And would you believe it? That stick-in-the-mud ole dry-as-dust lawyer, 'e put 'is flat foot right down on the thing and wouldn't 'ear of it, no how. I sez to 'im, 'You don't understand the importance of these investigations.' And 'e just grinned like a Cheshire cat, 'e did, and advised me 'very seriously,' 'e said, to get on with my work and mind my own business. What d'you think o' that? And to an expert like me! If 'e 'ad seen some o' the things I've seen, 'e wouldn't 'ave 'ad much grin left. I could tell you some things, Colonel . . ."

"Ah! Very interesting, Mr. Simpson. And here we are at Swaythling Court. Very glad to have been able to give you a lift. Do you mind standing clear while I put the reverse in? I'm afraid she'll hardly turn without risking the edge of the grass."

Offended by the Colonel's somewhat tactless interruption of his revelations, Simpson got out of the car rather huffily and clambered, with his parcels, up the perron without waiting to watch the Colonel drive off. Colonel Sanderstead swung his car into position facing the avenue again and was about to let in the clutch when his attention was attracted by the sight of Leake, the butler, who was approaching the house with the parrot-cage in his hand. The Colonel slipped his gear into neutral again. He thought he would like to have a few words with Leake.

"Had the parrot out for an airing?" he inquired, as the butler came alongside the car.

"Yes, sir. The bird has an hour or two out on the grass whenever the weather is fine enough. I believe the fresh air is good for its health."

"Is that so? I never had much to do with parrots myself. Rather treacherous brutes, aren't they?"

"Sometimes, sir."

"That one talks fluently enough, doesn't it?" demanded the Colonel, to keep the conversation going.

"Very fluently, sir. A great command of language—mostly bad."

"Yes, I remember hearing it once. Where did it get hold of that vocabulary?"

"I think it listened a good deal to Mr. Hubbard, sir. It certainly could imitate his voice wonderfully. Took in the dog completely when it chose, sir."

"Indeed. A dog usually knows its master's voice pretty well."

The Colonel was fond of dogs and disliked to think of any dog being taken in by a miserable parrot.

"The parrot gave Mr. Hubbard's dog a lot of trouble, sir. Used to call it whenever it saw it in the distance and make it think Mr. Hubbard was calling. Quite an amusing practical joke, it seemed to think, sir."

"Oh, very funny indeed," said the Colonel, crossly. "It must have been an excellent imitation."

"Yes, sir. I've often been deceived myself, sir. It had the very voice of Mr. Hubbard."

The Colonel looked at the shimmering green of the parrot's plumage and noted with distaste the intelligence in its eye. Leake still stood beside the car, holding the cage by its ring; but the Colonel had lost his desire to pursue his inquiries. The butler's precise answers left him without any reasonable excuse for prolonging the interview without obvious fishing; and he could think of nothing that would lead to anything better. So with a curt good-day he started his car and swept off down the avenue.

But in some inexplicable way the sight of the parrot had set something at work in his mind. All Simpson's nonsensical talk about the voice on the telephone came back into his mind coupled with the picture of that hatefully intelligent bird. The voice Simpson had heard was Hubbard's and yet not exactly Hubbard's. From all Leake had said, the parrot's voice would correspond to that. But the Colonel dismissed the idea as soon as he had formed it. How could the parrot have got into Swaffham's shop? And even if it had been there, how could it possibly have used the telephone?

"Rubbish!"

Colonel Sanderstead dismissed the parrot from his mind again. Things didn't happen in such weird ways as that.

Constable Bolam was emerging from the police station as the car passed; and, catching sight of him, Colonel Sanderstead pulled up.

"'Afternoon, Bolam! Nice weather."

"Yes, sir. Sort of Indian summer, almost. By the way, sir, I'd like to speak to you for a moment, if you please. It's about Sappy Morton, sir. He's been a little strange lately."

The Colonel's face showed his interest and Bolam took that as permission to continue.

"He's been very funny, sir. I don't quite know what to make of him. You've heard all this silly chatter about the Green Devil, sir? Well, I've been at some pains to trace it back; and it seems that Sappy was the one that did most talking. So I took it on myself, sir, to speak to him about it and try to get him to stop putting these lies about—upsetting half the kiddies in the place and making them afraid to pass a tree on the road. But, sir, he would have it that he'd seen the Green Devil himself. Described it to me, sir. I could make nothing of him. I haven't your way with him, sir, you know. But it's getting to be a nuisance, sir; he's given the children a regular scare. So I thought, perhaps, that you'd take him in hand yourself and persuade him to stop his lies, sir. Of course it's only his imagination—not downright lying—but it's having a bad effect, sir; and I think something will have to be done about it."

The Colonel nodded sympathetically.

"Poor Sappy! A hard case. One must deal gently with him, Bolam. I'll see what I can do next time I come across him. We must manage to put a stop to this sort of thing, anyway."

And as Colonel Sanderstead drove on, he made up his mind to get hold of Sappy at the earliest possible moment and stop the legend at its source.

14
THE GREEN DEVIL IN PERSON

ON THE FOLLOWING MORNING, Colonel Sanderstead made up his mind that his interview with Sappy Morton should be the first business of the day. It was useless to send for Sappy; the idiot's peculiar temperament would have made any such arrangement futile. If he came in answer to an order, he would arrive in a mental condition which would defeat the Colonel's aim immediately. The only way of effecting anything with Sappy was to come across him in an apparently casual manner. So in the forenoon, Colonel Sanderstead walked down to Fernhurst Parva and made a few inquiries as to Sappy's probable whereabouts.

Apparently the imbecile had been seen not long before, walking towards Carisbrooke House; so Colonel Sanderstead, whistling his dog to heel, set out in a leisurely fashion in that direction. Sappy was erratic in his movements; but the Colonel trusted to his having been attracted by something on his road; and he hoped to overtake his quarry before long.

He had passed the gate of the Bungalow and turned off towards the Swaythling Court lodge before anything out of the common attracted his attention; but shortly after leaving the Micheldean Abbas road he noticed three figures coming towards him; and a further glance enabled him to recognize two of them. Leake, the butler, walked in the centre; and the Colonel seemed to see something dejected in his gait. On one side Leake was flanked by Bolam, whilst at his left hand was a stranger who, the Colonel observed as they came up, wore constabulary boots. As the trio passed the

Colonel, Bolam saluted punctiliously but made no attempt to halt. The stranger looked Colonel Sanderstead up and down curiously, but gave no sign of recognition. Leake, more hang-dog than the Colonel ever remembered having seen him, walked past without a glance.

"'And Eugene Aram walked between . . .'" Colonel Sanderstead's memory threw up this fragmentary quotation from the literature of his early school-books. "No gyves visible; but the situation's clear enough. They've collared the beggar."

The Colonel paused and looked round at the dejected back of the butler as it receded down the road.

"I wonder what's at the bottom of this. It's funny that Bolam never mentioned the matter to me. It must be someone else's warrant. And that third man isn't any of our local lot, for I know the whole of them. Plain clothes, too. I must ask Bolam what it all means. Perhaps they've got more evidence and roped him in for the Hubbard affair."

Though frankly eaten up by curiosity as to the meaning of what he had seen, Colonel Sanderstead did not allow himself to be diverted from his self-appointed task. He walked on, keeping a sharp lookout on either side of the road; and at last, just beyond the lodge gate, he encountered Sappy Morton. The idiot was lying flat on his stomach by the side of a brook, watching intently the ripples which crossed the surface of the water. The Colonel was able to approach him without startling him.

"Well, Sappy? Nice sunny day this."

Sappy laboriously gathered himself together and executed his pitiful imitation of a military salute.

"Sappy likes sunny days. Dark frightens him."

"Oh, you shouldn't worry about the dark, you know. Nothing to hurt you then any more than in broad daylight."

The imbecile made a strongly dissenting gesture. "Dark frightens Sappy. Things in the dark. Frights."

The Colonel tried reasoning with his protégé.

"What is there to be frightened of? Things in the dark are just the same as in the daylight. You aren't frightened of your hand in the dark, are you?"

"Daylight keeps Things away. Keeps Green Devil away. Green Devil comes in dark. Sappy saw Green Devil in dark."

The Colonel had tumbled upon the very situation he wanted.

"Green Devil! You saw the Green Devil? Why, I've never seen it; and I've lived longer than you have, Sappy. Tell me all about it."

The Colonel would have scorned psycho-analysis if he had even heard of it; but he was unconsciously applying the psycho-analytic method. "Get the poor beggar to talk about it and I may be able to track down the thing that gave him such a scare." He assumed his most sympathetic manner—the Colonel could be very sympathetic when he chose—and began to elicit all the details that Sappy could furnish.

"How did you come to see the Green Devil, Sappy?"

"Looking for butterfly."

"Ah, while you were looking for butterflies? But butterflies don't come out at night. How could you see the Green Devil in daylight when you've just told me you saw it in the dark?"

The imbecile took some time to get at the Colonel's meaning; then he shook his head vehemently.

"Not butterflies. Butterfly. Hubbard's butterfly."

"Hubbard's butterfly? What about it?"

"Sappy heard—Hubbard—great lovely butterfly—wanted to see it."

"Oh, now I understand. It was Hubbard's butterfly you were after. Where did you hunt for it?"

Sappy pointed vaguely towards Swaythling Court.

"And how did you go about the business?"

The idiot scratched his head, thought for a time, evidently assembling his recollections as best he could, and then broke into a stream of disjointed phrases.

"Took candle—dark, don't like dark—climbed fence—creep, creep amongst bushes—front door—dog—Sappy likes dogs—patted it—dog follows Sappy—round house—window—Sappy took big stone—crash!"

He beamed on the Colonel. Even the mere recollection of that prodigious clatter of a broken window served to amuse him as he remembered it.

But now the Colonel knew where he was. This staccato story which he was hearing was a recital of the missing section in the Swaythling Court drama. Sappy, of all people, had been on the spot that evening; and that bemused brain, perhaps, held the key to the mystery. But first of all, it was essential to check Sappy's narrative; and that was a difficult matter. If he were pressed too closely, he might turn shy; and then it would perhaps be impossible to elicit anything from him at all. Colonel Sanderstead thought he saw a possibility; he recalled Sappy's interest in the church chimes.

"Oh, by the way, Sappy, are you still keeping a note of the time, like a good boy? Suppose you tell me what time it was when you broke that window."

Sappy Morton's great moon-face became contorted by the effort of memory. Some moments passed, while the Colonel waited on tenterhooks.

"Ding-dong, ding-dong, ding-dong, ding-dong! Dong . . . Dong . . . Dong . . ."

The idiot slowly counted up to nine strokes and then stopped short.

"Nine o'clock? All right! You're sure about that, Sappy?"

"Sappy quite sure."

"Nine o'clock," thought the Colonel. "That was when Hubbard was away at the Bungalow. So that would account for no one being disturbed by the smash when the glass fell in."

Sappy continued his tale without further prompting: "Climbed in—food!—chicken!—Good—ate it!" He gave a wolfish pantomime of ravenous eating. "Candle made light. Sappy brave. Into house. Door. Opened it. Big light in room. Hubbard. Sappy . . ."

"What's that?" demanded the Colonel. "Hubbard, you say?"

The idiot was taken aback by the Colonel's brusqueness and it required some little persuasion to get him to resume his story. At last he went on.

"Hubbard—asleep at table. Sappy looked round. Little bright thing near door—touched it—snap!—light out. Candle bright. Sappy brave, not frightened. Tiptoe, tiptoe. Glass cage. Butterflies. Lovely big butterfly. Sappy wanted it. Broke glass."

"And Hubbard didn't wake up?"

"No. Hubbard still sleeping. Sappy put hand in and take big butterfly. Lovely. All gold. Great wings. Pretty. Sappy look at it."

He mimicked his actions in taking out the butterfly, and then a sudden horror overspread his face. "Butterfly. Pin through it. Butterfly hurt!"

"Oh, yes, Mr. Hubbard pinned down his butterflies in their case, Sappy."

"Pin through it! Hubbard sleeping. Sappy tiptoe over. Sleeping. Big pin on table. Pin like this."

The idiot indicated a length of about a foot with his hands.

"Took pin. Stuck pin through *him*, so!"

He imitated the action of a vicious stab downwards. "Hubbard put pin through butterfly. Sappy put pin through Hubbard! Good!"

The Colonel was getting more information than he had expected, but what he had got only whetted his appetite for more.

"And then, Sappy?"

"Sappy sorry. Poor Hubbard. Pulled out pin. Threw it in fire. Sappy very sorry. Poor Hubbard."

"Did he cry out when you put the pin through him?"

"No cry. No wriggle. Just lay still. Sappy not like it. Not like sight of Hubbard. Took cloth. Covered up Hubbard. Turned round. Oh! the Green Devil! Great gnarled claws. Big angry eyes. Grabbed at Sappy. Sappy ran. Out of house. Away. Green Devil called after Sappy. Angry. Sappy frightened. Ran. Ran. Home at last."

One phrase in the idiot's description cleared up the Colonel's difficulties at a stroke.

"It called after you? By Jove—the parrot! What a fool I was not to think of that before."

Then Colonel Sanderstead turned to soothe Sappy, who was evidently overwrought by the mere recollection of his fright.

"Look here, Sappy, I know your Green Devil; he's quite an old friend of mine. Some day I'll take you up in daylight to see him; you won't be frightened of him then. You'll find him able to talk to you and make you laugh. Don't you worry about him in the dark. He's quite a nice Green Devil. Why, Sappy, he's only a bird—and a pretty bird at that. Lovely green feathers. You've never seen a parrot yet. Just you wait till you've had a look at him in daylight and then you'll laugh at yourself for having been frightened by him."

A fresh thought crossed the Colonel's mind.

"By the way, what did you do with the butterfly?"

"Lost. Fell out of Sappy's hand. Scrambling through bushes. Never found it again."

"That's clear enough. Well, Sappy, cheer up. Look forward to seeing the pretty bird. I'll take you up some day soon. And don't you worry about the dark, there's a good boy. Nobody'd hurt you."

The Colonel walked back towards Fernhurst Parva in a brown study. This new evidence worried him; for while it cleared up some parts of the Swaythling Court drama, it left the main problem still unsolved, and it seemed to conflict with other bits of evidence. If Sappy's tale were true, then Hubbard was dead before nine o'clock; and yet Mickleby had been very definite in his evidence that the death must have taken place about midnight. Again, if Sappy were accurate, then the whole story of Hubbard's visit to Jimmy Leigh at the Bungalow was false; Mrs. Pickering could not have heard the visitor, Lonsdale could not have come across him, the telephone call could never have been made, and, finally, Stella Hilton could not have heard his voice in the study at Swaythling Court.

Then the parrot came back into the Colonel's mind coupled with the butler's description of its imitation of Hubbard's voice.

"Of course, it might have been that infernal bird speaking. She would mistake it for Hubbard easily enough."

But that still left the evidence of the housekeeper, the gamekeeper and the clerk intact. And against these three witnesses what was there? Only the chance that Sappy had made no slip when he counted out the strokes of the chimes. Quite likely the imbecile had made a mistake. And there was no way of checking him. For a moment the Colonel thought of inquiring from Sappy's mother when the idiot returned on the night of Hubbard's death; but he recognized that there was not the slightest chance that the woman would remember anything definite about her son's movements on that particular night. That was a blank end, evidently.

Still, Sappy was usually wonderfully accurate in matters of time. Suppose that he were correct in his story. That still left it possible that Hubbard had either died by his own hand or had been poisoned by someone. Possibly Angermere's idea was right in essentials, even if the novelist had gone wrong in his full reconstruction of the night's events. Perhaps Leake was the murderer after all. And then the arrest of the butler came back to the Colonel's memory and he hastened his steps.

"Perhaps the police were on to him all the time and said nothing until they had collected enough evidence to lift him. I must see Bolam now and find out what the charge is."

A few minutes' walk brought him to the police station; and he was fortunate to find the constable still there.

"Well, Bolam, you've been arresting Mr. Leake, if I'm not mistaken?"

"Yes, sir."

"I heard nothing about a warrant."

"No, sir. It's the London police who are after him. They had it all fixed up, sir, without our hearing about it. A London man arrived here this morning with a warrant in his pocket, sir, and merely asked me to go with him to the Court."

"Ah! I suppose you know what the charge was?"

"Yes, sir. It seems Leake was a rank bad lot, sir. They'd been looking for him for a longish while; but he'd been lying doggo here and they hadn't managed to find out where he'd gone. A very bad character, sir. Mixed up in the dope traffic and White Slave business, the London man told me. He'll get a long stretch, sir."

"H'm! I always distrusted the look of the fellow. So it had nothing to do with the affair at the Court?"

"Nothing, sir. The London man was much interested to hear about Hubbard, sir. He asked a lot of questions about the case. It seemed to be fresh to him."

"And what happened to Leake?"

"The London man took him away, sir, by the first train. He'll be brought up in court in a day or two. They've got all the evidence filed, sir."

"We seem to have had a couple of discreditable characters in the village. Let's hope we get no more like them, Bolam."

"I hope not, sir."

"Well," the Colonel nodded his good-bye. "Let me hear if anything fresh turns up."

He turned away and walked leisurely through the village to his avenue gate; and as he went he pondered over this last piece of information which he had gained. Leake was a bad lot, evidently; and it seemed unlikely that Hubbard was in complete ignorance of his butler's past. If he knew of it, then that was the precise situation that Angermere had postulated: one scoundrel blackmailed by another. And if Angermere were right to this extent, perhaps he was right all through, except in details. Leake might have returned in the night, after Sappy's incursion, and cleared up the traces of poisoning, just as the novelist had suggested. And that would account for the motor-cycle belt-fastener.

But, as the Colonel turned the matter over and over in his mind, he still found himself unable to fit all the pieces of the jig-saw into place. The whole episode of the Bungalow and the matter of the telephone call refused to adapt themselves to the rest of the facts. Colonel Sanderstead found that the mystery still lacked a key, so far as he was concerned.

15
ANOTHER PART OF THE STORY

FOR WEEKS COLONEL SANDERSTEAD puzzled over the Swaythling Court mystery; but time brought no fresh facts to light, nor did the inter-relationship of the various pieces of evidence grow any clearer to his mind. It seemed that the 'plain mind of the ordinary man' was not the kind of instrument which was needed for the solution of this particular problem.

Jimmy Leigh was still absent; and no news of his movements came to the Colonel's ears. Stella Hilton's decree *nisi* was made absolute in the normal course; and preparations for her marriage with Cyril Norton had been pushed forward; for there was no reason to delay the ceremony.

One morning the Colonel had a visit from Cyril; and at the first glance Colonel Sanderstead thought that, for a man on the eve of his marriage, his nephew seemed anything but pleased. He looked as though he had an awkward affair on his hands.

"Stella sent me across to see you, uncle. She wants me to tell you something. I'd rather let it alone, myself; but she insisted that as you'd heard part of the story already, you ought to have the rest of it. She thinks it can be told now. I believe in letting sleeping dogs lie, myself; but she made it a point of conscience, so I gave in. And here I am."

"Why didn't she tell me herself?"

"I quite understand that; and you will, too, when I've told you the thing. It's not the sort of tale a girl would want to tell you herself.

Besides, I happen to have been the chief actor; so I suppose my first-hand evidence is better than her hear-say."

The Colonel thought for a moment.

"She told me something, once, about being blackmailed by Hubbard. Has it anything to do with that?"

"Yes. She says you heard half the tale and didn't ask any questions about the rest. But now she's marrying into our family she seems to feel that you ought to have the whole thing before you, so that you'd know she wasn't to blame in the matter. Keeping it dark might have made you think she's something to conceal because it was discreditable. It's nothing of *that* sort."

"Of course not. Stella's straight. Nobody would suspect her of anything underhand. And I quite understand how she feels about it. Not that I'd ever have believed anything against her, be sure to tell her that. Still, I suppose she wants to let me know that there was nothing wrong. Whatever it was, it seems to have given her a nasty jar at the time."

"It did," confirmed Cyril Norton, grimly.

He sat for some seconds looking at his uncle, evidently finding it difficult to select the point at which he should begin his tale. At last he plunged into it; and as he talked, his narrative flowed with increasing ease.

"It's no news to you, uncle, that this divorce has been difficult to get. We'd only a single case to go on; and we had to stake everything on that. And you know that Stella and I have been pretty circumspect ourselves. We've been careful to have no tittle-tattle going round. If it hadn't been for that, I'd have taken Master Hilton in hand myself long ago, physically. Well, once, as it happened, Stella and I weren't careful enough."

The Colonel's face betrayed his astonishment. Cyril saw the expression and frowned.

"I begin to think Stella was right after all. Even *you* seem to misinterpret things. I didn't mean we'd gone off the rails; Stella's not that brand. But once, quite innocently, we did make fools of ourselves. We wanted a whole day together by ourselves. Nothing in that to be ashamed of. Quite natural, I think."

"Perfectly."

"I arranged to take her away in my car for the whole day. Picnic somewhere and get back in the evening. Get away from everything, you know."

The Colonel nodded.

"As it happened, I needed some money about that time, so before taking the car for her I drove into the bank at Micheldean Abbas and drew something over £50 in notes. I can't remember how it came about. I suppose I was thinking of something else at the time—but anyhow, I stuffed my note-case into the pocket of my driving-coat instead of my jacket pocket; probably I meant to change it round when I got to the car. Anyway, I forgot all about it. Just remember that. It's important."

"Go on," said the Colonel.

"Everything went all right till we were on the way home. We'd had a fine day, everything first class. It had been a bit of a relief to get away from anything that could remind us of things. We'd gone farther afield than we intended and we'd got clean away from high roads. Then, when we were still a long way out, right in the middle of a lonely bit of the road, the steering-gear went wrong. And there we were—stuck.

"It was miles from anywhere, apparently. I got out the map; and it turned out that there wasn't a railway station anywhere within reasonable distance. We hung about for a bit; but there seemed to be next to no traffic on that bit of the road.

"We'd just made up our minds that it was a case for tramping, when the lights of a big car came round the bend. I stopped it and asked for a lift. It wasn't going our way; but that didn't matter. All I wanted was a lift to the nearest railway station on the road."

Cyril Norton paused in his narrative for a moment. The Colonel was still in doubt as to where all this was leading. Cyril continued.

"It was Hubbard's car. He recognized us, of course, and was effusively friendly, most anxious to help, and all that. He took us aboard and told his chauffeur to drive to the nearest station. But he took us to a branch line; and when we got down and his car had gone, we found that the last train had steamed out of the place ten minutes earlier.

"Of course there was nothing for it but an hotel. It was a miserable little town with only one decent pub in it; and that seemed to date from the coaching days. However, we went to it and got rooms for the night. Of course I see now that I ought to have walked the streets rather than go in myself; but one simply doesn't think of the things other people might think about. Anyway, I didn't even know where Stella's room was. I had a room two stairs up. It was a most rambling old place—all sorts of turnings and passages in it; and you had to walk half over the house to get from the top of the first stair to the beginning of the second flight.

"We had something to eat and then Stella went off to her room. I smoked for a bit and then found my way up to my den. By that time it was late. The whole place seemed to be deserted, everyone in bed.

"I'd just got ready to turn in when suddenly I remembered I'd left that £50 in notes in the pocket of my driving-coat. I hadn't been too impressed with the general look of the waiters and so forth in that pub. It was a second-class place. And I didn't like the notion of that money lying in the hall where anyone could pick it up. So I put on enough clothes for decency and wandered out to get the money. There seemed to be nobody astir in the place.

"I took my bedroom candle with me; but as I told you, the old place was a rambling one; and when I got to the bottom of my flight of stairs, I took the wrong turn and wandered along a passage. It came to a blank end at last, nothing but bedroom doors all along it. So I turned back to try my luck in the other direction.

"Just as I came out of the passage, I found I wasn't alone in the house at that time of night. One of the servants was coming along the corridor in the opposite direction. I explained that I wanted to get my motor-coat. The maid looked at me rather queerly, I thought, but she showed me the right road and I got my note-case without any further trouble. Then I went off to bed again.

"I think I told you it was an uncomfortable kind of pub. I was up pretty early next morning; and as I pulled back the curtains I found I was looking out on the main street. And who should I see but Hubbard's chauffeur loafing about. Of course I thought nothing about it at the time. Why should I? It was only afterwards that I had reason to put two and two together.

"Stella and I had breakfast together and she took the train home, while I went off to see about getting my car towed in for repairs. It had been rather an anti-climax to our day; but neither of us thought anything about it. That's the end of Act I."

"If that's all Stella was worrying about," said the Colonel, "she must have an extra clean conscience. Who could ever think anything of a mishap like that?"

"Wait a bit. Nothing did happen for a while. Before we had time to think of the thing again, something else happened. You remember young Eric Campbell, one of my subs?"

"Poor young chap who committed suicide?"

"That's the one. Well, I happened to come across him about that time—I was rather keen on the cub, you know—and he dropped some sort of hint about Hubbard. He'd got into a corner, it seemed, and somehow he seemed to be in deadly terror of Hubbard. He didn't tell me anything. It was only afterwards that I put two and two together. Anyway, the pup seemed to be up against it, hard, and I could get nothing out of him. He talked a lot about 'indelible disgrace' and so forth; and people who knew about things, and so on. I didn't take it as seriously as perhaps I ought to have done; but you know that at least fifty per cent. of youngsters think they've indelibly disgraced themselves at some time or other, especially the ones who've done nothing in particular but suffer from acute consciences.

"The next thing I heard was that he'd shot himself. I went to see his people. Decent old man, his father—quite heartbroken over the business—so fond of the boy, you know—only son—so proud of him. And the old man showed me a letter which didn't come out at the inquest. It was wild, rambling stuff; but knowing what I did, I could see what it all meant. The boy had been blackmailed for something or other; got the wind up; evidently thought he would disgrace his people; and so he took to the pistol.

"It was all clear enough to me, from what the boy had told me. Hubbard had blackmailed him and driven him to that. I don't know

what you think about things, uncle; but by my simple lights there's
not much difference between that and plain murder. If Hubbard
had shot young Campbell with his own hand he couldn't have finished him more certainly."

"Couldn't you have done something in the matter?" asked the
Colonel.

"Two reasons why I couldn't. First, I had no evidence except
the hints young Campbell dropped. Second, suppose I had made a
move, it would have meant stirring up all the mud of the case—the
very thing the cub had shot himself to avoid. That wouldn't have
been serving him well, would it?"

"I suppose not," the Colonel admitted. "But I'm delighted that
Hubbard came to a bad end himself. There's a certain justice in
things, I've always believed."

Cyril Norton regarded his uncle curiously for a moment and
then continued his narrative.

"The next thing was Hubbard's interview with Stella, the one
she told you about. Perhaps you can guess what it amounted to
now. It seems Hubbard had sniffed a chance of his blackmailing
game when he picked us up that time on the road. He'd deliberately taken us on to a station where the last train was sure to have
gone. Then, when he pretended to go off in his car, he really simply went round the corner and kept his eye on us. He and the chauffeur put up for the night at the next town; and in the morning he
sent the chauffeur in early to see that we'd really spent the night
at that hotel. That was how I happened to see him in the street."

"I don't see much foundation for a blackmail case in that,"
interjected the Colonel.

"No? That's because you don't know yet a thing that neither
Stella nor I knew ourselves until Hubbard interviewed her. By pure
bad luck and accident, we'd played right into his hands. I told you
I'd blundered into a passage that night, a cul-de-sac. As ill luck
would have it, Stella's room was in that passage and when that maid
saw me coming out of it, she drew her own conclusions, and she
repeated them to Hubbard when he interviewed her a day or two

later. It looked black enough. And that was the tale Hubbard had
to tell when he met Stella."

"Still I don't see much in it. You could have laughed at him if
he'd tried to spread a story like that. And there's a law of libel, too.
You could have muzzled him easily enough."

"Think so? Now I'll tell you something that puts a new com-
plexion on the affair. Stella had got her decree *nisi*. But until it
was made absolute, it might be upset. And *it could be upset by the
King's Proctor* if anyone informed him that she'd been up to any
tricks with me. Hubbard had only to drop a note to the King's Proctor—acting purely as an honest citizen trying to see justice done—
and Stella's divorce was in the soup. Now do you see where we were:
Would anyone have believed the true story in the face of the obvious interpretation of the facts? And we couldn't deny the facts."

The Colonel had to admit that it made a black case to go before
a jury who did not know the actors personally. Cyril Norton looked
glumly at the fire and remained silent for some minutes. At last he
made up his mind to say something.

"I was against this business coming out at all; but Stella insisted that you should be told. I hate stirring up things. It's like pitch-
ing a stone into a pool; you never know where the ripples will get
to before all's over. I know exactly what's going to happen next.
You'll begin putting two and two together; and before we know
where we are, you'll have got near the centre of the Swaythling
Court affair. You couldn't help doing that now, since you know so
much. I know you spotted Stella's car and kept that up your sleeve;
never told even me about it. What I don't know is how much else
you've collected."

"I certainly know some sides of it that probably you don't,"
Colonel Sanderstead admitted with a certain pride. He was getting his own back now for Cyril's ironical treatment of him on the
morning they had gone together to the Court.

"Well, I don't mind admitting that a lot of it's still a mystery so
far as I'm concerned. Some parts of it were outside my experience.
But I do know that you had suspicions of Jimmy Leigh. You showed

that quite clearly. I don't wonder at it, either. Jimmy's doings must seem a bit mysterious to you. And if you go on thinking, your suspicions will probably crystallize a bit further, after what Stella insisted on my telling you. Look here, Jimmy Leigh is coming back soon. Oh! yes, I've been in communication with him all along. He's coming back next week for the wedding. We'll both come up for dinner on Thursday; and you can ask Jimmy yourself what part he played in the affair of Hubbard. He'll trust you; and now that you know as much as you do, I can't see there's much harm in your knowing more. But I wish Stella had let well alone. I couldn't tell her to drop it because her brother was mixed up in it. She doesn't know that. And if I had forbidden her to talk, she'd have wanted to know why. And she must never know why."

16
HOW IT HAPPENED

DINNER WAS OVER at Fernhurst Manor; and the Colonel's guests were making themselves comfortable in the smoke-room. Cyril Norton selected a saddle-bag chair that fitted his size and, after dragging it towards the fire, sat down in it and began to fill his pipe. Jimmy Leigh, on his right, drew the cigarette-box to a handy position and then inspected his host, who was adjusting a piece of coal on the fire. The Colonel, looking round as he completed his task, found Jimmy's quizzical bright eyes fixed upon his face. He put the tongs back into place and sat down himself on Cyril Norton's left, so that he could see the faces of both his guests. Then, finding that no one volunteered anything, he turned to Jimmy Leigh.

"Well, Jimmy, what have you been doing all this time?"

"Me?" Jimmy Leigh's voice expressed a feigned surprise. "Me? What have I been doing? Oh, nothing much. 'just loungin' around an' sufferin'' like Brer Tarrypin, you know. Just loungin' around an' sufferin'."

"Well, then, where have you been, if you can answer that?"

"Me?"

"Yes, you," snapped the exasperated Colonel.

"Oh! I've been abroad. Places where nobody ever goes. *Exempli gratia*: Margate, Afghanistan, Broadstairs, Tung-king-cheng—all those places that you find on the outside edge of the map, you know. Take the first turn on the left as you leave Charing Cross and you get to them in no time."

"H'm! I suppose it's no business of mine," Colonel Sanderstead conceded, giving Jimmy up as hopeless. He swung round to his nephew. "Perhaps one could get something serious out of you, Cyril?"

Cyril Norton settled himself more comfortably in his chair before replying.

"This is going to be a longish tale, uncle. I'll give you the general outline; Jimmy can chip in when I come to bits that he knows most about; and perhaps you'll fill up the gaps that we happen to leave. I suspect that there are one or two points where you can enlighten us. As you'll see, I've been rather handicapped in my investigations and I don't profess to have cleared everything up even now."

"Very well," said the Colonel. "Go ahead and I'll do what I can."

"Jimmy knows all about the part I told you the other day, so we may skip that," Cyril began. "I'll start after Hubbard's interview with Stella. Of course, she came straight to me with the story; and when I'd heard it and realized what a nasty corner we'd blundered into, I got hold of Jimmy here and we talked it over. Perhaps I ought to mention that Hubbard had boasted to Stella that he had an alternative market for his goods—Hilton. If she didn't pay up, then he'd sell his news to Hilton, who would use it to break the divorce case. And I ought to tell you, also, that Hubbard had pitched his demands high; it would pretty well have bankrupted me to pay his price. He knew to a hair what I was worth, it seems."

Jimmy Leigh reached over and took a fresh cigarette. He was evidently following Cyril Norton's story closely.

"Jimmy and I talked it over, and we advised Stella to temporize. I didn't want to appear in the matter at all, for reasons you'll understand very soon. So, through her, we kept Hubbard in play as long as we could. But I may as well tell you that from the very first neither of us was inclined to stick at trifles in the matter. We'd both known young Campbell—you may remember that he was the boy who pulled Jimmy out of a hot corner the time he was chewed up—and we didn't suffer from any soft spots where Hubbard was in question. So far as I was concerned, Hubbard's mouth was going to be shut, one way or another. He'd as good as murdered young Campbell, and he'd blackmailed Stella. That was quite enough for me. Switch off that light over there, Jimmy. It's in my eyes."

Jimmy Leigh leaned across and snapped the switch.

"Thanks. We talked it over, Jimmy and I, and we could see no possible way of ensuring Hubbard's silence. If we'd paid him, there was nothing to hinder him selling his tale to Hilton all the same; and then Stella would have been back in the net again, tied to that brute once more. We were going to run no risks of that. And there seemed no way out of it. Who would trust to the honour of a black-mailer? Not I, certainly."

"Nor I," confirmed the Colonel. "It was an awkward affair."

"Spoken very gentlemanlike, Colonel," said Jimmy Leigh. "In my uncultured way I'd have called it a 'hell of a predicament.'"

Cyril Norton paid no attention to the interjections.

"It boiled down to this in the end: either two people's lives were to be spoiled or else this murderer Hubbard was to—disappear from the scene."

"My idea from the first," Jimmy Leigh explained. "Cyril had his scruples. When it came to choosing between Stella and friend Hubbard, the trouble was simply nothing, so far as I was concerned. He'd overreached himself; and I meant to see him pay up. Plank the double-blank on him! Domino! That was the way I looked at it."

"H'm! Logical mind you seem to have, Jimmy," commented the Colonel. "I don't say you're wrong."

"Young Campbell saved my life once," Jimmy Leigh retorted soberly. "I owed him something for that. So far as I was concerned, Hubbard wasn't going to cost me any pangs of conscience. Do you suppose the Public Executioner loses sleep over his job? Well, I was quite ready to play Private Executioner for Hubbard and lose just as little sleep over it. And glad of the chance, too."

The Colonel had never seen Jimmy Leigh so serious before. Cyril Norton rapidly took up the tale again.

"Jimmy and I put our heads together over the business. The usual trouble in a murder, it seems, is to arrange an alibi for the murderer. Jimmy had a stroke of genius and suggested that it would be just as easy to arrange an alibi for Hubbard; postdate the murder, you see, and then both of us could prove we'd been elsewhere at that hour. Hubbard's body wouldn't be found till morning, if we arranged things properly; so all the medicos would have to go on would be the drop in the body temperature after death. And in front of a hot fire, a body doesn't lose its temperature nearly so quickly as normally."

"Now I begin to see light," Colonel Sanderstead commented. "And I suppose you trusted to Mickleby not to be too clever?"

"We did," Jimmy Leigh interjected with a grin.

"The next thing was to arrange a cast-iron alibi," Cyril Norton went on. "It was Jimmy's idea. You know he's an expert on gramophones and dictaphones and all that kind of truck. So it occurred to him to fix up a wax cylinder record of a long conversation between himself and Hubbard—had the machine running while Hubbard paid him a visit—and reproduce it on a loud speaker for Mrs. Pickering's benefit that night. Then, to make things doubly sure, he got a dictaphone record of a telephone message from Hubbard to his clerk; it was taken that morning when you were down inspecting the Lethal Ray. That record also was filed for use. Between the two of them, we had enough evidence to convince anyone that Hubbard was alive and talking, long after the brute was really getting his deserts in the next world. See the point?"

The Colonel nodded assent.

"That scheme implied that Hubbard was left to me whilst Jimmy looked after the machinery. And then Jimmy had another idea: in case anything went wrong, why not supply a false trail leading to himself? And so we hit on the faked Lethal Ray."

"Faked? Why I saw Jimmy kill a rat with it myself!"

"How we are misunderstood!" drawled Jimmy Leigh. "What you saw was me electrocuting a rat with the help of the village main. It walked on to two plates in that shooting-gallery tube and got 250 volts d.c. through its spine. A complete fake, Colonel. Sorry to disappoint you, and all that; but that's the truth. There never was a Lethal Ray. But Flitterwick helped us to spread the glad news about it. A useful fellow."

"And all that talk of yours about cyanide in the stomach was rubbish?"

"Squidge of the worst."

The Colonel leaned back in his chair. He was ashamed to admit how completely Jimmy had taken him in and how much thought he had spent on the connection between the Lethal Ray and Hubbard's death. So far as he was concerned, the "false trail" had been a complete success.

"It took Hubbard in completely," Jimmy Leigh continued. "We needed to put him off his guard, so I approached him and asked him to finance me in the Lethal Ray affair. That made him think I knew nothing about the business of Stella and so I could fix up friendly meetings with him. We needed that for the plan. He took it that Stella had been afraid to tell me anything."

Cyril Norton took up his narrative once more.

"Then we hit on the notion of a fake blackmail case. That was to strengthen the false trail, supply some reason why Jimmy should want to get Hubbard out of the way."

"You weren't blackmailed at all, Jimmy?" demanded the Colonel. "*That* took me in completely, I admit."

"Character white as the driven snow, Colonel. See how the best of us are misunderstood. I wouldn't have swallowed a tale like that about you on such flimsy evidence."

The Colonel grunted non-committally. Jimmy's irony touched him on a sore spot.

"We faked up that correspondence I showed you," continued Cyril Norton. "Thank the Lord for the typewriter, it saves any bother about handwriting. We bought an extra shuttle for Jimmy's 'Hammond'; chipped a bit off the letters here and there—the defective 'd's,' you remember—to make it distinctive; typed out all the stuff on Jimmy's machine and stored the shuttle for future use."

The Colonel was seeing light on a number of dark places.

"So that's the explanation? I couldn't understand how Hubbard's letter to Stella had no defective 'd' in it."

Cyril and Jimmy Leigh exchanged a glance.

"You noticed that?" Cyril inquired.

"Yes. But I couldn't fit it in."

"H'm! We shouldn't have left that loose end, Jimmy."

Jimmy Leigh nodded acquiescence.

"We ought to have snaffled that letter to Stella, if we'd really been careful," he commented. "Well, no harm's done. We'll do better next time, perhaps."

"Any point I've missed, Jimmy?" asked Cyril Norton.

"The cyanide and the paraldehyde, I think."

"Oh, yes, they'd slipped my memory. I bought them in town. Quite untraceable, I'm sure." He reflected for a moment or two.

"No, I think that's all. I've given you the scaffolding of the scheme, anyway. The only thing that remained was to get at Hubbard when he was alone. We had a tip fixed up to manage that; but as it so happened, Hubbard himself played right into our hands. He wrote that letter to Stella. If I'd had any scruples before, that epistle washed them away. Anybody could see what he was after."

The Colonel's face showed that he understood; and Cyril Norton avoided stressing the point.

"That letter told us that Hubbard's staff would be off the premises at eleven o'clock. All we had to do was to make a few inquiries—easy enough in the village here—and find out exactly when the servants were leaving the house. That was an easy business. We found that after about 7.30 the coast would be clear. That meant running things fine enough; but we couldn't afford to miss the chance; it might not recur in a hurry. So at eight o'clock or a little before it, I was at Hubbard's front door, ringing like blazes to make sure of waking him up. I'd left my motor-cycle parked just off the road at the edge of the Swaythling grounds, near the turn-off to Micheldean Abbas. Under my overalls I had on a short coat and black tie, as I meant to go on to the Allinghams' and play bridge that evening."

Cyril Norton threw away the stump of his cigar and chose a fresh one with some care. Then he took up his narrative again.

"Hubbard came to the door himself; and that satisfied me he was alone in the house. I played the terror-stricken victim pretty well: just learned what was happening, would pay anything if only he'd keep his mouth shut, made it appear that he would be doing me a personal favour by almost bankrupting me. I think I did it fairly well, considering that it isn't a pose that came naturally to me just then.

"My throat got dry with talking—very soon; and I begged for a drink. (I ought to say I kept my gauntlets on all the time, too worried to think of the ordinary decencies, you see.) To show there was no ill-feeling, Hubbard got out a second tumbler and poured out the stuff for us both. As soon as he'd done that, I wanted to see the affidavit, of course; and while he was at the safe getting hold of it—he must have judged me a pitiable creature or he'd never have let me see where he kept his stuff—I tilted a stiff dose of paraldehyde into his tumbler. He took one long drink, and before I expected it he was asleep in his chair. That stuff acts like magic."

The Colonel was plainly puzzled by his nephew's story.

"What did you want with the paraldehyde? You could have put cyanide into his drink just as easily then and finished him."

"Quite true. But you must remember I had two things to think about: other people, and myself. I meant to make a clean sweep of all his compromising documents so that none of the poor devils who were under his thumb would suffer by my interrupting his career. That meant spending some time in burning his papers. But that meant the chance that someone might drop in and catch me at the work. Suppose someone *had* turned up, what would the state of affairs have been? Hubbard was asleep and I was burning his papers. Do you think he'd have dared to make a fuss and chance his blackmailing coming out? Not he. So I could safely go that length, so long as he was alive. But so long as he was alive he was a danger to Stella, so he wasn't going to wake up out of that sleep.

"To continue. I burned every scrap of paper in the safe. I piled up the fire until it was a regular furnace—heaped on coal as if I'd been a stoker. To tell the truth, I didn't much care whether I set the house on fire or not; it might have been better to do that, but then there'd have been the risk of someone rushing up and rescuing him. Then I left the fake letter on his desk—the one warning him I meant to apply for a warrant. And I clipped the fragmentary threatening letter to Jimmy into his 'Hammond' machine and sub-stituted the chipped shuttle for his own, which I put in the fire after breaking off the metal clip on it.

"That brought me near the end of things. I put out the killing-bottle I'd brought in my pocket—laid it on the desk handy for him. I collected his stick, the one with the silver name-plate on it, from his stand in the hall. And then I gave him a dose of cyanide solu-tion I'd brought in my pocket. I didn't want any struggle, so I gave him it through the nose with a rubber tube and a filler—forcible feeding, you see. He took it without a squeak—simplest thing in the world. And that was the end of Master Hubbard's career. That was about half-past eight—quick work, I think. By the way, I for-got to mention that I washed out my tumbler and put it back on the pantry rack before I dosed him.

"Now came the time when I had to hurry. This was the danger-period if anyone happened to come to the door. I left the light on in the study—a man doesn't switch off the light when he's going to suicide, you know—and I left the light on in the hall as well. Then I decamped, and made for the Bungalow, one-time."

Jimmy Leigh propped himself up in his chair and took up the narrative where Cyril Norton dropped it.

"And meanwhile, Colonel, where was our hero all this while? Dining with you, moving in the highest circles, and quite safe with an alibi. I can't say that I was exactly bubbling with animal spirits that evening; you may have noticed that I was somewhat *distrait*, wrapped in gloomy thought, so to speak, and *parlant à tort et à travers*, as our French pals have it. In fact, I was a bit worried and not feeling particularly rambunctious."

"I noticed it," confirmed the Colonel, "but I put it down to your coming interview with Hubbard at the Bungalow."

"At 8.30 p.m., I relieved you by taking myself off and buzzed all out for the Bungalow. Cyril arrived almost at once; and between us we put up a fine imitation of Hubbard coming to pay me a visit—for Mrs. Pickering's benefit. Cyril slammed Hubbard's stick into the stand in the hall—where she found it next morning according to plan—and then I dispatched her out to post a letter (see evidence under oath at inquest). As soon as she was out of the road, Cyril cut his stick and picked up his motorbike, which took him to the Allinghams' in nice time for the start of the bridge party."

Jimmy Leigh blew a long puff of smoke as though to put a period to this phase of the night's operations.

"Don't tell me that murder is an easy stunt. I know better. While Mrs. Pickering was out, I started the gramophone record of that long conversation I'd had with Hubbard; so when she came back again she heard it in full swing. I tell you, Colonel, it was a trying evening. I had to use that record over and over again; and I had to vary the running each time so as not to let it get monotonous, for fear she'd spot it. Between times, I eked out the record with a musical programme—arias and squeaks by James Leigh, the well-known basso-falsetto. I was supposed to be amusing Hubbard, of course. I

> Played him a sonata—let me see!
> *Medulla oblongata*—key of G.

I certainly remember singing Offenbach's Barcarolle, you know, 'Night of stars and night of love.' I thought that would impress itself on Mrs. Pickering; but the good lady never mentioned it in her evidence. Tone-deaf, probably—a sad case."

"Will you kindly get on with your story," interrupted the exasperated Colonel, not without reason.

"There, you've put me off—made me quite lose the thread," complained Jimmy, plaintively. Then, seeing that he had exhausted Colonel Sanderstead's patience, he continued:

"Well, about half-past ten, I heard Mrs. Pickering retire to her cubby-hole to prepare for rest. Ten minutes later, I gave her an imitation of Hubbard leaving the house, with me falling on his neck in pure friendliness on the door-step. I came in again and shut the door with a good bang."

"So that accounts for Lonsdale's Invisible Man!" commented Colonel Sanderstead, enlightened by the fresh facts. "Never mind about that," he added, "I'll explain what I mean later on. Get on with your story."

"The next thing was to put through that false telephone call and clinch the evidence of Hubbard's being alive at 11 p.m. I had tapped old Swaffham's wire as soon as his shop closed for the night—his line crosses my garden, you remember. And I had a dictaphone record of his voice, as Cyril told you. In fact, you were on the spot yourself when the record was taken, that morning when I swindled you over the Lethal Ray. It was dead lucky that I'm a whale on gramophones and so forth. It came in handy, didn't it? *Ave Scientia!* as Flitterwick would say.

"And now the labours of our hero were drawing near their close—like Lady Godiva at the end of that little spree of hers. All I had to do was to make as much rumbling as I could in here, to impress Mrs. Pickering with my presence. And I took the liberty of bracketing the Lethal Ray machine—I must have a laugh!—on Swaythling Court and adding the oriented map and compass just to top things off. I had hopes that good old Flitterwick would drop in, nose round in his usual way, and find 'em. Collateral evidence you know, to strengthen the false trail."

He lighted a fresh cigarette.

"Well, that's about all. Next morning I got up bright and early, scared Mrs. Pickering into fits with a sudden departure, galloped for the station and nearly missed the train through carelessness. I just managed to spring into a carriage as the thing slid out."

"Did you know your travelling-companion?" inquired the Colonel.

"Who? I didn't notice anyone in particular."

"Oh, Flitterwick will enlighten you," Colonel Sanderstead assured him, silkily.

Cyril Norton confirmed this with a nod.

"The laugh's on you, Jimmy, you'll see soon enough," he said. "Flitterwick thinks you're immoral. And now, uncle," he went on, "perhaps you'll kindly give us the rest of the thing. You see how I was placed. I'd left everything neatly arranged to represent Hubbard's suicide. Next morning I forced myself on you, because I meant to be on the spot when the discovery was made. I was afraid I'd overlooked some detail and I thought I might set it right if I got there along with you and Bolam. And of course I wanted to make sure that the windows were opened wide."

"What was the point in that, specially?" Colonel Sanderstead demanded.

"To make sure that Mickleby was put off the scent, of course. You remember that it was a very cold morning? Now Hubbard's body had been lying in front of a roaring fire most of the time since his death, and naturally the body-temperature hadn't fallen at anything like the normal rate. I wanted to impress the idea of normal cooling on Mickleby; and the obvious thing to do was to get the windows opened, let in the cold air, and trust that Mickleby wouldn't have the sense to remember there had been a huge fire on during the night. If you hadn't told Bolam to throw open the windows I'd have done it myself; but you saved me the trouble. And so when Mickleby came on the scene, the room was like an ice-house and he never thought of it having been any warmer. He just went home and looked up a book to find the ordinary rate at which a body cools after death, and then brought out the result in his evidence to prove that Hubbard died about midnight—post-dated the time by some hours, just as we wanted. Apart from that window business, the only thing that turned up was the belt-fastener you found on the floor. If I'd come across it myself I'd have pocketed it and said nothing."

"It was yours, then?"

"Mine. Must have dropped it out of my overall pocket that night. But you got it; and I saw it could do no harm anyway, so I made no fuss about it."

"You acted pretty well, that morning," commented Colonel Sanderstead. "You looked the most astonished of the three of us; and I would have taken my oath that you really hadn't expected what we found."

"No more I did," said Cyril Norton. "How would you feel if you'd left all the stage neatly arranged to point towards suicide—corpse included; and then you came back first thing the next morning and found somebody unknown had been at work after you and had staged an obvious murder—the very thing you'd done your best to avoid suggesting? Wouldn't you have had a shock? And who the devil could it have been? I can tell you there was no acting about it: I was far more puzzled than you were, I'm sure. And I must have looked it."

"I hadn't seen that side of it, of course," admitted the Colonel. "It's no wonder you were taken aback."

"You put it mildly," said Cyril Norton, dryly. "I can tell you I did quite a lot of worrying on the subject of that unknown re-arranger. And what made it worse was that I daren't try my hand at investigating the affair, except in the mildest way. I couldn't afford to do anything that might suggest that there was a mystery at all, for fear some other person might get excited over it. That's why I did my best to damp down your enthusiasm, uncle."

Colonel Sanderstead let this pass without comment.

"By the way," he inquired, "what about that bottle of paralde-hyde they produced at the inquest? Was that really Hubbard's; or did you plant it in the house as another bit of fabricated evidence."

"I forgot to mention that. Sorry!" Cyril Norton apologized. "No, it wasn't Hubbard's. I put it in his bedroom after I'd drugged him. Paraldehyde was sure to be found in the body, you know, if they did a P.M.; so one had to provide a supply on the premises if it was to look like a suicide case."

Jimmy Leigh broke into the conversation before the Colonel could say anything further.

"What about my moral character? I'd like to hear the evidence."

Cyril Norton swung round in his chair.

"I've gone into that business as far as I could without raising too much of a dust; and what I make out of it is this: There was a Mrs. Vane, Jimmy—I suppose she had as much right to the 'Mrs.' as to the 'Vane' and not much claim on either of them. She turned up in Fernhurst Parva that night. Stayed at the 'Three Bees.' She was a friend of Hilton's, I understand. They had a stormy inter-view on the road and, from Bolam's account, I infer that she was going to see Hubbard for some purpose and Hilton headed her off.

My reading of the thing is that Hubbard had learned of her connection with Hilton, had got into touch with her, and was going to double-cross everybody. He'd have sold his information to Hilton and got the divorce case smashed; then he'd have come to us, with this Vane woman, and offered us—for cash—enough evidence against Hilton to start a fresh divorce action. But that's only my interpretation of the affair."

"And where do my morals come in?"

"Flitterwick saw her waiting—for Hilton, probably—at the station next morning. You happened to travel in the same carriage as she did. That's enough to settle your moral character in Flitterwick's eyes. I understand she was the sort of female that rather draws the eye, you know."

"Oh," commented Jimmy Leigh. "I promise myself something out of this next time I meet Flitterwick. I wonder if I'd look best as the indignant slanderee or the repentant sinner. H'm! a repentant sinner ought to have sack-cloth. I can do the slanderee character in ordinary clothes. That settles it."

Cyril Norton turned round to his uncle.

"I think, now, we've told you everything we can, all that matters, anyway. But so far as we're concerned, there's a big hole in the yarn. Suppose you fill in the gaps for us, if you can."

Colonel Sanderstead, nothing loath, recounted the results of his investigations, but he was careful to omit all description of the various theories he had formed from time to time. He felt that in the circumstances Bolam's objective method would be the best model for his narration. As a collector of facts, he had scored to some extent; but as a theorist and a detective, he had not much to boast about. When he admitted altering the Lethal Ray machine's position, his guests exchanged a glance; and they received his account of his interference in Stella Hilton's affairs with unconcealed satisfaction.

When the whole tale had been told, Cyril Norton leaned back in his chair and turned so as to look his uncle full in the face.

"Well, now that you know the whole affair, may we ask what you are going to do?"

Colonel Sanderstead sat silent for a few moments, while the others watched him keenly. At last he condensed his reply into a single word:

"Nothing!"

"So we guessed," said Cyril Norton, "otherwise you'd never have heard the tale at all."

COACHWHIP PUBLICATIONS

ALSO AVAILABLE

THE TWO TICKETS PUZZLE

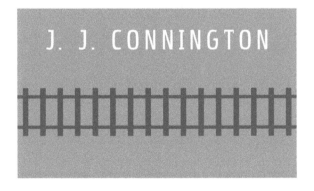

J. J. CONNINGTON

ISBN 978-1-61646-305-8

COACHWHIP PUBLICATIONS

COACHWHIPBOOKS.COM

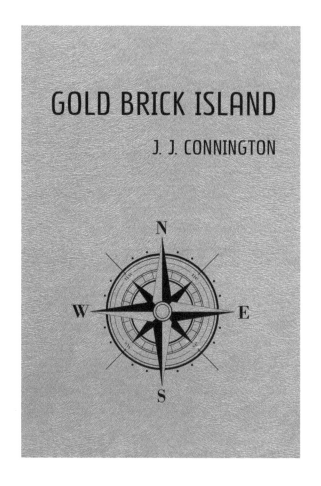

GOLD BRICK ISLAND

J. J. CONNINGTON

ISBN 978-1-61646-307-4

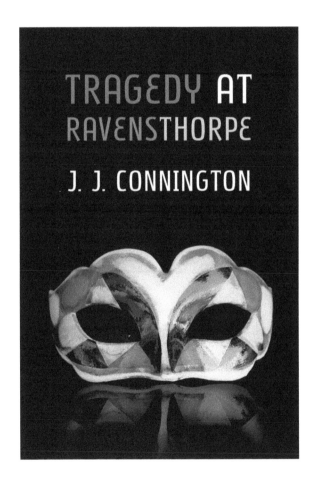

TRAGEDY AT
RAVENSTHORPE

J. J. CONNINGTON

ISBN 978-1-61646-308-2

COACHWHIP PUBLICATIONS
COACHWHIPBOOKS.COM

THE BOAT HOUSE RIDDLE

J. J. CONNINGTON

ISBN 978-1-61646-306-6

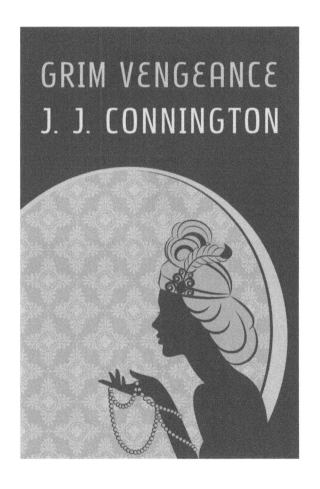

GRIM VENGEANCE
J. J. CONNINGTON

ISBN 978-1-61646-310-4

COACHWHIP PUBLICATIONS

COACHWHIPBOOKS.COM

J. J. CONNINGTON

THE
TAU CROSS
MYSTERY

ISBN 978-1-61646-115-2

ISBN 978-1-61646-113-6